"I promise you will both be safe. I'll guard you with my own life."

Cora closed her eyes and asked the Lord what she should do.

Within seconds, peace filled her and she felt confident that not only would Flynn look out for Noah but God would, too. Cora opened her eyes. "So, you are offering me the safety of your name?" she asked. "You don't expect anything from me?"

"Yes, in name only, nothing more."

"Are you sure about marrying me? Seems to me, I'm getting the better end of the bargain."

Flynn lifted his hand from her shoulder and touched the baby's soft cheek. "I'm as sure as a man can be with a marriage of convenience."

Noah grabbed Flynn's finger and smiled. He garbled something and then released his new friend, poking two fingers back into his small mouth.

"Looks like Noah has given his approval." A smile touched her lips. "I'll marry you."

BY REKOWO

Rhonda Gibson lives in Oklahoma with her husband, James. She has two children and four beautiful grandchildren. Reading is something Rhonda has enjoyed her whole life and writing stems from that love. When she isn't writing or reading, she enjoys gardening and making cards for her friends and family. Rhonda hopes her writing will entertain, encourage and bring others closer to God.

Books by Rhonda Gibson

Love Inspired Historical

Pony Express Courtship
Pony Express Hero
Pony Express Christmas Bride
Pony Express Mail-Order Bride
Pony Express Special Delivery
Baby on Her Doorstep
Wagon Train Wedding

Visit the Author Profile page
at Harlequin.com for more titles.

Wagon Train Wedding

RHONDA GIBSON

LOVE INSPIRED
INSPIRATIONAL ROMANCE

LOVE INSPIRED®

INSPIRATIONAL ROMANCE

ISBN-13: 978-1-335-47476-6

Wagon Train Wedding

Copyright © 2021 by Rhonda Gibson

This edition published by arrangement with Harlequin Books S.A.

For questions and comments about the quality of this book, please contact us at CustomerService@Harlequin.com.

Love Inspired
22 Adelaide St. West, 40th Floor
Toronto, Ontario M5H 4E3, Canada
www.Harlequin.com

Printed in U.S.A.

Be strong and of a good courage; be not afraid,
neither be thou dismayed: for the Lord thy God
is with thee whithersoever thou goest.
—*Joshua* 1:9

This book is dedicated to all the men and women who traveled the wagon trains west to create a better life for their families. Also, a big thank you to my husband, James Gibson, for all of your love and support. And, most important, to the Lord above for the talent that You have bestowed upon me that I might bring a little joy into the lives of others.

Chapter One

May 1867
Independence, MO

From the porch of the general store, Cora Grace Edwards looked out anxiously over the wagon train's busy preparations to leave Independence, Missouri, for Willamette Valley, Oregon. For the sixth time in less than ten minutes, her eyes passed over each wagon, counting the white canvases. From what she could see, there were five rows of twenty-five wagons each, plus one extra wagon. She was sure that each row had been given instructions as to when to fall into single file behind the other. One hundred and twenty-six covered wagons in all. That was, if she had counted correctly. Her attention kept wandering to the people around her and she'd had to start over again more than once. Still, the counting calmed her. That was why she kept doing it. As a schoolteacher, she'd always valued math lessons, where the answers were clear and straightforward. Nothing else about her life felt nearly as straightforward right now.

This wagon train was larger than others she had seen preparing to leave in the past few weeks. She wondered briefly if there was truth in the old saying, "More safety in numbers."

The nine-month-old baby she carried wrapped in a sling against her body squirmed. A whimper left his lips and little hands pushed against her. Holding tight to the one small suitcase she carried, she rocked side to side and cradled baby Noah as close as she could. She breathed in the sweet scent of baby powder. Raw, primitive grief overwhelmed her. It shouldn't be her comforting the baby—it should be his mother. But his mother would never enjoy that small pleasure again.

Caught up in the horror of all she had lost in the last few hours, she could no more stop the tears flowing down her cheeks than she could the sun rising each morning. Her home, her identical twin sister and the only life she had ever known, gone. Just like that, in one night, all was gone. If only she could tell the sheriff what had happened, how brutally her sister had been beaten, barely clinging to life long enough to go to Cora and hand over her son—but Gracie had told her not to tell anyone. Involving law enforcement could backfire, and Gracie's dying wish had been that Cora get her baby away from his murdering father.

"Ma'am, are you all right?"

Cora turned to face the man. He wore an apron and was bone thin. She recognized him as one of the local shop owners. With the edge of Noah's blanket, Cora wiped her tears away. "I'm fine. This is just a little overwhelming." Her gaze returned to the hustle and bustle of the covered wagons and people as they prepared to leave. Oxen bellowed and men shouted above the noise of people, animals and a band that had gathered to give them a proper send-off.

He snorted. "I wouldn't want to be heading out with them. There is rumor that the Indians are getting tired of their hunting lands being trampled by animals and wagons. This could be the group that ends up having to pay the price."

Fear gripped her at his words, but determination propelled her into action before she had time to change her mind. Carefully negotiating the wooden steps, trying to see past the baby in her arms, she hurried toward the covered wagons.

But even as she walked, she questioned. Why her sister, Gracie, had chosen the wagon train as a means to escape her abusive husband still mystified Cora. Surely there was another way? Had Gracie thought this through?

Cora's mind raced, searching for other possibilities to escape the man who had murdered her sister. But just thinking of Hank derailed all other thoughts. Did he know that Noah was with her? Was he already searching for his son? She could only hope that Hank would still be sleeping off the effects of last night's alcohol consumption until after she'd left town. In the past, he'd slept until well into the afternoon.

Frantic to get her nephew away from his dreadful father, Cora realized that time was of the essence and fear was a great motivator. She had been set on a course not of her own making but she would see it through. Her sister had made her promise to protect and care for Noah. And even though she would be leaving her whole life behind, this was one promise she intended to keep.

The sun, barely rising in the east, meant the wagon

train would be leaving soon. She had no time to fret about not going to the schoolhouse this morning or preparing lessons for her students. Those days were gone now. She had sent a note to the school superintendent, explaining that a family emergency had required her to leave immediately—and that she would not be returning. The children would soon have another teacher, and all would continue as normal in their lives. She would be forgotten. It would be as if nothing had changed for them in their world and yet everything was changing in hers. All within the last few hours.

Gracie's words echoed in her mind as she searched the covered wagons for a couple by the name of Mr. and Mrs. Clarkson. "Cora, you'll find them toward the end of the train. I've already paid for our food on the trail and everything you'll need to get started when you get to the valley."

In that moment, Cora had been so devastated by her sister's battered state and impending death that she'd barely comprehended the words. As close as the twins had been, she'd had no idea that her sister had planned to leave town, or that she'd arranged to join a couple on the wagon train. Gracie had kept it all a secret—up until the very end, when she'd pleaded for Cora to take her place. She had clasped the front of Cora's dress tightly, pulling her close. As she struggled for breath, she pleaded, "There is money hidden in the Bible. Please take care of my son… Promise you will get on the wagon train and get as far away from Hank as it will take you." She'd waited for Cora's nod of agreement, then pressed on. "I love you both very much." She'd kissed baby Noah on the cheek, taken another labored breath and then closed her eyes, never to open them again.

Cora had considered going to the sheriff and having her brother-in-law arrested for murder. Surely if Hank was in jail, she and Noah would be safe, and leaving town wouldn't be necessary after all?

But Cora knew Hank had presented himself as an honorable man and that he had a good reputation in town, so she felt the lawman would not believe her. Yes, Gracie was dead, but it would be Cora's word against Hank's as to what had caused that death, and in today's world, men tended to believe men more than women. Plus, she'd promised to take Noah and run as far away from her sister's husband as possible. Cora intended to keep her word.

Having never met the Clarksons, Cora had no idea how she would identify the right wagon. They all looked the same in the early-morning light. Their white canvas covers rocked gently in the early-morning breeze. She had read that out on the prairie they looked much like clouds from a distance.

Cora stopped and turned back the way she had come. Gracie had said they would be at the end of the train. But what if Gracie had been wrong? And which row represented the end of the train? What if they had been moved up front for some reason?

"It's about time you got here, girl. We are almost ready to leave. Hurry up and throw that bag in the back of the wagon with the missus and help me with this ox."

Cora startled and barely managed to hold back a tiny shriek. The man had to be talking to her, since his green-eyed glare was fixed on her face. Taking a leap of faith and deciding that this was the Mr. Clarkson Gracie had mentioned, she hurried to the back of the wagon and gently laid the bag inside, choosing to ignore his instruction that she throw it.

She could not take the chance that the one glass bottle of milk inside might get broken. If she lost that, she had no idea what she'd do to feed Noah. Earlier, she had rolled the bottle into one of the three dresses she'd added to the bag Gracie was carrying when she'd arrived earlier in the morning. Her sister had packed enough diapers and tiny outfits for Noah for the trip. The bag also held a couple of simple dresses for Gracie—dresses that would, thankfully, fit Cora, as well—and ties for her hair. There was also a small Bible, a journal and a pencil for writing. Nothing more filled the bag.

She was happy to see that baby Noah had settled down and seemed to be sleeping as she hurried to the front of the wagon to help Mr. Clarkson guide the ox to the harness where a second, larger ox awaited. Cora kept her hand against the first animal and watched the older gentleman quickly attach the animals to the wagon. She wondered how much Gracie had told the Clarksons about her situation. Gracie's strength had failed so rapidly once she'd reached Cora's door—she'd only had time to share the most pressing details. Cora had no idea how Gracie had found the couple, or what she had told them. Did they know that her sister was running away from an abusive husband? They must. Why else would they take in a young woman with a baby? But what if they didn't? What if she said the wrong thing and roused their suspicions?

As if he could read her mind, Mr. Clarkson narrowed his eyes and said, "So you decided to go ahead and make this long trip after all, did you? It'll be a rough journey, you know. But I suppose I can see why you'd need a new start. It's a sad day when a woman's man dies." He waited for her to say something. When she simply stared back at him, he continued, "As promised, as long as you help me and the missus, you're welcome to go with us all the way to Oregon."

Cora grimaced. Things just became a little clearer. Gracie had claimed to be a widow to explain why she was leaving. Her heart sank. Her sister had lied to this man and his wife. Cora knew she could not continue with the falsehood. She would have to set the record straight and hope that they'd still be willing to shelter her during the journey.

"Mrs. Edwards!"

A call, more like a screech, came from inside the covered wagon. Cora felt a moment of confusion. Edwards was Cora's surname, Gracie's maiden name. Had Gracie chosen to use her maiden name instead of her married name, Marshall? Another lie in order to avoid Hank's detection?

"Mrs. Edwards!"

"You best go see what she wants." Mr. Clarkson continued inspecting the harness, dismissing her with a wave of his hand. "I can handle this now."

Cora felt like a fish out of water. She walked to the back of the wagon. Should she climb inside or wait for Mrs. Clarkson to tell her what to do? If only Gracie had lived long enough to explain what was expected of her, what she'd agreed to do for this couple, or better yet, if only Gracie had lived. Tears pricked the backs of her eyelids and a lump tightened her throat. The urge was strong in Cora to run and not go on the Oregon Trail with total strangers.

The baby squirmed in his sleep, reminding her that nothing mattered more than her pledge to keep Noah safe. She would continue to fulfill her sister's last wish. She would have to be careful and do her best not to pile more deceptions on top of the ones that Gracie had started. Cora hated lying and this was the biggest lie she'd ever participated in. But she appeased her conscience by reminding herself that this was the best way to keep her precious nephew safe.

A young woman with bright red hair stuck her head out of the cover flap at the back of the wagon. Her green gaze ran over Cora with something akin to dislike. Why would she allow Gracie to join them if she felt such disdain as her look suggested? A heavy Irish accent laced her words. "Cora, why are you standing out there? Get in here and help me move these things. I'll not have them cluttering up my wagon."

Cora clumsily climbed over the wooden tailgate of the wagon before the words truly sank in. When they did, she paused, confused. Mrs. Clarkson had called her Cora. Her tired mind tried to wrap around the fact that Gracie had used her name as part of her disguise. It was a good thing that they were identical twins, or this would have been harder to explain. But while the Clarksons didn't seem to harbor any doubts, Cora herself was filled with them. Honestly, she felt as if she did not know her sister at all. She wouldn't have thought Gracie capable of this elaborate a deception. What other secrets or surprises had Gracie kept from her?

They had been separated for so long, due to Gracie's

husband's dislike for Cora. Thankfully, once Noah was born, they'd begun to grow close once more, despite Hank and his evil ways. Or at least, she'd *thought* they were close. Now she wondered how much her sister had kept from her.

Cora had never thought of Gracie as an outright liar. But now, in the last five minutes, Cora had realized her sister had lied not once but three times. She had said she was a widow, had used her maiden name and had allowed the Clarksons to believe her Christian name was Cora. How many more untruths had Gracie told? She had to have been desperate to lie. Gracie had always been as honest as the day was long; at least, that was what Cora had thought.

Baby Noah pushed against her as she stood. She silently prayed she would get better at moving with her nephew strapped to her like a second skin. Thankfully, during Gracie's many visits to see her, Cora had seen Gracie care for Noah enough to know how to get him into the sling and cradle him against her own body. But it was a bit more difficult swaddling him at nine months of age. Also, unfortunately for her, Gracie had still been breastfeeding. And other than the one-quart bottle of milk she was carrying, Cora had no means of feeding the child. She had already spoon-fed the baby some of the milk, and that seemed to satisfy him for now.

Mrs. Clarkson's Irish brogue pulled Cora from her thoughts. "I told Harold you'd only be a hindrance to us. You barely managed to get up here, with that kid tied to you like a sack of potatoes." She shook her head in clear disgust, then pointed to a haphazard mound of boxes and supplies. "I'm going to go visit with Mrs.

Grossman. I expect those to be evenly stacked beside that wall when I get back." She climbed out of the wagon with ease. Then she poked her head back inside the canvas curtain for one final remark. "I didn't want to bring you, so if you want to stay with us, I suggest you do everything I say, or you just might find your-self sitting beside the Oregon Trail instead of traveling it." After that, Mrs. Clarkson was gone.

A wave of apprehension swept through Cora. Panic threaded its way into her chest. It was hard to shake the feeling she'd dodged the frying pan only to fall into the fire. Cora bowed her head and tried to pray for strength, but at the moment, God seemed far away. She felt more alone than she'd ever been in her life.

If the woman's words were anything to go by, Cora would learn over the next several months what it meant to be a servant. Well, wasn't it in the Scriptures some-where that God said to have a servant's heart? At times like this, Cora wished she had studied her Bible a bit more. But this was not the moment to fret about that. Grimly, she began to stack boxes. A suddenly remem-bered verse stopped her in midstride. She whispered it aloud: "Cast your cares upon Him, for He careth for you." She knew those words were Scripture; her grand-mother had drilled her and Gracie on verses each night. And just like that, she felt a ray of peace and satisfac-tion shine in through her fear and sadness. Someone cared. He cared.

Flynn Adams pulled his prairie schooner up behind Harold Clarkson's wagon. A young woman with a baby in a sling turned to watch him. Her deep brown eyes expressed weariness and a sadness he couldn't quite identify. Turning his gaze from her, he looked about at the other wagons getting into formation. Each family had a story of sorrow or adventure to explain their place on this journey. Flynn looked back at the young woman and knew instinctively that hers was a story of sorrow.

He watched as her clear, observant eyes swept over him and past him to the area behind him. Her arms tightened around the baby. Flynn turned to see what had caught her attention. Seeing nothing or no one, he turned again. A frown marred her pretty forehead. Then she turned away.

What had she been looking at—or maybe looking for? Flynn shook his head. What difference did it make? He assumed she was Mrs. Clarkson, although she seemed a lot younger than her husband. He sighed. It was none of his business, and right now he was late for the meeting the wagon master had demanded each lead male wagon driver attend.

"What do you think the wagon master wants to talk to us about, Mr. Adams?"

Flynn grinned at the young man who had fallen into step beside him. "I imagine, Joe, that he wants to remind us of the rules and tell us what time to be ready to leave in the mornings."

Joe nodded. The oversize cowboy hat that sat on top of his head wiggled a little too much and the boy reached up and steadied it. "Yeah, probably." He fell silent for a moment, then spoke again. "Pa says you wish to hire a young man to help you drive. Is that so?"

Ah, the true reason why young Joe Philmore had approached him had come to light. Flynn nodded. "Yes, it is, but I require my helper to address me as Flynn.

'Mr. Adams' just sounds too formal." He turned his head to hide his grin from Joe.

"Uh, Flynn. Would you consider letting me work for ya?"

They were almost to the hedge of trees where they were supposed to meet with the other men. Flynn wiped the grin from his face and looked at Joe. "You don't even know what I'm paying."

Joe nodded. "True, but I'm sure it's better than what Pa is paying me."

"And what's that?"

A smile touched the young man's mouth. "Nothing."

Flynn slapped him on the back. "You're hired. We'll talk wages after the meeting."

"Thank you, sir." Joe ran back to his pa before Flynn could tell him he did not much care for the title "sir," either.

He had already planned on hiring Joe to help him drive the covered wagon to Oregon. Flynn and Joe's pa, James, had discussed it the night before over a cup of coffee. Flynn liked the Philmore family. James and Sarah were God-fearing people and were raising their children in the same manner.

Flynn had been reared in a loving home, too, but growing up had been a painful time for him. Thankfully, time had eased the memory of a lot of the sorrow he had encountered in his young life. Time had a way of doing that. He'd almost had a family, though that chance had been taken away from him once his selfish needs had interfered. As Flynn had done many times in the past, he pushed the thoughts away and focused on the scene in front of him.

"What do you mean I can't leave without a male driver to help me?" Harold Clarkson spit on the ground.

The wagon master, Samuel Tucker, shook his head. "Clarkson, I told you when you signed up to get another man to join you. We need each wagon to have two male drivers." Firm decisiveness filled the wagon master's voice.

"Well, I'm bringing my wife and that Edwards woman. They can both drive."

Even as Harold spoke, the wagon master was shaking his head. "Nope, has to be a man. We'll be crossing some rivers that only a man can get a team of oxen across." He held up his hand to stop any other protest forming on Harold Clarkson's lips. "I'll have no arguments. Find another man to help you drive in the next half hour or I'm leaving you here."

Harold Clarkson looked to each man, waiting to see if anyone else would protest. Seeing no support from them, he stomped off in a huff.

Flynn wondered where Harold would find a willing man to go all the way to Oregon in the next half hour. He shook his head. They had been told early on to get a second man as a driver, and Flynn himself had waited until the last moment. Only because it hadn't initially been his intention to join the wagon train at all.

He'd come to Independence on the same hunt that had driven him for the past two years—the search for the man who had murdered his fiancée. It was only the news that that man might have joined the wagon train himself that had led Flynn to sign up. He didn't know the killer's name or face—just his horrendous deeds and the trail of destruction he'd left behind him—but for all that, Flynn was determined to find him. Even if he had to chase him all the way to Oregon Territory. Thankfully, young Joe had been of age and willing to take the job or he would have been in Harold's position also.

He turned his attention back to the wagon master. As he expected, Samuel Tucker went over the rules, the terms used during travel, such as "form up" when it was time to leave. He told the men to remind their children and womenfolk to stay on the left side of their wagons while traveling and to keep their children away from the wheels. Flynn thought some of the suggestions and rules should not have to be spoken aloud, but he knew not everyone had common sense.

The wagon master turned to a young man who stood beside him. "This is Levi. He is our scout. Levi has been on this trip more times than I have fingers on one hand. He knows the land that we will cross and the people it belongs to. If he tells you to move, you move. Don't ask questions. It could save your life or the lives of your family."

Flynn's gaze moved over the faces of the men who stood around, all nodding their agreement. Was his man in their midst? Flynn wished he knew what the man he pursued looked like. All he had to go on was that the man was short and probably in his late fifties. It was strange that no one could give a more detailed description or even knew his real name. The last name he had used was Smith. Flynn shook his head at the unimaginative name. With so little to go on, he might not have even been sure they were dealing with one killer rather than a handful of separate men…but the

method of death had become the killer's calling card.
Every woman had been knifed in a very specific way.
And Flynn was going to make sure the man responsible was caught before any other woman fell victim
to his blade.

"We leave in thirty minutes. Make sure your wagons, livestock and families are ready to form up." Mr.
Tucker dismissed them by walking off and swinging
into the saddle of his horse that stood several feet away.
Levi did the same.

Flynn walked slowly back toward his wagon. Unlike the other wagons, his held no personal items to
build a new life in Oregon. All he'd brought were the
things he would need to get to Oregon—food, clothes,
bedding, tools for keeping the wagon moving and his
Bible. All practical, essential things—no heirlooms
or cherished items to remind him of home. He'd left
all of those behind when he'd started his manhunt two
years earlier.

His gaze moved to the men and women of Independence, Missouri, who were waiting for the train
to begin its long journey to Oregon. The local sheriff
stood in the center of the crowd and nodded. Flynn
made his way to the lawman—the man who had convinced him that Mr. Smith was on this train.

He motioned for the sheriff to join him, away from
the crowd. "Have you seen anyone who might be him?"
Flynn asked.

The lawman shook his head. "No, but I'm sure he's
here somewhere. I would help you search every wagon,
but I still believe if he sees me searching, he will give

us both the slip again. You will have a better chance of capturing him when you get out on the trail."

"Tell me again—how can you be sure our killer is on this wagon train?"

The sheriff sighed. "I can't claim I'm completely certain, but like I told you, one of the local gals said a man who fit Smith's description bragged that the easiest way for him to get out of this town was to take the Oregon train, today. Then two days later I found that gal in an alley behind the saloon with the same knife wounds you described from the other victims." The sheriff shook his head, looking regretful. "I blame myself for not taking her report more seriously. I thought the man was just doing some empty boasting. I should have paid more attention to how scared she was. He threatened her before they completed their business transaction. Told her he had killed women before, starting with a gal down in Texas for not giving him the goods, and he would do the same to her. Shortly after she talked to me, she was dead."

He fiddled with the gun on his waist. "If I could have caught him, I would have done so. He is slippery, Flynn. Now I understand why you've been after him for two years."

"Would you mind telling me again what the woman said he looked like?" Flynn hated having to ask the sheriff to repeat himself, but since she had been murdered, they only had the sheriff's memory of their conversation to rely on.

The sheriff sighed again. "He's short, gray-headed, and has light-colored eyes. She said he wasn't some saddle bum, more of a business-type man. It's not a lot to go on."

Flynn nodded. That description could be any number of men. "Well, it's more than I had a few days ago. No one has ever mentioned the color of his eyes. As far as I know, no woman has ever gotten that close to him and had him admit that he's killed before." But even with that added information, Flynn wondered how he would know the man if he did see him on the trip to Oregon. What would give him away—or would he manage to stay hidden? Would he kill again on the Oregon Trail? With the number of people on this train and the lack of privacy, Flynn didn't think the killer would attempt another murder. He seemed to kill his victims when they were alone. Flynn's thoughts turned to Miriam, his fiancée. She had been alone the night she was murdered, and it was all his fault.

His memories floated swiftly to that night. Them taking an evening ride in her father's carriage. His deputy riding out and telling him that they had cornered a set of cattle rustlers who had avoided the law for several months. Flynn had left with his deputy after Miriam assured him that she would be fine driving the carriage back to town. Only she had never made it home. They found her body the next morning, battered, bruised and with a knife wound that had taken her life. Dr. Shipman had said that her defensive wounds indicated that the man who had attacked her was not very tall. Flynn didn't understand how the doctor figured out such things, but he believed him.

Later, the man had struck again. The sole witness, a young boy about twelve years old, said he had only seen a short, older man running away from a woman who had been killed in exactly the same way as Miriam. Flynn had started following the bodies. So far, the man had killed a woman about every six months. Each time, Flynn had missed him. No one ever saw more than an older man, running from the scene.

The sheriff slapped him on the back, much like Flynn had done to young Joe less than an hour earlier. "Don't worry. You will catch him. I'm sure he is hiding in one of those wagons."

Flynn nodded. He shook the other man's hand and then headed back to his wagon. As he rounded the corner, he heard raised voices.

"Look, girl, I can't take you with us. Now that I've got a second driver, I don't have room for another person. So you need to go." Harold Clarkson set a box out onto the ground at the blond-headed woman's feet.

Her eyes moved to the box. "You promised if I paid my way, you'd take me and the baby." Panic filled her voice and pretty brown eyes.

"Things change. Tucker says I have to have another male driver, and that means no room for you and the kid." He took the box that his wife handed down to him and placed it with the others.

"But I have nowhere else to go."

Flynn expected tears—maybe of frustration or from anger—but all he saw was panic. He recognized it and cataloged it in his mind. What was she afraid of? Had someone hurt her? Was she running from something? One thing he'd always been good at was reading people, and this woman had his eyes narrowing speculatively.

The baby laid his head on her shoulder and sucked two fingers. His big brown eyes jerked from one adult to the other.

It was none of his business, but Flynn stepped in anyway. "Clarkson, you cannot kick her out of your wagon if she has already paid you to take her."

Harold stood to his full height of five foot seven. "She didn't pay me anything."

The young woman reared back as if she had been slapped. "What about the food, blankets and…well, everything else?"

"I'm giving you back the food and your personal belongings. I owe you nothing." Harold pointed to the boxes about her feet. He sighed. "Look, I don't like this any more than you do, but I have to get to Oregon, and if that means leaving you behind, so be it." He turned to get another box from his wife.

"Who is going to help your wife?" she asked, as if she hoped it would remind them that they needed her.

"She will have to fend for herself."

Flynn watched as the two women's eyes met. Both looked miserable. Once more, he stepped forward. "Ma'am? Do you have anyone else you can ride with?" He knew the answer even before he asked the question.

"No." It came out as a humiliated whisper.

"You can ride with us," Joe said.

Flynn looked to the young man. When had he arrived on the scene? And did his parents know he was offering their wagon to another person?

Her gaze moved to Joe. "That's very kind of you, but…"

"Joe, you should probably ask your folks first," Flynn reminded him.

Joe shook his head. "Not with my folks, Flynn. With us."

Chapter Two

❧

Cora realized that they had the attention of several of the closest wagon families. She watched as the man—Flynn, he'd been called—shook his head at the boy beside him. Mortification swept over her; she felt heat enter her cheeks and travel into her neck. The boy was old enough to know that his suggestion would be wholly improper.

"Yeah, Flynn, you take her." Mr. Clarkson snickered as he put another box down in front of Cora.

She kept her face averted from everyone, using Noah as an excuse to look down. This was getting so out of hand. What was she going to do?

"Now, see here. A lady cannot move into a wagon with a pair of single men." The protest came from one of the many women who now stood watching them. *They're just like a bunch of buzzards at the Last Supper*, Cora concluded, and then she mentally chastised herself for the mean thought.

"And I most certainly agree." The low voice came from behind the women.

Everyone turned to see who had joined in on the

conversation. Spotting the white collar around the latest speaker's throat, Cora sighed. A man of the cloth. Great. Just what she didn't need or want at a time like this. She looked about. A mixture of fear and shame consumed her at the amount of attention they had drawn. What if Gracie's husband, Hank, showed up—drawn by the crowd—while they were deciding her fate? Would he pretend she was Gracie and force her to go back with him? Would anyone stop him? Or would he just be grateful to get rid of her and Noah?

"Now, if you two were married, it would be a totally different story," the minister continued.

Cora jerked and said the first thing that popped into her head. "But I'm not Catholic."

The minister smiled. "Nor am I. I wear the collar so that others will recognize that I'm a follower of Christ." He touched the cloth at his throat as if that explained everything.

On the brink of hysterical laughter at this non-funny conversation, Cora realized it didn't matter what church he represented. She was not getting married. The very idea was ridiculous. She had enough problems without adding a man to the mix. Besides, she had Noah to think about. Even his own father couldn't be trusted to care for him; how could she expect a total stranger to do so? She had sworn to keep her sister's baby safe, and that meant not putting him under the power of anyone who might hurt him.

Not only that, but the man named Flynn hadn't spoken a word since the preacher's arrival. He probably felt the same displeasure at the idea of a hasty marriage that she was experiencing herself. She looked in his direction only to find his expression still and serious, as if he actually were contemplating asking her to marry him.

Deep blue eyes studied her face, searching for the correct answer. What that answer might be was beyond her. She could not leave, and she could not stay. She didn't know anyone on the wagon train and no one else had offered to help her. They were due to leave at any moment—there wasn't time to run from wagon to wagon in the hopes of finding someone else to take her in. What was she going to do? She became increasingly uneasy under his scrutiny. Noah began to squirm in her arms, forcing her to look away from Flynn's captivating gaze.

"Mr. Adams, is there a problem here?"

Cora felt like groaning out her frustrations. Another man stepping in to take over. She pressed Noah's head back into the crook of her neck and rocked her body back and forth, praying for a solution to her problem.

Flynn answered, "Depends. Mr. Clarkson just put this young woman out of his wagon and intends to leave her behind."

Cora looked up at the man on the horse. No doubt, he was the wagon master. She had seen him riding between the wagons checking on the men and visiting with the drivers. If that had not been enough to make his position clear, the way he held himself in the saddle screamed "I am the boss of this outfit."

"Does anyone have room for this young woman and her child?" He bellowed loud enough to wake the dead.

Feet shifted in the dirt; eyes looked anywhere but at her. No one answered his question.

He looked down at her and then at the onlookers. For a brief moment, his eyes softened, but he quickly dropped a nonemotional veil over them and shook his head. He raised his head and spoke again, his voice and look coolly disapproving of the situation. "Then there's nothing to see here, folks. Get back to your wagons. We'll be heading out in a few minutes."

Cora knew this man was the only one who could hold Mr. Clarkson to his deal. But that hope was quickly dashed.

The wagon master turned back to face them. "Now, Flynn, you know Mr. Clarkson has the right to leave her behind." Compassion filled his gaze as he looked to her once more.

Flynn Adams nodded. "But I don't have to like it."

The wagon master tightened his knees on the horse, turning him to the Clarksons. The look on his face as he glared down at Mr. Clarkson said he did not like it, either. "No, sir, Flynn, you don't. And neither do I, but Mr. Clarkson has the right to take or leave whoever he wants."

Cora's gaze bounced back and forth between the men. She pressed a hand against her lips to keep from crying out at the injustice of the situation.

The wagon master grabbed their attention once more. "If you want to take her with you, I suggest you hurry up and marry the woman so we can get started. Otherwise, she stays." He spun on his horse, leaving Cora, Flynn, the preacher and the Clarksons all standing and looking at each other.

Cora remained motionless as Flynn stepped closer. He paused, stretched out a hand and lightly touched Noah's head. She started to speak, but he stopped her with a raised hand.

He took her arm, gently urging her away from the

others. When they had a tiny bit of privacy, he finally spoke. "I know this is not the best of situations to find yourself in, but what do you say, miss? Want to marry a total stranger?" Flynn asked. He widened his stance, crossed his arms over his chest and offered a friendly smile.

"No," she answered, wishing for all the world that she could say yes.

He sighed and looked at her intently. "Can you stay here in Independence?"

She shook her head. Cora felt foolish. She was between a rock and a hard place. What would become of her and Noah? Would she be able to find another way out of Missouri without her brother-in-law catching her first? Cora didn't think so.

"Then come with me. We don't have much time." Before she could answer, he pulled her to the back of his wagon. "I want to help you, but the only way I can do so is if you marry me."

Was he insane? Why would he want to marry a complete stranger? "But we don't know each other."

His sentences were rushed as he explained. "True, and neither of us wants to be married. It's not the ideal situation. But I am willing to marry you in name only so that you will not be left alone here."

She didn't know what to say or do.

Since she didn't answer him, Flynn pressed on. "When we get to Oregon, we can annul the marriage and go our separate ways."

Cora heard the suspicion in her voice and wondered if he did, too, as she asked, "Why would you do this?" She tilted her head sideways and studied his face. Noah squirmed his little head about, too, as if asking the same question.

Flynn took his hat off and explained, "I left a woman alone once before and things didn't work out well for her. Maybe if I help you, it will atone for my not being there for her."

She noted that he refused to look at her now. Was he truly that guilt-ridden? Or was he hiding something more? Cora cleared her throat. "Are you a drinking man, Mr. Adams?"

Flynn met her gaze as he shook his head and answered, "No, ma'am. I don't touch the stuff. Never have."

Cora studied him as if he were one of her students. Compelling eyes, firm features, his face bronzed by the sun. The set of his chin suggested a stubborn streak. Oftentimes when someone lied, they would look away, but he did not drop his gaze nor look away when he assured her of his abstinence. Instead, his expression held a sheen of purpose and an independence of spirit she'd not seen in a long time. Flynn's eyes were a deep blue that gleamed like glass, sharp and assessing.

She wondered at Flynn's reasoning. Was he using her? If so, how and why? "Can I ask you one more question?"

One side of his mouth tipped up. Those pretty blue eyes teased. "Just one?"

A short nod was his answer. Cora wanted to know much more about him than could be covered with one question, but she also knew they didn't have much time—and she didn't have much choice. Still, she felt it was important to ask him this. Maybe it would help her decide whether he could be trusted.

"Go ahead, then. Ask it."

She wrapped her arms more securely around Noah. This information was important for both their futures. "Why are you going to Oregon?"

He hesitated for a moment. His gaze swept over the area before returning to her. Flynn pulled a badge from his front shirt pocket and showed it to her. He lowered his voice. "I'm a lawman looking for an outlaw, a murderer."

Cora knew shock filled her face. His answer could explain how this marriage would benefit him. With a wife and child, Flynn would look more like a family man and less like a lawman, which might make it easier for him to capture his target. But now she had a new question: Was Noah in danger? "You think he's on this wagon train?"

Flynn placed a soothing hand on her shoulder. "Honestly, I don't know for sure. But my last lead said it was possible. And since I don't know any of these people, it's important that you not tell anyone I'm a lawman."

"I won't tell anyone, but is Noah safe here? Will he be safe with you around?"

"I believe so." He moved closer, his voice low and reassuring. "I promise, I'll guard you both with my own life."

She had to take him at his word. Noah definitely wasn't safe in Missouri. At least on the Oregon Trail the baby would have two adults looking out for him. Cora closed her eyes and asked the Lord what she should do.

Within seconds, peace filled her and she felt certain that not only would Flynn look out for Noah but God would, too. She knew, with the confidence of a per-

son of faith, that the baby would be safe. She realized
she would have to draw on that faith often during the
months to come, if this morning's events were a sign
of the turmoil that was to come.

Flynn cleared his throat, reminding her without a
word that time was of the essence.

Cora opened her eyes. He tipped his head toward
her, then raised his brow. She asked faintly, drawing a
step nearer to him, "So you are offering me the safety
of your name? You don't expect anything from me?"

Flynn tucked his badge back into his pocket. "Those
are more questions." He touched his forehead slightly
in a mock salute. "Yes, the marriage will be in name
only, nothing more. I'll ask nothing of you. Unless..."
A warning voice whispered in her head, as she waited
for the rest of his statement. "...you don't mind cooking. I can cook, but a woman's touch makes every meal
much tastier than anything I come up with."

For the first time that morning, Cora bit back a grin.
Baby Noah started to fuss, so she buried her smile
against his little head. She managed to control her expression before looking up to answer. "I don't mind
helping at all, but are you sure about marrying me?
You don't know me. You don't even know if I can cook.
Plus, I can't keep Noah from crying at any given time
of the day or night. Seems to me I'm getting the better
end of the bargain, while you're getting a handful of
headaches." Cora grew serious. She'd just given him
several reasons to back out of his offer. Would he take
them? She sucked her bottom lip between her teeth
and waited.

Flynn lifted his hand from her shoulder and touched
the baby's soft cheek. "I'm as sure as a man can be with

a marriage of convenience. Between the three of us, we should be able to keep this little boy amused and busy throughout the day. By nightfall, he'll be so tired he'll sleep sound."

Cora almost laughed, more than sure that Flynn knew nothing about babies. Instead of commenting on that, she asked, "The three of us?"

He nodded. "Yep. Joe got us into this, and he'll help us make it work. Even if that means entertaining this little guy."

Noah grabbed Flynn's finger and smiled. He garbled something and then released his new friend, poking two of his fingers back into his small mouth.

"Looks like Noah has given his approval." A smile touched her lips. "I'll marry you."

"Form up!" The shout came from the front of the wagon train. It echoed from wagon to wagon.

Flynn grabbed her hand and they hurried to where Joe and the Clarksons waited. The minister had already returned to his wagon. "Joe! Help her get her stuff in the bed of the wagon, while I catch up to the preacher." With an encouraging squeeze, he let her hand go.

Cora watched him disappear around one of the wagons beside them. Was she doing the right thing? She wasn't sure…but she was well aware that she didn't have time to doubt her decision at the moment.

Joe didn't waste any time. He was already putting boxes into the back of the wagon.

"Wait." She hurried to assist him. "I'll climb inside and get the boxes packed away, if you don't mind handing them up to me." Cora didn't give him time to answer. She quickly took the baby from his sling and set him into the bed of the wagon and then climbed in after him.

She looked about the tight space. It appeared empty in comparison to the Clarksons'. There was no oversize furniture, not many cooking supplies and no crates or chests full of who-knew-what. The wagon didn't even have a mattress or sleeping pallet. Other than the pillow and a pile of blankets, there were no other sleeping luxuries in Flynn's.

Cora took Noah and moved him to the middle of the wagon, where he wouldn't fall out of the front or the back. Then she began moving boxes around the baby to fence him in. A bit of a late bloomer, Noah wasn't pulling up or walking yet, but he could sit up on his own. She figured that was a good thing, at least for now. If she could keep him corralled and out of trouble, that would be great.

Her only reason for accepting Flynn's marriage offer was to keep Noah safe, and for now, the baby was safe from his father. She saw a wooden spoon and a tin cup sitting at the front of the wagon. Cora quickly picked them up and handed them to the baby, who looked as if he were about to cry in the center of his boxed-in area. He took the items and gave her a big grin. She returned his smile as he began to beat the two together.

While she worked to the sound of the baby's banging, Cora noted that other than food items, clothes, neatly stacked blankets with a pillow on top, and tools, the wagon was mostly empty. Would Flynn allow her to rearrange the wagon? If so, she could organize the space so that the baby would stay inside the wagon and out of sight during the daytime hours.

"That's the last of them." Joe slid her bag into the wagon. "We'll be heading out in a few minutes."

"Thank you, Joe." She smiled at the young man.

He returned her grin. His cheeks turned a soft pink as he confessed, "I hope you didn't mind my interference a while ago. Between you and me, I knew Flynn would not leave you behind. He's a good man." With that, he jumped down from the wagon bed and disappeared from sight.

Noah fretted.

Cora pulled him from his pen and sat down. "We are going on a grand adventure, Noah." She prayed her words were true and that Joe had been right in his assessment that Flynn Adams was a good man. The idea of getting married and being indebted to the man didn't sit well with her.

"Form up!" Joe echoed the yell. The wagon shifted to the left as he climbed up on the wagon's seat.

Cora wondered if Flynn would be riding his horse beside the wagon as they traveled. Clutching the baby close as the wagon jerked forward, she moved closer to the front so she could see outside. She watched over the young man's shoulder with undiluted excitement as Joe maneuvered their wagon behind the Clarksons', confidently cracking the whip over the oxen's backs.

Good decision or bad, Cora Edwards was on her way to Oregon. She silently asked the Lord to help her in this new phase of her life.

"Look at that." Joe spoke in a voice filled with awe and respect. Cora followed his gaze and her mouth dropped open in surprise. As far as the eye could see both in front and behind them, white canvas tops billowed back and forth as they moved in sync. Children

laughed as they attempted to outrun their own wagons, and Cora's smile turned to a chuckle. Who knew
oxen could move fast enough to stir up a little dust?

Cora quickly climbed into the wagon to escape the
dirt. She waved to Joe to alert him of her actions and
then pulled the wagon canvas shut. The baby snuggled
into her chest and she eased into a sitting position to
better accommodate him. Before they'd left her house,
Cora had changed into one of Gracie's dresses, which
still held the light scent of her twin sister's perfume.
She'd hoped the baby would be comforted with something familiar from his mother. Even so, Cora felt sure
that Noah knew the difference between his mother and
her. She prayed that Noah wouldn't put up too much
of a fuss when he realized his mother wasn't around
anymore.

Tears welled up in her eyes. Gracie was gone, her
life's breath snatched away at such a young age. She'd
never get to see this little fellow grown up. She would
miss all the rest of Noah's firsts. In the privacy of the
wagon, with only Noah for company, she finally allowed herself to grieve for the loss of her sister. Hot
tears ran down her face unbidden. There were so many
things that Gracie was going to miss out on. This adventure to Oregon, for one; Noah's growing up; and
freedom for herself from her abusive husband. All
taken from her because Hank couldn't control his
drinking or his temper.

With the steady rocking of the wagon, Noah fell
asleep against her. Cora leaned over and pulled the
pillow and a blanket from the pile toward her and the
baby. Holding him close, she made a small pallet on
the wagon floor. Since she hadn't slept the night before,

Cora chose to sleep now. She wiped the tears from her face and settled down to rest. The wagon wasn't the most comfortable bed she'd ever slept in, but between emotions and exhaustion, it wasn't long before she felt her body relaxing and her eyes closing.

"Is the baby asleep?"

So much for sleeping, Cora thought drowsily. She sat up and looked toward Flynn.

"Yes."

He climbed onto the tongue of the wagon, then threw his leg across the wagon's back gate to ease into a sitting position beside her, the thrust of the wagon jarring him as he sat down. "I hope you don't mind, but I thought I'd tell you the plans."

"All right." She covered her mouth with the back of her hand and yawned.

"When we stop today for lunch, it will only be for an hour. Mr. Wright, the minister, said we can have a short wedding ceremony then." He swallowed hard. "If you are still sure you want to marry me. We aren't that far from Independence. I still have time to take you and the baby back if you've changed your mind."

So he was having second thoughts, just like herself. But Cora also knew there was no going back for her and Noah. She prayed Flynn would understand when she said, "I haven't changed my mind."

He nodded and a reassuring smile touched his lips. "Good. Then I'll let you get back to your nap." He stood and balanced with his legs firmly locked against the swaying of the wagon. He lowered his voice. "I think we should keep the marriage-of-convenience part of our arrangement to ourselves while we are on the trail. Don't you?"

Cora nodded. "That might be for the best." It wouldn't suit either of them to draw too much attention to themselves. With her, it was because she didn't want to be too memorable in case Hank came looking for them. With Flynn, he probably wanted a low profile to avoid spooking the killer he hoped to catch.

Flynn studied her face for a few moments and then nodded once before going to the back of the moving wagon and jumping out. Cora waited until she saw him mount his horse that he'd tied to the wagon earlier before she lay back down beside the baby. The squeak and creak of the wagon lulled her into a much-needed rest.

Flynn grunted as he pulled up onto his horse, Winston. Winston had been his buddy for the last five years. The horse knew every movement Flynn made and what it meant. Flynn could even sleep on Winston and not worry. The two of them knew each other so well that at times Flynn thought he didn't need any real friends.

"Well, if it isn't Flynn Adams, as I live and breathe."

That voice. He recognized that voice immediately. So much for thinking everyone on the wagon train would be strangers. Oh, he'd made friends with the Philmore family but no one else. Flynn looked to his right and realized he had ridden up to the Clarksons' wagon. "Doc?"

"Yep, it's me in the flesh." Dr. Shipman sat on the wagon seat with a big smile on his face. His gray eyes sparkled with mischief. "Come sit a spell." He scooted over so that Flynn could join him. "I can see you are surprised that I took this job with Mr. Clarkson. I'd actually planned to travel with a different family, but they decided against coming at the last minute. When Clarkson was looking for help, we found each other at just the right time."

Flynn could see that both of the Clarksons walked ahead of the wagon. Mr. Clarkson watched the ground, making sure to kick loose rocks to the side in front of the wagon. Mrs. Clarkson looked annoyed but walked with him. He eased his horse up to the wagon and dismounted to join the doctor on the wagon's seat. He held on to Winston's reins and the horse walked along beside the wagon. He clasped hands with the doctor. "It's good to see you. How long has it been?"

"Two years. I left shortly after Miriam's death." The older man focused on the oxen.

Flynn felt the loss of his fiancée again. It wasn't the heartbreaking hurt of two years ago. No, it was more a feeling of guilt. He didn't want to dwell on those feelings. "Did you retire from doctoring?"

"For a year or so, I did. I lost my drive. Lost my will to heal." He looked at Flynn. "You know, a doctor has a calling, much like a preacher. It has to motivate you above all else. You know…that Hippocratic oath and all." He slapped the reins calmly across the oxen to speed them up a bit. "For a while now, I've been itching to start up again, and when I ran into an old friend in the saloon, he suggested I make a fresh start in Oregon. Well, I thought on it, rolled it round in my noggin a few minutes, then decided that Oregon is as good a place as any to open a new practice. And then when that friend backed out just as Clarkson found he needed another man, it seemed like everything fell into place like it was meant to be."

A new start. Wasn't that what most of the people

on this trip were looking for? Why not a doctor? "I believe you're right that Oregon will be a good place for all these people to start a new life." Flynn glanced back at his own wagon. Mrs. Edwards was looking for a fresh start. He realized he probably needed to learn her given name before they got married.

The thought unsettled him, slightly. After Miriam's death, he'd vowed never to marry. But in a few hours, he would marry a woman he knew nothing about, save the fact that she was a widow and had a small child. She was also beautiful, with big brown eyes and a plump mouth that curved lovingly when she kissed her baby's head. Flynn knew he was helping her to escape from Independence, but he was also using her to make sure no one suspected he was a lawman.

"What are you doing on this trail? Still looking for Miriam's killer?" Doc asked as he arched a bushy, graying eyebrow.

Despite their friendship, Flynn felt it was best to stick to the cover story he'd prepared. After all, you could never be sure who might be listening. Even though they were sitting on the wagon, their voices could be carried on the wind or anyone could be walking beside the wagon at any given time. "I'm looking for a new beginning, too, Doc. As you can see, I'm not wearing the badge any longer. I guess you heard I'm getting married here in a few hours." It wasn't a lie: the sheriff's badge was in his pocket, not on his vest as it had been in the old days. His deputy had been keeping his town safe, but soon they'd want him to return. Even he had to admit two years was a long time to be gone.

The doctor chuckled. "Sure did." He slapped the reins across the oxen's backs. "Not sure it's a love match, though. I was here when you proposed and then sneaked to the back of your wagon to persuade the soon-to-be bride to marry you."

"Aw, she's a pretty little thing. I have had my eyes on her since early this morning." Again, he wasn't lying. He had seen her several times.

Dr. Shipman looked up at the sun. "So, about three hours ago?"

Flynn laughed. "I reckon about that long. Long enough to know she needed me, and I need her."

"I hope you find the happiness you deserve, Flynn." The doctor bumped shoulders with Flynn. "Maybe Oregon is just what we both need to get on with our lives."

Was it? Would Oregon give Flynn the peace he had been asking for from God? Did a man ever truly get over the losses in his life? Especially when it was a love loss. As Flynn examined his life, he realized for the first time in two years he felt an excitement about what his future would hold. Maybe it was hope. Not because of the marriage per se, but because he soon would put his fiancée's murder behind him. To let go of all the focus he'd put on one single thing for such a long time would be a mighty change, indeed. He shrugged his shoulders, lifting and twisting, and it was then he realized his load had lightened somewhat. The heaviness that usually settled in his neck had lessened. A new beginning. Something new to experience. To look forward with eagerness to what was offered. Yes, Dr. Shipman had said it well… It was time to get on with their lives.

Chapter Three

News traveled fast on the wagon train. Any thoughts of having a simple, quiet wedding floated away on the noonday breeze as Cora stepped down from the wagon bed and into the midst of five women. "Um, hello, ladies."

Flynn rode around the back of the wagon. "Ladies." He tipped his hat at them from atop his horse.

"Mrs. Edwards," one of the women said, stepping forward. "I know you don't know any of us, but we're going to be spending the next five months together, and well, we would like to help you with your wedding." The woman was tall, with blond hair and blue eyes. She looked to be about thirty years old. When she smiled, Cora could see the wide gap between her front teeth.

Cora offered what she hoped was a friendly smile. "I appreciate—"

"See? I told you she wouldn't mind, Sarah. You always make too much of everything." The gap-toothed woman waved her hand in the direction of another woman, who Cora guessed to be about ten years older than Cora's own twenty years.

Sarah stepped forward. "Mrs. Edwards, please forgive my sister Abigail's rudeness." She stared at her sister for a full half minute before returning her attention to Cora. "My name is Sarah Philmore. I am Joe's mother, and this—" she waved in the direction of her sister "—is Mrs. Abigail Moore, my baby sister. She means well, but Pa always said Abbie is like a bull in a china closet. She always charges into every situation headfirst—and she has no filter. Whatever comes up comes out."

Cora couldn't help but smile at the expressions on the sisters' faces. How many times had she and Gracie acted the same way? Gracie being the impulsive one and Cora the more restrained. "It's all right. I'm sure Mrs. Moore meant no harm."

"My friends call me Abbie. Sarah only calls me Abigail when I'm right." She wrinkled her nose at her sister, daring her to argue with her further.

Sarah chose to ignore her sister and pointed to a woman in her forties. "This is Mrs. Mable Young."

"Nice to meet you, Mrs. Young." Cora felt overwhelmed as the ladies smiled at her.

"Please, call me Mable." She twisted her apron in her hands.

Sarah continued with the introductions. "Beside Mable is Mrs. Ella Blackstock and Mrs. Opal Murphy."

Cora smiled at them, wishing they'd tell her what they wanted to do so that they could get on with it. Butterflies filled her stomach and doubts swirled in her mind. Was she doing the right thing for Noah, for herself? "It's nice to meet you, Mrs. Blackstock and Mrs. Murphy."

Both women responded, "It's nice to meet you, too."

Mrs. Blackstock pushed her bonnet back, revealing black hair. "Please, call me Ella."

Mrs. Murphy nodded. "And I'm Opal. We decided not to be formal on the trail." Opal's wrinkled face broke into a smile. "We're going to need each other, and formality isn't going to make us feel comfortable."

Cora nodded. She hadn't thought about making friends on the trail—but it was nice to feel a little less alone. There were so many things that she hadn't thought of, and she knew there were many things that she would think of later. It would be useful to have support and people she could turn to for help. "Then you ladies need to call me Cora." She glanced up and saw Flynn smile before turning his horse away. Had he stuck around to protect her? Or just to see how she would handle herself with the women? Either way, he seemed pleased by how things were going. And for some reason, Cora felt good about that.

"I brought you a necklace to wear. If you already have jewelry you planned to wear, I understand." Ella handed her the simple chain with a clear teardrop-shaped stone.

Cora touched the stone. "It's beautiful. Thank you, Ella. I would love to wear it."

"I brought you something also." Abbie held up a cream-colored ribbon. "If we pull your hair up, we can weave it about the bun."

The bun? Cora smiled. "That sounds beautiful." She honestly had no idea how it would look, but she wanted to be polite.

"I've brought you something that my grandmother gave me." Opal took a thimble from her pocket. She extended it out to Cora.

Cora took it, admiring the short thimble that was blackened with age. "Thank you, Opal. It looks very old."

Opal's eyes rested on the thimble, seriousness lining her face. "It is. It belonged to my grandmother's mother." She raised her gaze to Cora's. "My grandmother told me that a thimble protects a woman's fingers as she pushes a sharp needle through material, which is just what a husband does for his wife. He protects her from the sharp things in life."

Cora nodded. "But there is more, isn't there?" She knew instinctively that there was more.

Opal smiled. "The thimble also allows the user to create something beautiful. Grams said when we get married it is like sewing a beautiful quilt or dress. We build a family, and if we allow our husbands to protect us, then we create a beautiful life for ourselves, our children and the man we love."

Cora closed her hand over the thimble. "Thank you. I'll make sure you get this back."

Sarah stepped forward. "Well, my gift is something I've made but haven't worn." She held up a dress. It was light purple with small white flowers. "I think it will fit you if you want to wear it." She smiled.

Cora looked to each woman. Joy shone in their eyes, knowing that they were going to be a part of her special day. "I don't know what to say, other than thank you." She reached out and touched the dress. What would these women think if they knew this was a marriage of convenience? She dropped her hand from the dress. "I'm not sure I should use these things. Flynn and I were just going to have a simple wedding."

Opal touched her arm. "We know that this isn't a

love match, Cora. Lots of women have married out of necessity or because their parents arranged the marriage. But that doesn't mean love can't blossom between you. Give your marriage a chance. You may find that Flynn is the perfect man for you and your little boy."

Cora didn't want a marriage without love. But she also knew that love came with ties. And sometimes it even came with ties that bound, and not in a good, loving way. Gracie had paid the price for loving Hank. She had allowed him to ruin her life and then cause her death. That was not going to happen to Cora. She wouldn't let it. Not when Noah needed her. Flynn might not be Hank, but how would she know? Cora felt sure her sister hadn't expected Hank to turn into the man that he was today. Instead of sharing those thoughts and feelings with the other women, Cora simply nodded and smiled.

Ella said, "The other ladies on the train are preparing a meal for everyone to share after the ceremony. It will be simple but good."

Her chest tightened as Cora realized that these women were offering friendship in the only ways they knew how, through gifts and food. Too surprised to do more than nod and offer a brief "Thank you all" at such open kindness, Cora gave each lady a brief hug. She hoped that expressed to them what their thoughtfulness meant to her.

Sarah tucked Cora's hand inside her arm and said, "Come on. Let's get you ready for your wedding."

"Wait! Noah is taking a nap. I can't..."

"Don't worry about him. My daughter Martha has agreed to look after him. My youngest is about the same age, and Martha watches him all the time. I think the children will get along just fine once your baby wakes from his nap." Sarah patted her hand, nodding toward a tall young woman standing at the tailgate of the wagon. Cora guessed that Martha might be somewhere between sixteen and eighteen years old.

Martha inclined her head. "I love babies. I'll take good care of him for you."

Cora didn't want to leave Noah but felt uncertain how to turn down the women's generosity without hurting their feelings. Eventually, she smiled in agreement, but was quick to say to Martha, "Please, come get me the moment he wakes up."

"I will," Martha promised. She pulled herself up into the bed of the wagon and grinned down at Cora. "He's such a darling little thing."

"He is that." Cora felt her worry lessen as she watched the adoring look light in Martha's eyes.

The women tugged her around the wagon and away from baby Noah. Things were changing so fast in her life. Last night, she was planning a test for her students; this morning, she'd said goodbye to her sister and had taken on custody of her nephew. Now here she was, about to promise to be a wife to a stranger. Could things get any more catawampus? How had she lost all control over her own life? What in the world would she face next? Should she admit to herself that a tiny bit of excitement stirred in her breast at just the thoughts of the marriage she was about to begin?

Flynn walked about the prairie, picking the little purple, yellow and white flowers that covered the area. Every bride should have flowers on her wedding day.

Once more, he asked himself if this had been a wise decision. He had not taken the time to pray about it; he had simply reacted. Would he regret this act? Flynn hoped not.

He bowed his head and prayed. "Lord, please bless this union. Help me to be a good husband, even if it is for a short time. Keep us safe as we travel to Oregon." He thought about asking for help with catching Miriam's killer but suppressed the thought. Over the last two years, he had asked for help more times than he could count. God's answer had been to bless him with the patience and determination he'd needed to continue his search.

But for this, for his marriage, he could only hope the Lord would lead him to the right choices for himself and the wife and child who would be in his care for the next several months. He looked up at the clear blue sky. "Amen."

The flowers held a soft, sweet scent. He continued to pick them until he had a large bouquet in his hands. He hoped his soon-to-be wife liked them. If so, he planned on keeping her in fresh flowers for as long as they were in season.

Flynn glanced toward the covered wagons that were now arranged in a circle. The animals were in the center of the circle. He could see children playing and women working over firepits that had been left behind by earlier wagon trains.

Joe leaped over a wagon tongue and came rushing toward him. He stopped short of running into Flynn. "The preacher says they are ready for you now," the boy huffed.

Flynn's heart accelerated. It was one thing to think

about the wedding but another thing to actually say the words that would put them together as man and wife. He pulled his shoulders back and nodded. "Then I guess we shouldn't keep them waiting."

"Nope, I guess not," Joe agreed. He walked alongside Flynn. "Do you really want to marry her?" he asked.

Did he? Flynn nodded. "I would not have asked her if I didn't."

"That's good. I was worried that I had put you in a bad position with my interfering." Joe pulled a blade of grass from the earth. "She sure is pretty."

Flynn couldn't argue with that. Cora had big brown eyes flecked with a ring of gold that were unlike anything he had ever seen. Since he'd met her, he'd seen them filled with some indefinable emotion. Maybe he'd learn what that was as they spent more time together.

Her long eyelashes curled up at the end, reminding him of a deer's eyes. He had seen his fair share of deer. Their eyes were pretty but always filled with caution or panic, much like Cora's had been earlier this morning. He gave an impatient shrug, pushing the thought away. It was just the lawman in him making assessments. There was no way he could name the emotions in Cora's eyes after knowing her all of three hours.

"I'm glad you asked her to marry you." Joe stuck the grass between his teeth.

He couldn't imagine why Joe would care one way or the other. "And why is that?"

The boy's cheeks flushed red before he admitted, "If you hadn't, I was going to."

"You like her that much?" Flynn asked. Would Joe's infatuation become a problem?

Joe shrugged. "I don't know her, and I don't want to get married just yet, but I don't think I could have left her in Independence. There's something about her that makes me want to protect her and little Noah. I believe she's scared of something or someone there."

With a deliberately casual movement of his hand, Flynn managed to say offhandedly, "So you aren't sweet on her?" He didn't mind if it was just protectiveness that Joe was experiencing. He understood that feeling all too well. Hadn't he offered to marry Cora for the same reason?

Joe laughed. "Naw. Ma says I am too young to be sweet on anyone. She said I need to make something of myself before I start getting all dewy-eyed over a lady." They walked along in silence for a few moments more. "Besides, she's too old for me. If I was going to go all dewy-eyed over a girl, it would be Ruby Harper. She's the prettiest girl on the wagon train and she's almost my age." He cut his eyes at Flynn.

Flynn knew the boy expected a good ribbing, but he didn't say anything. Joe would get enough of that from his family, no doubt.

Joe's cheeks turned red, and he said, "I'll go let them know you are on your way."

"Thanks, Joe." Flynn watched as the young man ran back to the wagon train. He walked faster himself. His and Cora's wedding would be simple and to the point. At least, that was what he hoped. Who knew what the ladies had cooked up? With long, purposeful strides, he covered the distance between them.

He stepped over the wagon tongue and stopped short. Cora and the preacher stood in the center of the circle. It looked like the whole wagon train had turned out for the event. Kids sat on the dirt at their parents' feet and all eyes were turned on him.

"You better hurry, Flynn! You're gonna be late for your own wedding," Bob Blackstock called from the sidelines, garnering a few snickers from the men around him.

Flynn ignored Bob. He straightened his back and walked to where Cora stood. Her cheeks were flushed as she looked up at him.

"I'm sorry," she whispered.

He handed the flowers to her and leaned down and whispered so that only she could make out his words. "Don't worry. I'm sure you didn't plan all this." Flynn placed a light kiss on her cheek before standing.

"You're supposed to wait until you're hitched before the kissing begins!" another male voice called out, followed by an "umph."

Flynn hoped that the last sound came due to the rude commenter's wife putting an elbow in his ribs. He ignored the laughter that followed and turned to the minister.

Taking his cue, the minister began. "Dearly beloved, we are gathered here today to unite this man and this woman in holy matrimony."

Flynn glanced sideways at Cora, who stood with the flowers held steady in front of her and her head high. He wondered if her insides were shaking as badly as his. Was she questioning her decision to marry him?

As if she felt him gazing at her, Cora turned to look at him. Her hair was piled high on her head. Ringlets framed her face. Her brows furrowed and big brown eyes clung to his, analyzing his reaction. Her gaze was penetrating, searching—and unrelenting. She almost seemed to be challenging him to be the man she needed him to be—one she could rely on and trust. One who would soothe those fears he still saw lingering in her eyes, nearly hidden behind her strength and resolution.

What was she afraid of? Him? Their future together? That he would not keep his word and set her free at the end of their journey?

Flynn didn't know and there was no way he could ask her now. The preacher's voice droned on in the background. Silently, he tried to convey to her with his eyes that he would protect her and Noah with everything he had in him. If she would let him, he would wipe away Cora's fears and make the trip to Oregon safe for her and Noah.

Then Flynn asked himself, could he live up to those promises? If Miriam's killer was on this wagon train, would Cora be safe? Would any of them?

Cora sighed as she put the baby down to sleep for the night. Thankfully, their wedding had gone smoothly. Flynn had turned her from the prying eyes of the rest of the wagon train and gently tilted her head and kissed her cheek. Then he'd released her so that they could turn and greet their well-wishers. As the crowd of people pressed forward, he'd kept her close to his side with a protective hand. Following that, they had all quickly finished lunch before returning to their wagon and the Oregon Trail once more.

Now that they were stopped for the night, dinner had been eaten and babies put to bed, she could hear the fiddle playing a merry jig and knew Flynn waited in the firelight for her to join him for their first dance. Why had she agreed to attend the festivities? Her body ached along with her heart. She missed Gracie so much. Cora knew it was expected of her to celebrate her wedding; that was the only reason she had agreed. Still, it would have been nice just to curl up on the sleeping mat she had created earlier for her and Noah. It had been such a wearying day—and she felt so distant from the woman she had been just one day before.

"Is the baby asleep? Joe's sister Martha has offered to watch him."

She turned and looked at Flynn. He looked as tired as she felt. Was the stress of the day weighing heavily on him, too? Cora offered what she hoped was a sweet smile. "He's just dozed off. Would you mind if I stay with him for a few moments longer? I want to make sure he's sleeping soundly before leaving him."

The wagon shifted as Flynn pulled himself up into it. "I think that's a good idea. I wish we could join him." He looked down at the baby, who had two fingers between his bow-shaped lips.

Cora yawned. "Me, too. This has been a long day."

"You know, you don't have to come to the dance. I can make your excuses." Flynn squatted beside the baby. "He really is a cute little tyke."

She smiled. "He is, isn't he?"

Flynn studied her face as if seeing it for the first time. She recognized the questions in his eyes. He wanted to know about Noah's father, wanted to ask why she was so insistent on coming with the wagon train. And the biggest question of all—could he trust her?

Cora wasn't ready to answer the unspoken questions. She searched her tired mind for something else to talk about. She realized she had not thanked Flynn for bringing her with him. Cora broke eye contact with him by reaching for the baby's blanket and covering him up. With her eyes on Noah, it was easier to speak. "Thank you, Flynn, for rescuing us and marrying me today. I know that wasn't what you had planned when you woke up this morning, but I don't know what I would have done otherwise."

When he did not reply, she continued, "We should get to that dance. I would hate to disappoint the ladies who helped me get ready for our wedding. They all seemed so excited about joining us for our first dance." She turned her head and moved closer to him. "You do know how to dance, don't you?"

A smile touched his lips and a dimple in his right cheek made an appearance. "Do I know how to dance?"

She chuckled. "That's the question."

Flynn took her by the hand. "Come on and I'll show you."

Cora tiptoed across to the wagon gate with Flynn. They were careful not to jostle the wagon. She realized that she wanted Noah to stay asleep because suddenly she felt like dancing with her new husband. Cora had to admit that she liked his lighthearted joking.

Flynn jumped to the ground, then turned to help her down. As soon as her feet touched the ground, Cora withdrew from his hold and turned toward the music. Her skin still tingled from where he'd held her hands.

"Mrs. Adams, I'll take good care of the baby while you are gone," Martha said, climbing into the wagon.

"Thank you, Martha. I'm sure he'll be fine." Cora hoped the baby would continue to sleep. She knew very little about her nephew and even less about his sleep patterns.

Flynn extended his elbow and smiled down at her. "Ready?"

She placed her hand in the crook of his elbow. From the sounds coming from the dance floor, everyone was already enjoying themselves.

They walked to the sidelines and stopped. Cora saw several young couples dancing merrily, along with a few older men who had no trouble keeping up with the fast beat. Their smiles and laughter were contagious, and she found her face stretching into a smile, as well.

The beat slowed and everyone moved to the sidelines.

Joe called from across the way. "We've been waiting for you to lead us in the first slow dance."

Flynn placed a hand on Cora's back. "Ready?"

She swallowed. Dancing was not her strong point, nor was she comfortable with having every eye on her. Gracie had been the outgoing twin, not her. She shifted from foot to foot. Taking a deep, unsteady breath, she stepped forward.

They walked to the center of the circle of people and faced each other. Music filled the night air, slow and sweet. Flynn gently took her into his arms, and they moved in unison around the dirt dance floor. Cora felt like she was floating. After several moments, others joined them.

Her husband whispered against her ear, making a shiver run down her spine. "That wasn't so bad, was it?"

She raised her eyes to find him watching her. His breath fanned the hair on her forehead, making her aware of just how close they were. "No." Her voice came out in a whisper. "Not bad at all. In fact, I quite like dancing."

Flynn chuckled and stood straight once more. He expertly turned her into a dip, causing a tingling in the pit of her stomach that had nothing to do with lack of balance. His gaze was as soft as a caress. They both remained motionless for a moment. Then he seemed to collect himself and brought her back into the circle of his arm. He pulled her closer to him and she felt the deep breath he inhaled. So she wasn't alone in feeling the electricity between them. But how could that be? They'd just met earlier this morning. She remembered her mother saying she fell in love with their dad at first sight, but she had never believed in it herself. Whatever this was between her and Flynn wasn't love—couldn't be. They were both overtired and that was the reason they were feeling romantic. That and the fact that they had just gotten married.

He inclined his forehead and touched it to hers. She tilted her chin up and his warm breath mingled with hers. "Cora?"

"Yes, Flynn?"

"I promise to care for you and keep you and Noah safe."

The intensity in his lowered voice and the security of his arms had an indefinable feeling of rightness.

Chapter Four

Flynn listened to the baby's soft cries and the sooth-ing sound of Cora's voice as she attempted to comfort him. Noah had woken when they arrived back after their dance. Sadly, the baby had not settled down yet, despite crying for nigh to an hour. The music continued in the distance. He could make out Martha and a young man dancing. He'd seen them earlier and wondered if there was a relationship brewing. She had looked at the young man with so much joy on her face. Such a con-trast to Cora, who carried such sorrow in her eyes. She must have loved Noah's father very much to be griev-ing so hard for him. Only for a moment had he seen the flush of happiness on her face—when they'd danced together. He wondered when or if he'd see it again.

Mrs. Philmore stepped out of the darkness. "He's not settling down, is he?"

Flynn stood taller. "No, ma'am."

She made a soft tsking sound. "He's probably fussy because of all the changes." She held out her hand. "Here, this might soothe him some."

Flynn accepted the small, cone-shaped item. He

brought it closer to his face. The fabric covering it was thin, but he couldn't quite tell what was inside. Mrs. Philmore had tied the top with some sort of twine. "What is it?"

The smile lines around her bright blue eyes crinkled up as she grinned. "We call it a sugar treat."

"It has sugar in it?" Flynn frowned, unsure what it was for. "Um, what am I supposed to do with it?"

Mrs. Philmore laughed and shook her head. "It's for the baby. Tell Cora to chew on the end and get it damp enough for the boy to suck on."

He must have wrinkled his nose or shown some other sign of disgust, because she laughed harder than she had before. "It's perfectly natural, Mr. Adams, for mothers to soften things for their children. The sweet will calm the baby down and then you'll be able to get some rest tonight. You have a lot to learn as a new father." She shook her head and started to walk away, then stopped. "Oh, and just in case she's never used one before, tell her to make sure not to let the lad keep it in his mouth after he's asleep."

Flynn nodded. "Thank you, Mrs. Philmore."

She nodded and then continued back to her own wagon.

Flynn pulled himself up into the wagon. It shifted slightly under his weight. Cora's troubled gaze met his. He held out the sweet for her to take. "Mrs. Philmore brought this. She says it will help the baby sleep." He still didn't see how giving a baby sugar would help it sleep but prayed it would be effective. Both he and Cora needed to sleep.

Cora took it and turned it over in her free hand. She clutched the baby in her other arm. "What is it?"

Flynn felt his face scrunch up as he said, "She called it—" he paused "—a sugar treat."

"Oh, I heard a couple ladies talking about making them one day at the general store." Cora stuck the tip between her lips. A smile touched her lips after she pulled it out. "Would you get me a little water in the bottom of the dipper?"

"She said you're supposed to chew on the tip until it's damp," he explained, happy that he knew something she didn't.

Cora nodded. "I know, but it will be faster to wet the end."

Noah shrieked at the top of his lungs, setting Flynn into action. He hurried out the back of the wagon to the water barrel and grabbed the dipper. Flynn's heart pounded in his chest at the child's obvious distress. He filled the bottom of the oversize spoon and then climbed back inside. He held the water out to Cora, who dipped in the end of the cone.

She rocked and cooed to Noah. Then when he opened his mouth to let out another bloodcurdling scream, she slipped the sweet treat inside. A single drop of water dripped from its tip onto the infant's tongue.

For a moment, Flynn held his breath and silently prayed the baby would understand and stop his howling. Noah opened his little eyes and met Flynn's gaze. He closed his lips around the sugar treat and sucked greedily, his lips smacking. Flynn released the air from his lungs and grinned at Cora. "It worked."

Cora's shoulders relaxed and she cradled the baby close to her body. "Thank the Lord."

"Mrs. Philmore said that will help him nod off but not to let him keep it in his mouth once he's sleeping."

Flynn watched as Noah's little eyes began to drift shut as if to confirm the older woman's words.

"Flynn?"

He turned his attention to her. "Yes?"

She ran her fingers across the baby's forehead. "Do you think we can get a milk cow at the first fort?"

Flynn shrugged. "Maybe. Why?"

"He needs milk." She kept her head bowed and didn't look up. Whether she was embarrassed or ashamed, he couldn't tell.

"How did you feed him today?" Flynn asked, painfully aware they were talking about a sensitive subject. He didn't dare ask why she needed outside means to feed her baby.

"I had a glass jar with milk inside. But it's empty now." Her voice sounded as if she were about to cry.

Flynn swallowed. Like most men, he hated to see a woman cry. He considered for a moment, then asked, "Have you thought about asking one of the other young mothers to help us, until we get to Fort Laramie?"

"I've thought about it but…" Her voice cut off and she didn't seem to be able to get out any more words.

He laid a soothing hand on her shoulder. "Maybe Mrs. Philmore can help us with this problem, too. You can ask her first thing in the morning. Until then, why don't you lie down with the baby and get some rest? This has been a long day for all of us."

Cora looked up at him. Her eyes swam with unshed tears. "Thank you, Flynn. I don't know what I would have done without you today."

Flynn merely nodded and hurried to leave. He scooped up his bedroll and climbed out the back of the wagon. The weight of the day rested heavily on him as he spread the bedroll under the wagon. Crickets and other insects sang as the camped wagons settled in for the night. What had he done? How had the direction of his life changed so drastically? And why wasn't he more upset about that? His focus should be on finding a killer, not on buying a cow so a baby who wasn't even his would have milk.

Inside the wagon, Cora was hoping and praying that Flynn wasn't plagued with the uncertainties she felt herself. Approaching Flynn about her inability to give the baby milk had scared her spitless. What must he be thinking? Had he figured out that Noah wasn't her child? Why else would she not be breastfeeding the baby?

Cora wished for her soft bed as she lay down on the hard wooden floor of the prairie schooner. The baby made a sucking sound against his small fist. She closed her eyes in order to silently pray and ask the good Lord above to supply a means of feeding the baby. She would try him on small pieces of mashed-up egg in the morning with a bit of mush. Hopefully that might hold him till milk could be found. She'd seen her sister popping little bits of different types of food in his mouth when he was barely six months old, so it wasn't like he'd never tasted solid food—but she didn't know for sure what he'd had and what was safe for him. So many things she'd need to learn about Noah; and what about herself? She'd only ever worked at teaching. Could she handle all the tasks expected of a wife till they arrived in Oregon? Would she always feel this tired at the end of the day?

The wagon jerked, waking Cora from a sound sleep. She looked about in confusion, certain that no more than a few minutes had passed. Why were they leaving in the middle of the night? Noah continued to sleep on her chest, sucking his small fist.

She eased into a sitting position, keeping the child cradled against her. The sounds of men calling to their animals and women's voices carried on the breeze. Cora looked through the wagon's entry and could see sunlight through the tarp flap. Her gaze swung to where Flynn had retrieved his bedroll the night before. It rested against the pile of blankets. How long had she and the baby slept?

Her hand flew to her lips and she gasped. What about breakfast and breaking camp? Had Flynn gone without rather than wake her and the baby? Heat filled her face. Had the other women noticed how lazy she had been? That she hadn't taken care of her campsite or new husband? Were they talking about her right now?

Noah squirmed against her. She gently laid him down and swaddled him tightly into a soft blanket. Then Cora finger-combed her hair. Once she had her hair up in a light bun, she stuck her head through the wagon slit and found Flynn driving the oxen.

He glanced her way. "I'm sorry. I had hoped you would be able to rest a little longer." He scooted over on the seat and motioned for her to join him.

Cora awkwardly climbed onto the seat beside him. "Thank you, but the wagon isn't conducive to sleeping when it's moving. I wish you had awakened me earlier. I could have fixed you and Joe breakfast."

Flynn leaned over until their shoulders touched. "You and Noah had a rough night. Besides, Joe brought me over a hot biscuit with fried bacon in it." He grinned at the sound of her stomach growling in response to his description of the breakfast he had enjoyed.

Heat filled her cheeks at her body's betrayal of hunger. The day before, she'd been too nervous to eat much. "Well, I'm glad you both had a hot breakfast. I'll have to thank Sarah when we stop for lunch."

He reached under the seat and handed her a lumpy parcel wrapped in a piece of cloth. Cora smiled in happiness. "Breakfast?"

Flynn nodded. "Yep. Sarah didn't forget you."

Cora opened the cloth and pulled out a warm biscuit. "Thank the good Lord." She silently did just that and then sank her teeth into the best biscuit she had ever eaten. Before she could finish chewing, the baby cried.

Flynn stated the obvious. "He's up again."

She wanted to groan but didn't. To do so would seem very unmotherly. Instead, she took another quick bite of the biscuit and bacon, then handed the rest to Flynn. "I'd best go get him. He'll need to be changed."

He took her breakfast and rewrapped it in the cloth with one hand. "This will be here when you are done." Flynn placed it back under the seat.

"Thank you." Cora hurried to Noah, who was now in a full-fledged snit. She felt sure the whole wagon train could hear his cries. If he was half as hungry as she'd felt a few minutes earlier, Cora could understand his frustrations.

She gave him the sugar sweet and quickly changed his wet diaper for a clean one. The baby continued to fuss when the sugar sweet didn't sate his hunger. Maybe if she sat with him on the seat, he could look about and would momentarily forget his empty belly.

Cora opened the front flap. "Would it be all right with you if I brought Noah up there?"

Flynn nodded. "Hand him to me and then come on up." He extended one arm out.

Cora wasn't sure if handing the baby off was a good idea. She met his gaze. "Promise you won't drop him."

He chuckled. "He's not the first baby I've held with one arm, Cora. Trust me. I won't drop him."

Taking a deep breath, she handed Noah to him.

Flynn wrapped his arm around the baby's middle and pulled him close while Cora climbed back onto the wagon seat. By the time she was settled, Flynn had tucked the baby into the crook of his arm so that Noah could lean against his body and look around.

Noah had quit fussing for the moment, but Cora didn't think his calmness would last long. The baby was hungry.

Joe's sister Martha ran up beside the moving wagon. "Mrs. Adams?"

Cora heard Martha's voice calling someone, but she continued to focus on Noah and the problem of what to feed him. She wished Gracie had written some notes on how to care for the baby. Then she felt guilty for the thought. Gracie hadn't planned on dying, so why would she have written notes?

Flynn cleared his throat to get her attention. "Cora? I believe Martha is talking to you."

She jerked her gaze from Noah. "What?"

He indicated his head toward Martha, who was walking beside the wagon, waiting for her response.

Cora turned to look at the teenager. "Oh, I'm sorry, Martha." Only then did it dawn on her that Martha had indeed been calling her. "I'm not used to my new married name. Please, call me Cora."

Martha smiled up at her. "I understand." She held up a small wooden bowl and spoon. "Here. Ma thought the baby might like some warm cornmeal mush for breakfast."

Cornmeal mush! How thoughtful of the woman to share it with her—and how embarrassing for Cora that Sarah knew she'd need the help since she'd slept the morning away. Cora leaned over and took the bowl and spoon. "Oh, Martha, thank you so much."

"You're welcome. Ma also said that when we stop for lunch, she'd like to have a short visit with you."

Cora's voice was resigned but courteous. "Tell her I'll come over as soon as I clean up our lunch."

Martha nodded and then turned to go back to her parents' wagon.

Cora called after her. "And, Martha, please tell Sarah I said thank you, for everything."

"I will." Martha picked up her skirts and ran back to her mother, who waved from the seat beside her husband.

"That was mighty nice of Mrs. Philmore." Flynn turned the baby so that Cora could feed him.

She answered Flynn with a voice filled with gratitude. "It was exceptionally nice of her. In fact, I think she just may be one of the nicest people I've met so far. I'll be sure to thank her personally when we stop." She began feeding a very hungry Noah.

Noah smacked his lips and grabbed for the spoon. Cora gently moved it out of his reach, guiding it to his mouth. He reminded her of a baby bird, opening his tiny mouth wide for his next bite. Cora filled his little spoon time and again till the mush was gone.

Cora heaved a sigh of relief. Her baby was fed, his little tummy stretched tight. She owed Mrs. Philmore a great debt.

For the rest of the morning, Cora alternated back and forth between worry and excitement. The scenery held her captivated and she heard hope and expectations in the conversations around her.

Right before they were to stop for lunch, Noah's eyes began to close, but he twisted and turned, fighting sleep. Cora wondered if nine-month-old babies were supposed to sleep as much as Noah seemed to. Whom could she ask? She was afraid to ask anyone. As his mother, she was supposed to know everything about her baby's habits already.

She remembered that Sarah had asked her to stop by during their lunch break. Her thoughts and fears taunted her. Did she plan on lecturing her about getting up early enough to feed Flynn and Joe? Or worse... had Sarah guessed that Cora wasn't Noah's ma? Had she told her husband? Or Joe? Or Martha? Anyone?

Chapter Five

At the wagon master's command, the wagon train
came to a slow stop. Dust boiled as one by one the wagons circled up. Cheers from tired travelers and bark-
ing dogs made conversation difficult to be heard, so
Flynn circled his wagon per the hand signals from Mr.
Philmore until he finally was able to leap off his seat,
to the ground. He stretched and walked a few steps,
trying to get his land legs back.

Flynn helped Cora down and then placed baby Noah
in her extended arms. He paused. "Would you like me
to take him with me?"

She shook her head. "No. I need to learn how to
take care of him and prepare meals for us at the same
time." Cora's gaze met his. "I'm certain that's what
Mrs. Philmore wishes to share with me."

She sounded as if she was trying to convince herself
as much as she wanted to convince him, and he saw
the now-familiar caution in her eyes. She seemed to always be on edge. She reminded him of women whose
husbands had abused them, always looking over her

shoulder. Always fidgeting. What was she so afraid of? Could she have been the victim of spousal abuse?

He knew it was too soon to ask such personal questions. Right now, questions about her past would likely cause her to panic, and maybe even bolt. It didn't take a lawman to know that even now Cora was running. He realized that he had been staring down at her for longer than she was comfortable with. "All right, but if you need help, let me know."

A small smile parted her lips. "Thank you. I will."

He started to walk away when she called his name. He turned back to her, a brow raised in question.

Cora took a step back as if she feared he would get too close to her and the baby. "You don't have to act like you care about Noah. That wasn't part of the deal." She suddenly seemed to realize how that sounded and closed her eyes and shook her head. "I don't mean to sound ungrateful for your help with Noah… I just don't want you to feel it's expected of you."

He fought the urge to wrap her in his arms and tell her that things would be okay. That, together, they would get to Oregon. That he would take care of her and the baby. But he'd already told her, so he didn't waste his breath repeating himself. It would take time for her to believe him.

Instead, Flynn fingered a loose tendril of hair on her cheek. "I seldom say or do things that I don't mean." He noticed Mr. Clarkson headed their way. He turned to greet the man, hoping whatever he wanted to discuss wouldn't take long—he had chores to do himself. In case he needed a reminder, the oxen began to paw at the ground and make bawling noises in their throats.

Flynn smiled and patted the nearest one on the rump. "All right, boys."

"These beasts wait for no man." Mr. Clarkson stepped around the edge of his wagon.

"I understand what you mean." Taking the words as permission to see to the animals as they talked, Flynn unhooked the oxen from his wagon.

Mr. Clarkson removed his hat and scratched his head. "That seems like a lot of work you're going through. We'll be leaving shortly and you'll just have to hook them right back to the wagon."

Flynn shrugged. "They need to eat and drink, too. The way I figure, letting them graze and drink from the river now will refresh them and they will pull better this afternoon."

"You don't know much about farm animals, do you, Mr. Adams?"

Flynn unhooked the last of the yokes and then rubbed the nose of the nearest ox. "Mr. Clarkson, I grew up on a ranch. Animals are not that different from people. They need to eat, drink and rest just as we do. Giving them time to rest goes a long way with them."

"They are beasts of the fields." Mr. Clarkson spit on the ground.

Flynn wondered if this conversation was going anyplace. "Yes, beasts that have to get us all the way to Oregon. My fellas here will work harder for me if I treat them with kindness and avoid whipping them." He started to tug them away from the circled wagon and tried not to show his surprise when Mr. Clarkson followed. "Think of them like your legs—if they stop working, you're going nowhere fast."

Joe jogged up beside them. "I'll take care of the

oxen, Flynn. Mr. Tucker, the wagon master, would like a word with you and Mr. Clarkson."

Flynn grinned at Joe. "Thank you, Joe." He handed the reins to the young man and then turned to Mr. Clarkson. "Looks like we've been summoned. We better not keep him waiting."

Mr. Clarkson nodded as they walked back to the wagons. "I'll stop and let the missus know where we're going."

Flynn smiled. "How long have you been married?"

"Not long. We're still getting used to it, but we're doing just fine."

There was a new twinkle in the older man's eyes when he talked of his wife. He truly loved her. Maybe Mr. Clarkson could teach him how to have a happy marriage. And if the older man would listen, perhaps he could return the favor by teaching him how to respect his animals and other people. "I better do the same. Cora will need to know I'll be a little late for lunch."

Flynn parted ways with Mr. Clarkson and walked to where Cora had already started a small fire and was mixing a bowl of what looked like dough. She looked up as he approached.

"The wagon master has asked to see me. Want me to take the boy now?" His gaze moved to where she had set four boxes and placed the little one inside the protected space they created.

Cora smiled. "I was wrong earlier. You are welcome to take him anytime you want to, Flynn."

He didn't know why, but showing that she trusted him with the baby sparked a happiness in him. "Then I think I'll take him to his first meeting with the wagon master." He scooped Noah up and placed him in his arms so that the boy could look about.

The baby puckered his small lips as if he were going to cry but seemed to change his mind. He tilted his head back against Flynn's chest and looked Flynn in the eyes. Could a child this small judge the character of a man? If so, Noah seemed to deem Flynn worthy of his trust, because he grinned. Flynn returned the smile and then proceeded to his meeting with the wagon master.

Someone ran toward him, the slap of feet against the earth alerting Flynn to their approach. Flynn shifted the baby to his side and instinctively reached for the gun strapped to his hip. He forced himself to turn his head and look at the man running toward him. Seeing Mr. Clarkson, Flynn relaxed his hold on Noah and moved his hand from the gun handle.

Huffing and puffing, the older man announced, "I told Doc to walk our oxen down by the water with yours. I hope you don't mind."

"I'm glad you changed your mind about leaving them hitched up during the lunch break. It's going to take all we have, both man and beast, to get to Oregon." Flynn continued to where he saw the wagon master and most of the men gathered under a cluster of trees.

Clarkson shook his head. "Doc wasn't pleased but he did it. You know, sometimes I wonder why he agreed to come with us. He doesn't want to do anything but drive the wagon. Although, I did hear him telling the ladies that if their families needed a doctor, he'd be happy to help them."

Flynn tried to remember if Doc had done more than doctoring when he'd lived in Texas. Until the night Miriam had died, Flynn hadn't paid much attention to the doctor. It was only after Miriam's death that he'd turned his attention to the man, seeking his insight from the examination of her body to see if it had yielded any clues that might lead to her killer.

The wagon master's voice caught Flynn's attention, pulling him from the past. "We'll give the rest of the men a few more minutes to get here." He turned to the scout and proceeded to chat with him in low tones.

Flynn took the time to search the features of each man who stood about chatting. If he were wanted for murder, Flynn didn't think he'd look as relaxed as these men did. But he also wouldn't be stupid enough to allow his unease to show, either. If his killer was easy to capture, it would have happened long ago. Flynn was dealing with a wily, careful man. Discovering his identity would take time and might require him to get to know each man personally.

"I see the wife has already got you taking care of her son for her."

Flynn turned to find John Hart, the owner of the wagon traveling in front of Mr. Clarkson's. Mr. Hart was a big man with a copper-red beard and matching hair that stuck out from under his hat like a scarecrow. His age was likely midtwenties to early thirties, but he acted like an old soul. He was not only tall but also built much like a water barrel, given his wide chest. His arm muscles bulged, as well. His bright green eyes sparkled, and his lips curved as if always on the verge of laughter.

"Well, friend, he's my son, too, now, so I thought I should act like it and bring him to a men's meeting." Flynn heard the defensive edge to his words and wished he could have sweetened them a little. It would not do for folks to think he took offense easily.

Mr. Hart chuckled good-naturedly. "I know what you mean." He turned so that Flynn could see the toddler clinging to the back of his vest.

Laughter floated up from Flynn's throat. He extended his hand and Mr. Hart clasped it securely, still chuckling.

"Is this your first child, too?" Flynn questioned, his curiosity piqued.

"Oh, no, this is number six." Mr. Hart didn't seem bothered by the number of kids he had, so Flynn figured he wouldn't mind a few questions.

"Well, I'll know whom to ask if I run into problems with this one."

Mr. Hart harrumphed. "Not *if*," he stated matter-of-factly, "just when. Once a man has kids, there will be problems till that child is grown." He seemed to ponder what he was saying. "And even after they're adults, they sometimes cause problems."

Flynn noticed the man's expression hadn't changed from the pleasant one of previous moments. "That doesn't seem to bother you overly much."

"Nope, it doesn't. Children make a home. Gives a man something worthwhile to invest in. Take me, for example. I have four sons. I'm teaching each one of them to work hard, to be honest, to care for those around them, and most of all, I'm instilling everything that's important to me into them. My faith and my love for their mother and for them and their sisters."

Flynn viewed the man in front of him with new respect. "And I guess your wife will teach the girls."

"That she will, but so will I. It's important that they

learn how a man should treat a lady, and they will learn that by the way I treat their ma."

Flynn's mind boggled at the wisdom of John Hart. "I guess there's more that goes into parenting than I first thought."

Mr. Hart laughed heartily and slapped Flynn on the back amiably. "You'd be correct on that, my friend."

"How do you know if you're doing it right?"

"You'll never know for sure, so all you can do is be the best man you can be yourself. Believe strongly in God, follow His teachings, and your children will grow up knowing truth. They won't be easily deceived if they've been taught right from wrong."

"Gather round, men. I think everyone is here." Samuel Tucker, the wagon master, motioned for them to move closer. Once everyone moved forward, he climbed on the tongue of a wagon so everyone could see him. He asked, "Did we have any problems this morning that need to be addressed?"

They all shook their heads.

"Good. You will soon learn that our noon break is a time of rest. It's also a time to fix any minor problems you have with your wagon or family. Men, try to rest, especially at the beginning of our journey. Later, when things get rough, we might have to do some major repairs on our wagons, deal with exhausted, crying women, or mourn the loss of a friend or a loved one. This is not an easy trip, so if you and your family are having second thoughts after this morning, you need to let us know now. There's no shame in turning back." He waited while they all thought on his words. The wagon master met each man's gaze.

He nodded. "Since you have decided to press on,

there are a few things I will expect from you. Now that we are a few miles from Independence, we'll each do security duty. Last night, Levi and I stood guard. Starting tonight, three men will take the first watch and three the second watch. If you have the second watch, I expect you to try and sleep until time for your watch. We need you alert—the wagon train's safety will be in your hands. Also, until we get to Oregon, I expect you to help each other. Anyone who causes trouble will answer to me."

Flynn watched the men's reactions. They nodded their understanding of what the wagon master said and seemed to accept him at his word. Flynn wondered how long their current camaraderie would last.

"Does anyone have any questions before we part?"

Again, heads shook negatively.

Except for Mr. Clarkson. He asked, "Who has watch tonight?"

Mr. Tucker nodded. "That's a good question. I almost forgot. Jones, Greene and Miller have the first watch. Adams, Hart and McDougal have the second." Again, his gaze found the eyes of each man that he'd just named.

Flynn nodded his acceptance of the assignment. He already knew that the second watch was from midnight to four in the morning. Being a lawman, he knew to take sleep where he could get it. There had been many a night that his job kept him awake all night.

The big man next to him slapped him on the back. "Looks like the two of us will be keeping the watch together."

Flynn nodded. "I suppose we should get our children to their mas and give them the news." He smiled. "I'll see you in a few hours."

Mr. Clarkson walked with Flynn as they returned to the wagons. "Would you like me to take your watch?"

It was nice of him to ask but Flynn refused. "Thanks for the offer, but I'll be fine."

"I just thought being newly wed and all, your missus might not be too happy about you getting the first night's watch." He took his hat off and rubbed his forehead. "I never did thank you for taking her in the way you did."

Flynn stopped and looked at the man, unsure how to reply. He'd understood why Clarkson needed a second driver, but surely one more person traveling with them wouldn't have been that big a hardship on the Clarksons. So why had they put her out like that? "Care if I ask why you did it?"

The old man shrugged. "Well, Dr. Shipman wasn't exactly prepared to go to Oregon when I asked him to join us. But we didn't have much time to get more supplies. I'm ashamed to say it, but we figured a slip of a girl wouldn't eat much, and so I let the missus talk me into a new dress and hat when I should have used the money to buy extra rations."

"Are you telling me you spent Cora's money on a new dress and hat for your wife?"

He sighed heavily. "I reckon I am."

Flynn shook his head. "So how were you going to feed her?"

"I'm a fairly good hunter."

He didn't much care for the whine in the older man's voice. Flynn turned to return to camp but then stopped once more. "Doc didn't bring any supplies with him? No food? No coffee?"

"Nope, and by the time we convinced him to join us, we didn't have time to buy extra. The train would have left without us if we'd stopped to buy more supplies." He continued walking. "Doc says he'll help me replenish our supplies and buy his own supplies when we get to Fort Laramie."

While joining the Clarksons' wagon had been a last-minute decision, Doc had said that he'd planned to go on the wagon train with someone else. So why hadn't he prepared any supplies? The lack of preparation seemed odd and not in line with what he believed to be the doctor's character. Maybe he didn't know the man as well as he thought.

Cora finished frying the bacon and placed it between two flapjacks. She had made such a mess of lunch that she wanted to sit down and cry. Cooking on a stove was so different from cooking over an open flame on the trail. Clearly, it would require lots of practice.

She would just have to face him and let him know that she'd tried her best. Even though the biscuits she had attempted to make were hard and burnt on the outside while still being doughy on the inside, the Millers' dog thought they were great eating. She hadn't given them to the dog intentionally; truth was, he had managed to steal some of the biscuits from the stump she'd placed them on to cool. She prayed Flynn wouldn't be too upset at her meager, poorly made food offering.

Cora placed the flapjacks and bacon on top of a box where she could watch them and then straightened her back. Standing over a fire would take some getting used to also. Her lips tightened. She would learn how to cook on the trail just like she'd learned everything else in life. She might not have succeeded quite as she'd hoped, but she refused to be defeated.

She saw Flynn returning. He seemed deep in thought, with Noah turned to face outward, his little eyes taking in everything at once. Cora prayed Flynn would be distracted enough to not notice what a horrible campsite cook he had married. She quickly put two flapjack sandwiches on the only plate she could find in the wagon.

When he noticed her waiting for him, Flynn smiled. Cora couldn't help but notice how handsome he was. And when he smiled, she found it impossible not to return the gesture.

"I hope you like flapjacks and bacon." She took Noah from Flynn and handed him the plate.

"Thank you. Have you eaten already?" Flynn sat down on the stump.

Cora didn't want to lie to him, so she shook her head, then watched as he took the first bite. No matter how hard he tried, Flynn couldn't hide the fact that this wasn't his favorite meal. He chewed and chewed and then chewed some more. "You don't have to eat it, Flynn. I know it's not good."

He swallowed. "No, it's fine." Flynn looked at the flapjack sandwich and took another bite. Again, he chewed for several moments before swallowing. "You'll get the hang of cooking outdoors soon enough. If you want, I can even help you. I have a little experience with it myself."

Cora felt tears burn the backs of her eyes. She should have tried the flapjacks before serving them to him. "I have more bacon, if you want to just eat that for now. I'll ask Sarah for help. I'm so sorry, Flynn."

He pulled the bacon out and bit into it. "This is good bacon," he offered.

Martha walked up to their campsite, carrying a covered bowl. "Hi, Cora, Mr. Adams. Ma made extra bacon and beans for lunch and wondered if you would like them."

"See, Cora, the good Lord supplies all our needs." Flynn smiled at Martha and took the bowl. "Thank you, Martha."

Cora felt her cheeks flame and silently vowed to herself to get the hang of cooking over the open flame so that no one else would have to take care of her family for her. Flynn had practically jumped at the chance to take the food. Cora chanted silently to herself, *I will not cry, I will not cry.* She cleared her throat and said, "Yes, thank you, Martha. I'll bring your mother's bowl to her in a few minutes."

Martha nodded. "May I take Noah back to our wagon? I made some cornmeal mush for him and little Daniel. I think Daniel will eat his mush more happily if he has someone to share it with."

She knew the mush she'd made was probably inedible, too. It sat beside the fire, thick and lumpy. Cora had planned to add water to it to try to thin and smooth it. She realized Martha was waiting for an answer. "Only if you have plenty."

"Oh, we do. I made too much. Ma is teaching me how to cook, and I tend to make too much of everything." Martha reached out for Noah, who went to her willingly. That was two people he seemed comfortable with. Flynn and Martha. At least she'd get a break every now and then. It had been one of the concerns that plagued her mind. To go from looking after only herself to a helpless baby depending on her twenty-four hours a day had been a lot to contemplate.

"Thank you, Martha, and be sure to thank your ma."

Cora picked up the water bucket when Martha left. "I will be back shortly," she called to Flynn, who was eating from the bowl Martha had brought.

She walked to the bank of the creek and sat down on the root of a giant tree. She closed her eyes, feeling utterly miserable. What was she going to do? Her cooking skills were horrible. She'd messed up both Flynn's and Noah's lunches. Her own stomach growled in hunger. Add to that a sense of complete loss over her sister's death, and she felt herself losing control.

Chapter Six

Flynn hadn't been at the campsite when she'd returned from the creek. Cora lifted the water bucket and re-filled the barrel on the side of their wagon. She ate the beans and bacon he'd left in Sarah's bowl, gathered up the rest of the dirty dishes and washed them in a pan of hot water. At least she knew how to boil water, she thought bitterly as she finished drying the bowl Martha had left. Once her campsite was cleaned, she walked to the Philmores' wagon.

Sarah looked up from her own dishwashing tub and smiled. "How are you today, Cora?"

She thought about lying and saying she was fine but knew that would not be the right thing to do. "I'm tired and the day isn't half over."

"I know what you mean." Sarah handed a bowl to one of her daughters who was helping do the dishes. "But we'll get used to this life soon and it will seem as if we've been doing this forever."

Cora didn't think she'd ever get used to the new life that stretched out before her for the next few months— and what about when it was over? She had no idea what she would do once she got to Oregon. Staying married to Flynn would be the best option for her, rather than having to figure out how to support herself and Noah on her own, but that wasn't what they'd agreed on and it was too early to even think along those lines. She realized her quietness could be mistaken for rudeness and said, "Perhaps you are right."

Sarah smiled. "Perhaps." She motioned for Martha to join them. "Martha, keep an eye on the kids and lend a hand with the washing up while Cora and I walk down to the river."

"All right, Ma." Martha placed Noah inside a tent with another baby who Cora assumed was Daniel. Then she proceeded to help her younger sister finish the dishes.

Cora followed Sarah away from the wagons. She wondered why the older woman had summoned her but sensed it would be better to let Sarah get to her reason on her own time. Oftentimes in the past, the parent of one of Cora's students would ask to speak to her, and she'd learned it was easier to wait them out and let them speak their minds instead of trying to coax information from them before they were ready to share.

"You must be wondering why I asked to speak to you," Sarah began. She pulled a blade of grass from the ground and proceeded to shred it between her fingers.

Cora smiled. "It had crossed my mind."

Sarah walked to a small grove of trees and leaned against one. "Please, don't think ill of my Martha. She is curious, and while taking care of the baby before your wedding, she noticed that you and Flynn don't have the supplies you need to make this journey."

How could she respond to that statement? It was

true—Mr. Clarkson had skimped on her supplies. They didn't have the flour, sugar and some other things that they needed. Once she'd had a chance to inventory the supplies, Cora had also realized they were short. Now she understood why Sarah was sending food to their wagon. Martha had told her that they didn't have enough. Cora had planned on talking to Flynn about their need this afternoon. "She's right. We don't."

"What are you going to do?" Sarah's face held the grimness that Cora felt.

She crossed her arms. "I'll have to talk to Flynn first, but I expect we'll pick up more supplies at Fort Laramie."

"That's a good plan. Do you have enough to get you that far?"

Cora nodded. "I believe so." If she didn't burn everything up.

"We brought plenty, so if you need anything, please feel free to ask," Sarah offered. Her gaze searched Cora's.

It was a very nice gesture of friendship that demonstrated the depth of Sarah's kindness. "Thank you." Cora sucked her bottom lip between her teeth. Pride fought her need to ask for help. She didn't want to confess that she didn't know how to cook over an open flame. Women were supposed to know how to be good homemakers. Cora had always thought her mother was a natural at being the woman of the house. She seemed to know how to do everything and anything without having to ask anyone how. But if that was a natural trait, she had not inherited it from her mother. She was capable enough to get by in a real kitchen, but she didn't have the kind of deeper understanding that would let her adapt her cooking techniques to this very new situation.

"Is something wrong?" Sarah pushed away from the tree and took two steps toward her, then stopped.

Cora released her bottom lip. "It's embarrassing."

"Many things in a woman's life are. What is embarrassing to you today?"

Tears welled in Cora's eyes. She swallowed hard. "I don't know how to cook over a campfire." The words sounded as if they had stuck in her throat before pushing their way out. Heat filled Cora's face, and no matter how hard she tried, she couldn't keep the tears at bay.

Sarah was at her side in an instant. "Oh, child. That's nothing to cry about." She tucked Cora into a tight hug. "Martha and I can teach you that. And since our menu is limited, there really isn't that much to learn. You'll be making biscuits and such in no time."

Cora hadn't been comforted in so long that she couldn't stop crying. There were so many things to cry about. Her sister's death, not knowing how to properly care for Noah, her fear that her brother-in-law would catch up to her and take the baby away, her anxiety over getting to Oregon and not being able to find work or shelter. So many doubts and fears that she couldn't contain any longer.

Sarah gently led her deeper into the tree line and out of sight of the camp. "Come along, Cora. I believe you and I have a lot more talking to do."

Cora found herself spilling everything to Sarah. Her sister's death, her running from her brother-in-law, not knowing what to do to supply Noah with the nourishment he needed. The only thing she didn't confess was that her marriage to Flynn was a marriage of convenience only—and one that would end once they reached Oregon. There was no way to share that without explaining Flynn's reasons, and she wouldn't betray his confidence.

"Please don't tell anyone else that I'm not Noah's mother," she pleaded.

Sarah handed her a handkerchief from her apron pocket. "As far as I'm concerned, you *are* his mother. Nothing you've shared here today will go any further." She waited for Cora to wipe her face and blow her nose. "I have a plan to help you and keep the other women from asking lots of questions."

Cora searched her face. "All right."

"Martha wants to be a schoolteacher. Last night at the dance, she talked to a girl who used to be one of your students—but she had to quit school and didn't know that you'd gotten married and had a baby. Ever since she learned that, Martha has been working up the courage to ask you if you will teach her how to become a teacher."

Cora hadn't realized a former student was on the train. But they were a large group and she hadn't really had time to interact with everyone yet. She could only be grateful it wasn't a more recent student who would have questioned Cora's identity as a widow and a mother when she'd been unmarried and childless just days before. "I'll be happy to teach her what I know." She felt giddy at the thought of teaching—of tackling something she actually knew how to do. She loved her work and had been saddened at the thought that her time of teaching was over. Knowing she'd be able to teach again, if only for a few months, gave her something to look forward to.

Sarah held her hand up. "You're not going to make it that easy for her."

Confused, Cora asked, "I'm not?"

Shaking her head, Sarah answered, "No, you are not. Her job will be to help you with Noah during the day in exchange for you going over lessons with her in the evenings, if that is acceptable to you." Sarah crossed her arms over her ample bosom.

"But don't you need her assisting you with Daniel and the other kids?" Cora didn't want to take Sarah's help from her.

A grin covered Sarah's face. "I do, but this is going to work for me, as well. Martha will also watch her brothers and sisters during the day while she's watching Noah—plus teach them their school lessons."

"That seems like a lot to ask of her," Cora protested.

"Not really. She was going to be doing all of that anyway. All we are doing is adding one more child for her to watch and giving her training to help with the teaching tasks. You'll have your days free to learn everything you need to know about how to manage your tasks on the trail without having to worry about childcare. And if your brother-in-law shows up during the day, Noah will be at our wagon, not yours." She smiled. "How many students did you teach at a time?"

"Anywhere from ten to twenty a day."

"And what ages were they?"

Cora allowed herself to go back in time and think about her students. It seemed as if she'd been out of her schoolhouse forever, but in truth, it had only been two days. "From five to eighteen."

"The way I see it, Martha will learn what it's like

to teach children of several different ages at a time."
Sarah began walking back toward the wagons.

"But having two babies will make it harder on her."
Cora walked beside her.

Sarah nodded. "True, but Martha isn't just training
to be a teacher. Someday she will have a family of her
own and she'll probably have at least two young'uns to
take care of once the older ones are ready for school-
ing. And more than likely they will be a year apart, unless she has twins and then they will be the same age."

Just before they got back to the Philmore wagon,
Cora admitted, "Sarah, I don't know how to feed Noah.
He needs milk that I'm not able to give him."

"We have several milk cows. I'll tell Mr. Philmore
that we need to sell one to Flynn so the baby will have
fresh milk. The other ladies will understand that the
stress of going on this trip and being newly widowed
and even more newly married has caused your milk
to dry up."

Heat filled Cora's face once more. She looked to her
wagon, where Flynn had begun to pack up the meager supplies she'd pulled out. "Thank you. I better get
Noah and then head back to my wagon and help Flynn."

Cora walked the rest of the way to Sarah's wagon
to collect the baby. She wasn't sure Sarah's thinking
process was solid, but the other woman was certainly
doing a better job raising kids than Cora, so she'd trust
Sarah's wisdom. Whether this worked or not, she could
use the extra help with Noah, and in time, she'd learn
how to cook over a campfire.

Flynn watched Cora and Sarah return to Sarah's
wagon. He couldn't help but wonder what the two

women had talked about. Had Sarah asked about their marriage? Did she have wifely advice to give? Or had she noticed that Cora wasn't cut out to travel the Oregon Trail and was telling her there was still time to turn back?

Lunch had shown him that Cora had no idea how to cook over an open flame. He would never tell Cora that her flapjacks were tasteless or that the bacon had been too stringy, but they were. Even so, a smile touched his lips. Her cooking left much to be desired, but over the last two days he'd come to appreciate his new wife's grit and determination. While the events of the past few days must have rattled her considerably, she'd consistently maintained her poise and her compassion, showing concern for his and Noah's needs before ever thinking of herself. He admired his lovely new wife and looked forward to seeing how she'd rise to the various challenges the journey would offer.

Joe, back from tending to the oxen, slapped him on the back. "Looks like Cora's gonna be busy with Ma for a little longer. We might as well finish packing up."

Flynn grinned. "Then you are just in time. This is the last pan to be put away." He placed the pan into the wooden crate at his feet.

The teenager laughed. "I believe you are right."

He looked to the young man. Could he trust the boy with his new family? Flynn told himself he could and then said, "I have guard duty tonight. Do you mind sleeping under our wagon while I'm gone?"

Joe grinned. "I was hoping you'd ask. It's a lot quieter here than at our wagons."

Wagons? Flynn set the wooden crate they'd been

using for a chair into the wagon. "How many wagons does your family have?"

"Two." Joe poured water into the cooking pit to make sure no sparks were left in the circle of rocks.

Now, why hadn't he known that the Philmores had more than one wagon? He'd only known of the one that Cora was visiting.

"We have the bigger wagon at the back of the train. It has all the store supplies in it," Joe continued as he put the bucket away. "Pa says we're going to need everything in that wagon, if we are to make a decent start in Oregon."

Flynn had known the Philmores planned to open a store but hadn't considered they had more than one wagon to get all the necessary supplies there. "I'm surprised your pa let you help me despite having two wagons."

"Oh, that's because my brother Charlie and his friend Mark are taking care of the second wagon."

Once more, Joe had revealed how little Flynn knew about the Philmore family. He placed his hands on his hips and grinned. "Joe, how many brothers and sisters do you have?"

Joe laughed. "Seven. Charlie is the oldest—he's twenty. And Daniel is the baby—he just turned one."

Flynn whistled low between his teeth. "That's quite an age difference."

"Yep, but Pa says God gives children when He's ready and not a minute sooner." Joe grinned. "I'll go get the oxen and get them teamed up. You do want me to drive this afternoon, don't you?" He waited with a serious look on his face. Now that he was talking about the job he was hired for, Joe looked older and more responsible.

Tying the flap closed on the wagon, Flynn nodded. "Yes, but I think we'll start walking along beside the team instead of riding. Our extra weight doesn't seem that much for the animals to pull now, but as we journey, and they start to wear out, lightening their load just that small bit could make the difference in making it to Oregon or not."

Joe nodded his agreement. "Pa and Charlie were saying the same thing last night. I suppose all the men will be walking soon." The boy turned and headed to where the oxen were staked out, eating fresh spring grass.

Life on the Oregon Trail was definitely different from when he was traveling alone on the trail of a bad guy. Here Flynn had to think about others and how his actions would affect them.

His gaze moved about the camp. Women, men and children busily packed their things back into the wagons. He could see and hear the herds of cattle being rounded up and driven into position to leave. Somewhere nearby, chickens squawked and clucked. Flynn wondered if the birds would make it to Oregon or if they were intended for the cooking pot somewhere along the trail.

He looked over at the Philmore wagon once more. Cora hurried toward him with Noah on her hip. The little boy looked sleepy. His little head rested on Cora's shoulder.

When she got close enough to him, Cora exclaimed, "I'm sorry, Flynn. I meant to be back in plenty of time to put away camp."

"No harm done. How was your visit with Mrs. Philmore?" He admired the sprinkling of freckles across her nose.

Cora smiled. "It was good. She has agreed to teach me how to cook so that you don't starve to death on the trail."

How did a man answer that? If he said he was glad, she might take offense and think he thought her cooking was bad—which it was, though he wouldn't say that. If he told Cora that she didn't need the lessons because her cooking wasn't that terrible, she might take him at his word and he'd have to eat whatever she dished up. Flynn decided to answer with what he thought his own father would have said to his mother to get out of trouble. "If that's what you think is best, then good."

"I do. You weren't the only one who had to choke down that lunch." Her eyes sparkled happily for the first time since he'd met her. A dimple showed in her left cheek when she smiled broadly.

Flynn liked this relaxed, smiling Cora. "Do you mind if I walk with you this afternoon? We have a few things to talk about, but first I need to help Joe with the oxen."

"I would like that." Her words had come out soft and she ducked her head, but not before he saw pink color enter her cheeks.

"Good. I'll join you and Noah as soon as we get going."

He found himself hurrying through his work. He and Joe had worked side by side as they prepared to leave camp. He retied the canvas flaps to keep dust from billowing into the wagon. Then he checked the ropes that held the water barrel onto the side of the wagon, surprised and pleased that Cora had filled it to the brim. Not that they had used much of it thus far, but still, she had contributed to the work.

His thoughts strayed to the talk he planned to have with Cora. Would she have the answers he needed? Was she just as concerned as he about their future? Flynn worried about their provisions and pondered what to do about the problem. If he understood correctly, it could take a full month to get to the first fort, where they would be able to stock up.

Thirty minutes later, he heard the "move out" call come down the line. He joined Cora beside the wagon as Joe maneuvered the oxen into line. She had put the baby in the sling and cradled him in front of her. Her hair looked freshly combed and she'd put it up in a knot on the back of her head. The style made her look younger. For the first time, he questioned how much younger she was than his twenty-five years.

Cora placed a soft hand on his forearm. "Everything all right?" When he glanced down at her hand, she hastily drew it away, coloring fiercely.

"Right as rain." In an effort to relieve her embarrassment, he reached for her hand. He gestured to those walking in front of them. Couples holding hands, laughing, spirits high. He slowed his steps to match hers. A feeling of rightness he couldn't explain stirred in his chest. She squeezed his hand gently and all the worries and fears fled right out of his mind. He decided right then and there that he'd live in the moment and let the rest take place at will.

His gaze moved to Noah. The baby slept soundly in

his mother's arms. "He's nine months, right? Isn't he a little old for that sling?"

Cora shook her head. "No. Thankfully, Noah is small for his age, so he fits nicely, but I'm not sure for how much longer. He's already pulling up when I set him down. He will be walking in no time. He's already a pretty good crawler."

"And running will come not long after. If I remember correctly, my little sister ran our ma's poor legs off when she started walking good." He missed his family and wondered what they would think if they knew he'd married. Flynn had sent a letter off before leaving, telling his parents he was headed to Oregon, but that was before he'd met Cora and married. His sister had married last summer and, thankfully, lived close to his parents. Flynn had always worried that he'd have to stop being a lawman and work his father's ranch once his pa got too old to work it. Now his brother-in-law worked side by side with Pa and learned whatever he needed to inherit the family ranch.

"You have a sister?" Sorrow filled Cora's voice, as well as curiosity.

Flynn wondered at the sadness in Cora's tone when just a few moments before she'd been happy. "I do. She's five years younger than me. Do you have any sisters?"

She started to nod and then shook her head. At his confused look, Cora answered, "I did, but she died recently." Her throat sounded as if it had closed on the word *died*. Grief filled her face and eyes.

"I'm sorry." He saw Joe coax the oxen to turn the wagon along with the others. The young man was doing a fine job.

Cora cleared her throat and sniffled. "What did you want to talk to me about?"

So much for learning about her family. But his curiosity wasn't as important as talking about their supply situation. As a lawman, he was used to eating dried jerky and beans, so the thought of preparing full meals hadn't been his goal when he'd bought his supplies. Now, with a family, it was obvious they'd need more. "I noticed that we are low on supplies and wondered if you had noticed it, too."

She inhaled and released the air in her lungs. Was she relieved to learn the reason for their talk? If so, why? What had she thought he wanted to talk about? Flynn turned his attention back to her.

"I did notice. We have plenty of salted bacon, beans and coffee, thanks to you, but our rice, flour, spices, cornmeal and sugar are trivial. Mr. Clarkson gave me enough for one person but did not consider you or baby Noah. Also, we have no dried fruit, eggs, nuts or milk. So desserts are out of the question at this time."

Flynn sighed. Just as he'd figured. He had been so concerned for her and the baby that he hadn't noticed what Mr. Clarkson had thrown at her feet. Now he knew it wasn't much. "Well, we will make the best of it. I'll see if I can't buy a milk cow from one of the other families."

"You might ask Mr. Philmore. Sarah said something about telling him to sell us one." She lifted the baby slightly as if to take some of his weight off her shoulders.

So that was one of the things she and Sarah had talked about. Flynn should have known Cora was in search of a means to get the baby more nourishment. "I'll do that this evening."

"With a milk cow, the baby will have milk to drink and I can hang some on the side of the wagon in the mornings. Sarah says the jostling will make butter during the day and we can have it with our dinner. She also suggested that I make extra beans and meat at the evening meal so that we can have leftovers for breakfast and lunch." She moved the blanket closer to Noah's face to block out the sun.

Flynn realized he had his hat to shade his face, Noah had the blanket, but Cora wasn't wearing a bonnet like the other women. He worried her face would sunburn. "Do you have a bonnet?" The question seemed to take them both by surprise.

"No. I looked in my things, but I guess I forgot to pack one." Again, her face filled with color and she looked away. Was she lying to him? How did one forget their head covering? His hat went everywhere with him, except to bed.

The thought came to him that Cora might have to ask one of the women for a spare bonnet. Probably Sarah Philmore. While he was grateful for the Philmores' kindness, it grated at Flynn to feel like he and his family were so ill prepared. They didn't have proper supplies for this trip. If only he'd known he would have two other people to take care of, Flynn was sure he'd have brought more staples for the journey.

Chapter Seven

Cora sighed with weariness. Four weeks had passed since they'd left Independence and she was sick of eating beans, biscuits and bacon, but she thanked the Lord that the quality had improved, if not the variety. Her baking over the campfire was getting better: the biscuits could now be eaten completely and not just the tops. At first, Flynn had tried to eat the burnt bottoms, but even he had to admit they were too charred to consume.

She walked beside Martha, who pulled her thoughts away from her sadness over the meals they had eaten.

The young woman fussed. "I can't get the older kids to take me seriously and the younger ones' attention spans are about as long as a lightning bug's flash."

Cora grinned. "That's pretty good."

Martha frowned at her. "What is good about that? Nothing I just said is good. The kids are wild. They don't listen to me."

"The comparison between their attention spans and the lightning bug's flash, that was very good." Cora tried to get the girl to smile but it was no use. Martha was tired and her siblings weren't helping her, with their unwillingness to focus and learn.

Martha sighed heavily. "Maybe I wasn't meant to be a teacher. Maybe I should work on my sewing skills and open a dress shop next to Ma and Pa's store."

Cora nodded, knowing it would help Martha if she took her young friend seriously. "That's a thought. Do you enjoy sewing?"

Martha shrugged. "Not as much as I like learning and teaching new things."

"Hmm…" Cora paused. "Well, maybe what you should do is establish some rules. When I was teaching, I had rules—and consequences if my students broke the rules. They either took their punishments or I spoke to their parents."

Martha laughed bitterly. "My students' parents are my parents. Ma would just say it was my problem and that I need to deal with the kids. She'd say she wouldn't be around when I'm actually in a schoolhouse."

They continued walking in silence. The clouds overhead were darkening as the afternoon progressed. Cora hoped it wouldn't rain until after supper. She looked to the miserable girl beside her. "Have you started their lessons at the same time each evening?"

Martha shook her head. "No. By the time I get them settled, we've wasted a good thirty minutes. Then it's never long before Pa says it's time for everyone to be in bed, so we're not getting much teaching or learning time in."

Cora realized that Martha hadn't been following their original plans. She'd been taking care of Noah and the other children but hadn't been using her time wisely and thought she could cram lessons in after supper. She smiled. Martha's sisters knew when their pa would stop the lessons each evening, and they'd obviously figured out that if they played around long enough, they wouldn't have to be in school long. "I have an idea. Instead of walking with me in the afternoons, can you walk with me in the mornings?"

Martha looked at her curiously. "I'd have to check with Ma, but I don't think she'd mind. Why?"

"Well, if we discussed your teaching in the mornings, then you could teach the children in the afternoon. You'd have to make a game of it and ask your ma to make sure the kids know that afternoons are now schooltime. Then, in the evening, those who didn't pay attention during schooltime would have to make up their lessons, giving up their playtime." She watched as a streak of lightning crossed the sky. A few moments later, thunder sounded in the distance.

Martha's gaze followed hers to the darkening sky. "Looks like we might get rained on."

Cora prayed they wouldn't. "Let's hope not."

"What kinds of games would I play? I'm sure Ma will ask." Martha balanced her paper and book as they walked. She held a pencil over her paper, waiting for Cora to answer.

"How about you sing the alphabet, then maybe stop for a moment and draw with your fingers whichever letter you are working on in the dirt. You could then catch up to your wagon and play a game like 'I spy.'" Cora's mind raced with other possibilities, but she needed to go slowly so that Martha could keep up as she wrote.

"What's 'I spy'?" Martha asked, looking up from her writing.

"Really? You've never played 'I spy'?"

The girl shook her head.

"Okay, we'll play right now. Let's say we are working on the letter *N*. I spy with my little eye something that starts with the letter *N*. Now you look around and find something that starts with the letter *N*. If you guess what I spy, then you get to spy something new that starts with the letter *N*. Stay focused on the letter *N* throughout the game."

Martha nodded. "I see." She looked about and then grinned. "My nose?"

Cora laughed. "No. Try again."

"The back of Mr. Adams's neck?"

Cora shook her head. "No. Try again."

Martha then laughed. "Noah?"

"Yes, Noah. See how fun that is? You had to think of the letter *N* and words that began with that letter." Cora cradled the baby to her. He was growing, thanks to the milk and corn bread, cornmeal mush and other soft foods he was eating. As a result, Noah was getting heavier each day.

"I like that game." Martha scribbled more notes in her notebook.

"You can also add the letter *N* to people's names. You could ask each child what their name would be if it started with *N*. Like, mine would be Nora and yours would be Nartha." She grinned at the girl.

Martha chuckled and wrote that in her notebook, as well. "Daniel's would be Naniel. That's funny."

"Right, and it should keep the kids' attention. Games are a great way to educate children. Now use your imagination and start thinking of ways you can get them to learn the other lessons you are teaching them."

When Martha nodded and turned her attention back to her teacher's journal, Cora focused on Flynn.

He walked several feet in front of them beside the oxen. Over the past several weeks, he'd bought them a cow, bartered for eggs, and even come home the night before with a small bag of dried fruit. As he'd promised, he'd taught her how to make the fire so that it wasn't so hot that it burned everything, but not so low that their food was undercooked.

Martha laid her hand on Cora's sleeve. "Cora, I think I'll go walk with Ma a spell. She'll be happy to know that you are helping me address the kids' attention problems."

Cora smiled. "I'm glad I could be of help."

She watched as Martha hurried up to her parents' wagon. The night before, Mr. Tucker had moved everyone's position in the line. The Philmore wagon now was three ahead of theirs. The general idea was to keep one set of wagons from having to take up the rear all the time. She dreaded when their wagon would be assigned to the end. Dirt and animal droppings from all the wagons ahead of you were a problem if you weren't careful.

Sarah turned and waved at Cora. It was fun teaching Martha, but it also served as a reminder that being a teacher herself wasn't an option any longer. No town council would hire a widow with a baby to be their schoolteacher. She tried to imagine other work she might be able to do in Oregon, but she struggled to come up with possibilities.

Cora also worried that her brother-in-law, Hank, would catch up with them. Every evening she had gone to bed with a small sense of relief, knowing he hadn't caught up with them that day. She prayed he wasn't looking for baby Noah, but deep down, Cora didn't believe that for a moment. Out of meanness alone, Hank was out there looking for the boy. What was she going to do if he ever did show up?

Later that night, Flynn lay on his back in the wagon, listening to the rain crash against the white canvas. Thankfully, their canvas wasn't leaking. Lightning flashed, revealing Cora and the baby sleeping on the other side of the wagon. The interior wasn't a very big space, and most of it was taken up by supplies, but Cora had realized the rain was coming, and during one of the few breaks they'd taken earlier in the afternoon, she had created a sleeping space for the three of them.

Flynn folded his hands behind his head and thought about the changes he'd seen in his wife. Her cooking had improved, and she'd made several friends. One of them had even traded her a bonnet in exchange for a small bowl of blackberries Cora had found beside the river. She was a good forager, often finding nuts and berries for them, and she'd proved to be adept at trading with the rest of the group for other little things they found themselves needing along the way.

Her appearance had changed, as well. The freckles across her nose were a little darker than the day he'd met her, revealing that even the slightest sun would cause them to show up even more. She smiled often and laughed with Martha as they discussed lessons and talked about how to teach Martha's sisters. But Flynn still saw fear in her eyes several times a day. Would she ever confide in him what caused her such distress?

Thunder shook the wagon just as lightning flashed once more. His gaze moved to Cora and the baby again.

Her voice whispered across to him. "Do you think the storm will last all night?"

He whispered back, "I don't know. I'm sorry the thunder woke you. How's Noah doing?"

"He's sleeping soundly."

Flynn heard her moving about. "Thank you for making us a dry place to sleep tonight. I'd hate to be under the wagon in this weather."

"No need to thank me. I'm glad you are in here with us. I have never liked storms, even though Pa always told Gracie and me that storms were God's way of making sure that the earth didn't dry up and blow away and that there was nothing to be fearful of."

He looked up at the canvas and grinned. "Did that help you fear them less?"

Her voice quivered. "Not really, but then he'd tell us the story of Noah and the ark Noah and his sons built. Pa named off different animals that were saved from the flood and had us name a few. That always made us forget about the storm for a while." Cora's voice had calmed in the telling of her past.

"Is that why you named your son Noah?"

Silence filled the wagon. Flynn waited for her answer as thunder sounded in the distance. The rain stopped pounding the canvas and became a steady light dripping.

Just when he thought she wasn't going to answer, Cora said, "The baby was named after our pa. His name was James Noah Edwards."

Flynn heard her yawn. "That explains why he enjoyed the story of Noah's ark."

"I suppose so."

He waited for her to say more and then decided

she had fallen to sleep. He thought about what she'd said and wondered that her maiden name and married name were the same. But then, Edwards was a common name—it could have been her husband's as well as her father's. Or maybe she'd decided to go back to using her maiden name for some reason? That fear in her eyes…it made him wonder if her marriage had been an unhappy one. Perhaps she'd wanted to leave all associations with her husband behind.

When he heard the rifle shots announcing it was time to start the day, Flynn rose slowly. He didn't want to move the wagon too much and wake the baby.

Cora yawned and stretched beside Noah. "I don't hear rain," she offered as she pushed back the small blanket she and the infant slept under.

"No, it quit shortly after you fell asleep." Flynn scooted to the foot of the wagon and pulled on his boots. "I'll start the fire for you this morning."

"Thank you. I gathered wood and twigs yesterday. They are behind the boxes to your left."

Flynn looked back at her. She was brushing out her hair. "You gathered wood yesterday?"

She wrapped her hair up into a knot on the back of her head. "I gather wood and store it in the wagon every day. It saves me time in the mornings and ensures that the wood is dry, making the fire easier to start." She paused and looked to him. "Doesn't everyone do that?"

Flynn shrugged. "I don't know."

Cora laughed. "Well, I hope they do. If they don't, it's going to take longer to make hot coffee this morning."

He looked behind the box and saw that Cora had

a nice supply of wood and kindling. She was right—
dry wood would make starting the morning fire easier.
Most everyone would be eating leftovers, as they did
every day, to shorten the time needed for breakfast,
but everyone enjoyed a hot pot of coffee first thing in
the mornings. How many people would be drinking
water this morning and looking for dry firewood for
later in the day? Could he use his fire to reach out to
those around him and maybe catch the killer in their
midst? Over the past few weeks, he'd tried to get to
know the other men in the wagon train, but the need
to stick close to his wagon for most of the day meant
that he really only became friendly with those posi-
tioned around him. This was a chance to widen his net.

Flynn worked fast and began brewing coffee. When
his was about ready, he turned to Joe. "Joe, pass the
word that we have a fire and anyone that wants fresh
coffee this morning is welcome to use our camp."

Joe grinned. "Pa will be glad to hear that." He did
what Joe always did when he was in a hurry. He ran
to his parents' wagon.

Flynn chuckled. The boy would spread the word
and soon everyone would be using the fire and making fresh coffee.

"Looks like you are the only one with dry wood to
make a fire." Doc walked around the back of Flynn's
wagon.

"Probably not the only one, but I'm willing to share
with those who need it. Think Mrs. Clarkson would
like to bring her coffeepot and make coffee?"

The doctor laughed. "No, she'll sleep for the next
half hour." He held up a tin coffeepot. "But I wouldn't
mind a fresh pot."

Flynn motioned him forward. "Come on over. Better work fast—we'll have more folks here in a few moments."

"Thank you." The doctor set his coffeepot next to the one Flynn had placed on the grate over the open fire. "That storm last night was wild."

Flynn looked at the doctor. He looked wet and tired. "Were you on guard duty?"

The older man nodded. "Yeah, and I don't mind telling you it was miserable. I felt like a rat in a city gutter."

Ben Witmore and his wife, Emma, approached. They were a pleasant young couple whom he'd recently met a few days earlier. Ben's brother, Stuart, was traveling with them. Ben and Emma had spoken of starting their family on farmland in Oregon, while Stuart had other plans. The Witmore couple had big dreams.

"Joe tells us you have a nice fire going and that we can warm up our coffee on it," Ben said as he shook hands with Flynn.

Flynn nodded at Emma. "Sure do, and you are more than welcome to use it."

He watched as Emma set their coffeepot on the grate. She looked up at him and smiled. "Thank you."

Before he could answer, Cora climbed out of the wagon and then turned to get Noah. Cradling the baby close, she scolded, "Flynn, I would have started the coffee." She sniffed appreciatively and smiled. "But I'm glad you didn't wait for me. It smells wonderful."

He poured her a cup, handed it to her and took Noah from her arms. Noah fussed for a moment but settled when he realized it was Flynn who had taken him from his mother. Flynn had noticed the baby seemed unsure of most people. Noah puckered his lips every time someone besides Flynn or Martha took the baby from Cora.

He looked to Cora and grinned. "I hope you don't mind, but I've invited everyone who didn't have dry wood to come use our fire to make their coffee."

She smiled at Emma. "Of course I don't mind. Good morning, Emma."

The other woman returned her smile. "Good morning. I didn't get a chance to thank you yesterday for helping me with my wash, so I'll say it now. Thank you."

"It was my pleasure."

Ben shook his head. "I can't believe I was foolish enough not to gather the firewood last night."

Emma laid her hand on his arm. "It was my fault."

While the young couple discussed who was to blame for not collecting the wood, Flynn leaned down and whispered in Cora's ear, "I'm not sharing the firewood, just the fire. We may have another shower tonight and need dry wood in the morning."

Cora nodded her head in understanding. Flynn stepped back and gazed into her pretty eyes. She had secrets, but he didn't think they were the kind that would harm him or the baby. Whatever pain or trouble she carried from her past, he just prayed someday she'd confide in him.

"She really is a jewel, Flynn. I'm glad you found her." Doc rocked on his boots.

Flynn smiled. "Yes, she is." He pulled his gaze from her and confessed, "If it wasn't for her, we'd be drinking water this morning and gathering wood as we traveled today."

Cora's cheeks turned a soft pink and she ducked her head. It seemed to Flynn Cora ducked her head often and normally when her cheeks were pink. They'd been married for a month and she still blushed on a regular basis, often trying to hide it from him. He didn't know why she felt the need to hide. Did she not realize how charming he found it?

"Noah, you ready to go get your milk?" Flynn asked the little boy. He took a small bucket that hung on the side of the wagon. "Cora, we'll be right back. Doc, would you like to go with us?"

The doctor shook his head. "No, thank you. I believe I'll wait right here and then take this fresh coffee to Harold. He's a bear before he's had his coffee." He laughed as if he were making a joke.

Flynn waited for her nod and then carried Noah toward the cows that were corralled just outside the circle of wagons. Several young men took turns attending the animals. It amazed him how well the wagon train was maintained. Charlie Philmore waved to him. Flynn waved back and continued toward the young man.

"Ready to milk ole Mertle?" Charlie had already put a rope around the cow's neck and pulled her to where they now stood under a big maple tree.

Flynn nodded. "We sure are." He started to hand Noah over to the young man. Noah seemed so calm and content—maybe this time, the handoff would go smoothly…but no.

Noah grabbed Flynn's shirt with both hands, his face turned red, and he let out a scream that Flynn was sure Cora could hear at their wagon. "There, there, Noah." He awkwardly patted the baby's back, trying not to hit him with the pail.

"How about I milk the cow?" Charlie offered as he took the bucket from Flynn.

Flynn continued to rub Noah's back. The baby clung to him like a second skin. "I don't know why, but this little man isn't ready to socialize with others just yet."

The sound of warm milk hitting the side of the milk bucket and baying cows filled the morning air. Noah settled down and hid his little face in Flynn's shirtfront.

Charlie glanced over his shoulder. "Nothing's wrong with him. He's about eight or nine months old, right?"

Flynn nodded. Amazement filled his voice. "Cora said he's ten months old this month."

Charlie turned his attention back to the milking but spoke loud enough that Flynn could hear him. "That explains it. Babies his age aren't real sure of what's going on around them, so they cling to their parents for comfort when something don't feel right to them."

Flynn stared at Charlie's back. "How do you know so much about babies?" he asked, feeling very uneducated when it came to children. Between Cora and Martha, Noah's needs were handled so capably that he'd had to do very little for the boy over the past few weeks.

Charlie stood and handed him the half-full bucket. "I have little brothers and sisters, remember. Plus, Ma wants me to be a doctor, so she has been filling my head with all kinds of practical things about what little ones need at different times."

Flynn walked back to the wagon. Noah began to cry halfway back and Flynn could only guess that the baby was hungry. Lately, there were so many things he was learning that he hadn't previously known. Where women were concerned, he'd always been in the dark. Despite growing up with a mother and a sister, he hadn't felt prepared in the slightest to start a life with a woman—much less a woman with a child. Cora's past and moods definitely had him stumped, and now that he was a husband and parent, Flynn felt even more inept. He pulled his shoulders back and silently vowed to learn more about his tiny family, even if they were going to be a family for only a few more months.

Chapter Eight

Cora and Flynn walked beside the Little Blue River after lunch. The wagon master had given them a day of rest, which she was thankful for. The plains were flat and the wind oftentimes blew until one was sick of hearing it and feeling the dirt it carried scratch one's face.

Noah slept in his sling across her chest. The little boy was becoming more active every day and she enjoyed these quiet times. She lovingly brushed his bangs across his forehead and breathed in a happy breath. Gracie would have been so proud of the way Noah had adjusted. The first week had been hard on the little boy, but now he seemed to be more content with her and Flynn as parents. She wondered how much he understood, if he knew what he was missing. For herself, Cora knew her heart would forever long for her twin, but the pain was less sharp than it had been at the start of the journey.

"Did I tell you Noah said 'Mama' this morning?" Flynn asked. He knelt beside the water and scooped up a few rocks.

Cora shook her head. "He did?" Had he been calling for Gracie or her?

Flynn skipped a rock across the river water's surface. "He did."

Cora watched the rock sink. Her heart felt like sinking, too. During the last couple of weeks, she had managed to not dwell on Gracie's passing. Sadness enveloped her once more at the loss of her sister.

Flynn glanced her way. "I thought you'd be happy." He searched her face as he walked back to her and the baby.

She swallowed the lump in her throat. "I am." A tear slid down her cheek.

He stopped in front of her and wiped the moisture from Cora's face. "So this is a happy tear?"

Cora wouldn't lie. "No, it's a sad tear."

The look of concern on his face mingled with a look that said he'd never understand her. Cora offered him a smile. "Don't worry. I'm fine. My emotions are all over the place, that's all." When he didn't respond, she continued, "I'm glad Noah is talking." She cradled the baby to her.

Flynn took her free hand and tucked it into his elbow. "Let's walk this way." He led her away from the river's edge to the meadow and away from the group of kids who had decided to swim in the river.

Wildflowers dotted the green grass with wonderful splashes of color. "This place is beautiful," Cora said, still fighting the urge to cry like a baby over the loss of her sister.

His gaze met hers, and he said, "Very beautiful." Then he looked away quickly.

Cora had the feeling he wasn't talking about the

flowers but about her. *That's crazy*, she told herself. They'd been married almost two months and he'd never told her she was pretty, let alone beautiful. She searched for something else they could talk about, anything to take away the uncomfortable feeling she was now feeling.

He broke the tense silence. "How are Martha's lessons coming along?"

Noah wiggled about, trying to get more comfortable. He pushed an arm out of the blanket.

"Very well. She's smart and has figured out ways to amuse her baby brother and Noah while teaching her sisters their lessons." Cora tucked Noah's arm back into the sling.

"Good." Flynn stepped away from her and began to pick wildflowers.

Cora trailed behind him. She thought of the day they had met and how he had told her he was a lawman on the search for a killer. Funny that when things were peaceful, she'd think of that. Silence continued to hang between them for several minutes before Cora looked about to make sure they were alone and then asked, "Have you figured out if the killer you are chasing is on our train?"

He turned to face her and held out the flowers for her to take. "Not yet. I've met every man traveling with us and none of them seem like the killer type."

She took the flowers and sniffed them. "Thank you. These are lovely."

Flynn smiled like a little boy who'd just been told he'd passed a test. "You are very welcome."

Cora couldn't help noticing how handsome her husband was. She pushed the thought away. He wasn't going to be her husband forever. "What are you going to do if you can't find him?" If the killer wasn't on the wagon train, would he desert her and Noah when they got to the fort so he could go back to Missouri and resume his hunt?

He sighed. "I'll keep looking. There are several men who match the man's description. Maybe I just haven't gotten to know them well enough yet." Flynn looked deep in thought.

Cora frowned. Hadn't Flynn said the killer was a short, older man? What if he was short but had disguised himself to seem more elderly? Or what if he was really looking for a woman who was disguised as a man? "Flynn, are you sure he's an older man?"

Flynn nodded. "The sheriff in Independence had a woman report to him that she'd entertained a gentleman who claimed to have killed several women."

Even though the day was bright and warm, Cora felt a chill crawl up her spine. How awful to have to entertain men for a living—especially dangerous men. To have one confess himself a murderer must have been terrifying. She sucked her bottom lip between her teeth.

Flynn placed a hand on her shoulder. "There is no reason for you to fret over it, Cora. I'll find him."

How was it that he could read her emotions so well? Did they show on her face? Cora decided it was because he read people's faces and body language as part of his job. "The women on this train know everyone. Maybe I could…"

Flynn gently squeezed her shoulder, putting a stop to what she was about to say. "No. I will not have you putting yourself or the other women on this train in harm's way by asking questions that might spook a dangerous man. I will take care of this. You worry about learning how to prepare meals."

Cora felt as if he'd just slapped her in the face. She ducked her head to hide the hurt his words had inflicted. Did he really think she needed more cooking lessons?

A few minutes later, Flynn left Cora at their wagon with the excuse of checking on his horse, Winston. He wished he could take back his careless words. The thought of Cora putting herself in danger to help him had scared him and he had said the first thing that popped in his head. Her cooking was improving every day and he'd not meant to insult her. But insult her he had.

Cora had nodded and then hurried back to the wagon with him walking slowly behind. Anyone watching must have been able to tell they'd had words.

Flynn had no idea how to fix his mistake. He'd already picked her flowers, so a gift of flowers wouldn't be special. No, he'd have to tell her he didn't mean that the way it came out.

Cora was climbing out of their wagon when he approached her. He knew without being told that she'd laid the baby down so that he could rest better.

Flynn gently pulled her into his arms and hugged her. "Cora, I'm sorry. I didn't mean to hurt you. In my haste to keep you safe, I said the wrong thing." He pulled back and looked deeply into her sad eyes. "Your cooking is wonderful and…"

The sound of a shotgun blast and a woman's scream cut through whatever else he'd intended to say. Flynn released her. "Stay here. I'll be back as quickly as I can." At her nod, he turned and ran toward the sounds, worried about what he'd find. Dire thoughts raced through his mind as he ran for the wagon at the end of the train.

He stopped short when he arrived. Ben Witmore lay at the back of his wagon, and his wife sat beside him, weeping. The shotgun was lying next to Ben. Flynn quickly concluded that Ben had been pulling the gun from the wagon, barrel first, when it had gone off, catching him in the chest.

Flynn jerked his shirt off and pressed the material against the gunshot wound. More blood pooled under the young man, telling Flynn the shot had gone all the way through. "Ben, you're going to be all right. We'll send for the doctor."

The man gasped for breath. "No, I'm dying."

"Ben, please don't say that," his wife begged as she stroked his face with one hand and cradled her rounded belly with the other. "You can't leave me."

He reached up and grabbed her hand. "Emma, listen to me. You have to go on to Oregon. Look for Mr. Young." He gasped for air. "He has the deed to our farm."

She shook her head. "No, we'll do that together." Tears coursed down her face and dripped off her chin.

Joe and several other men arrived. They stopped short of the trio. Several of the older men shook their heads and then left. Probably going to tell their wives and drivers what had happened.

Flynn motioned for the boy to come to him. When Joe was close enough, Flynn ordered, "Go get Doc."

Joe nodded and took off running.

Ben's brother, Stuart, came around the wagon at a

run. He slid to a stop behind Emma. "Oh, Ben" was all he said.

Ben looked up at his brother and tried to smile. "Looks like I did it this time." He winced in pain. "Take care of Emma."

Stuart nodded. His eyes filled with tears.

Flynn watched it all play out in a daze. He'd seen men die from gunshot wounds before and knew that Ben would likely soon be dead. He swallowed hard as he watched his clean white shirt soak up the blood and turn red.

The doctor arrived and knelt down beside him. "Here, let me see."

Flynn stood back and watched while the doctor examined Ben's chest and then turned him to look at the exit wound in his back. His gaze moved from Ben to his wife. She held her hands over her face and wept. Her brother-in-law, Stuart, laid a big hand on her shaking shoulders.

"Let's move him inside the wagon," Doc said, looking to Flynn and then to Stuart.

Stuart helped Emma to stand and then moved to take her place. Flynn stepped forward once more and helped lift Ben into the wagon. As soon as they had him lying on a pile of quilts and blankets, Flynn and Stuart left Ben in the capable hands of Emma and the doctor.

He turned to Stuart. "If there is anything we can do to help, please don't hesitate to ask."

Stuart took his hat off and ran his fingers through his blond curls. "He's not going to make it, is he?"

Flynn didn't think it looked good for Ben, but only the good Lord really knew. "I've seen men walk away with worse injuries. He might."

They walked a little farther away from the wagon. Flynn didn't want Emma to hear their conversation. He watched the wagon sway as the doctor and Emma moved about inside.

Stuart sighed. "I guess I'll go on to Oregon and help Emma with the farm."

Flynn remained silent and waited, knowing the other man needed to talk out his thoughts. He heard Emma sobbing. He hated what the woman was going through and prayed Cora wouldn't have to go through anything like it with him.

"I promised Ben I would take care of her should something happen to him along the trail, but I never dreamed I'd really have to. I'd planned on going to California once they were settled on their farm." He sat down on a crate and looked off into the distance.

Life could change so suddenly. Flynn looked at his own life. Hadn't he gotten married despite having never planned to do so after losing Miriam? He sighed. He and Cora had planned to part ways when they reached Oregon, but if something happened to Cora on the trail, he knew that he'd take care of Noah for the rest of the boy's life. Until this moment, he hadn't thought that far ahead.

Flynn's attention was captured the moment Doc stepped out of the wagon. His grim face broadcast that news wasn't good.

Stuart stood. "How is he, Doc?"

The doctor shook his head. "He's gone. I couldn't stop the bleeding." He looked down at Flynn's shirt in his hands. Then he lifted his gaze to Stuart. "Do you know any of Emma's friends? We need someone to comfort her while we take care of his body."

Stuart nodded. "I'll go ask the Ingles woman. She and Emma have spent many a days walking this trail together." He lowered his head and walked away.

"It's a crying shame." Doc wiped at the blood on his hands. "Ben said the gun went off when he pulled on the barrel to get it out of the wagon."

Flynn nodded. "I figured as much." He wished he could go back in time and warn the man, but it was too late. This wagon train had its first member to bury. He silently prayed he wouldn't have to bury Cora or baby Noah. Just the thought caused his heart to hurt.

Chapter Nine

After two months of traveling, Cora had never been so happy to see a fort in all her life. Fort Kearney had been torn down and so the travelers had carried on to Fort Laramie. Wagon wheels busting had delayed them, but finally the fort was in sight. She was bone weary and looking forward to a hot bath.

Her eyes widened as they got closer. The pile of left-behind things that rested outside the far wall of the fort was enormous. It had everything from cookstoves to pianos. How could people not know they shouldn't take such things with them? Still, the temptation to see what others had abandoned was great. Perhaps she would find another frying pan or something else useful.

She'd heard that people left food items there, too. But this morning, the ladies were all grumbling that with the rain the night before, any food that may have been left was waterlogged now, sinking Cora's hopes that God would supply them with free food supplies to continue the trip.

Sarah hurried into step beside her. "I still say we should see what we can find, wet or not."

Cora smiled at her friend. Without Sarah and Flynn, the trip this far would have been miserable. "Are the others going to look through it?"

She shook her head. "No. Mrs. Chandler has them all convinced that last night's rain ruined anything worth using."

"And they believe her? Even Abigail?" Cora couldn't believe how much influence Mrs. Chandler had over the other ladies.

"Every one of them, especially my sister. I don't know what hold Mrs. Chandler has over those women, but it might work out for our good." Sarah shrugged. "She might be right, but I think it's worth a look-see."

Cora sighed. "Well, I don't see why we should listen to her. Let's go inspect what's there as soon as we can and then I want a hot bath. Flynn says that he'll watch Noah for an hour and let me soak."

"Sounds wonderful. I'd love a hot bath but I don't see me getting one anytime soon." Sarah had made sure the kids had a weekly bath, but as far as Cora or anyone else knew, she'd only taken sponge baths and washed her hair in the river.

After all Sarah had done for her, Cora wanted to see the woman get a little break. A hot bath would make her feel like a new woman. She decided to ask Flynn if they could treat the woman to a hot bath also.

One of the Philmore children ran up. "Ma, Pa says he needs you at the wagon." Then she turned and ran back the way she'd come.

Sarah sighed. "A woman's work is never done. Do not go looking without me, promise?"

Cora nodded. "I promise."

Keeping that promise was the hardest thing Cora

had done in a long time. For the next two hours, she set up camp, fixed the noon meal and waited. She watched as other women left in small groups or with their husbands to go to the fort.

Flynn walked toward her. He'd been at a meeting the wagon master had called. He grinned as he approached. Cora marveled at how handsome her husband appeared. He'd grown a short beard and his hair had grown over his ears, giving him a wild look that for some odd reason set her heart aflutter.

His eyes sparkled with anticipation. "Ready to go to the fort?"

She shook her head and rocked Noah on her hip. "I promised Sarah I'd wait for her."

His grin slid from his face. Was that a hurt expression?

"Well, I guess it's just us boys going in, then." He reached for Noah. "That's if you don't mind me taking our little man with me."

Cora smiled. Flynn took the role of stepfather seriously. He involved Noah as much as he could in everything he did. Noah smiled and reached for Flynn. She wondered if Flynn realized how hard it was going to be for him to leave the baby behind when they got to Oregon.

"I don't mind." She handed Noah over and lowered her voice. "See that pile of stuff beside the fort?"

Flynn looked in the direction she was looking. "Yep. Some of the men thought they might find some extra tools in there, but their womenfolk told them not to bother looking because of the rain."

Cora felt her face scrunch up in disbelief. "And?"

Surely the men knew that tools and such wouldn't be that affected by some rain?

"And so they aren't looking."

"Flynn Adams, are you telling me you aren't looking, either?" She placed both hands on her hips.

He laughed and tweaked her nose. "Aren't you going to look?"

She felt a flush enter her cheeks. "Well, yeah."

"So, if you find something good, get it or come get me and I'll haul it back to the wagon."

Cora shook her head. "You knew Sarah and I were going to see what we can find. It was your plan all along to let me do the tool hunting for you. Let the wife go dig in the wet stuff and pretend that taking care of the baby would help out." She laughed at his bemused expression.

"Me taking Noah doesn't help you look for treasure in them there hills?"

His jokey Southern accent brought another smile to her face. "Yes, it will be a great help."

Cora decided now was a good time to ask for a favor. "Flynn, Sarah has been so wonderful to me. Do you think we could treat her to a hot bath, also? I know it would make her feel so much better."

He leaned down and kissed Cora on the cheek. "One of the things I like about you is that you are always thinking of others. I'll be sure to pay for two ladies' baths. All you have to do is get her to go with you when you go." He stood up straight once more. "Come on, Noah. Us menfolk are going to go look for a new harness for Big Blue and Big Red."

Sarah arrived, a little winded. Joe stood beside his mother, grinning. Sarah said, "I'm sorry, Cora. I tried to be here earlier but you know my bunch—if you want them to hurry up, they drag their heels, but if I had wanted them to sit around the fire as a family and visit, they would have all rushed through the meal. It never fails."

Flynn laughed. "Ladies, if you don't mind, I'm taking my leave now." He bowed at the waist as if he were exiting a grand ballroom.

"Oh, go on." Cora laughed.

He tucked Noah against his side. "Let me know if you need any help." He turned to Joe. "Ready to go?"

"Sure am." The boy took two steps toward Flynn when his mother's words halted him.

"Oh, no you don't, Joseph David Philmore. You are coming with Cora and me." Sarah gave her son a stern look.

Cora could see the boy's disappointment, but instead of arguing, he just gave a respectful nod. Thinking the boy might be in trouble with his ma, Cora decided to be quick with her examination of the left-behind things so that he could join Flynn or any of his other friends. Going inside the fort was a treat, something she didn't want Joe to miss out on.

Flynn smiled. "I'll see you inside, Joe." Then he left, tossing Noah in the air as he went. The baby's laughter warmed Cora's heart even as it almost stopped each time the baby took flight. She trusted Flynn but still worried.

Sarah tugged on Cora's arm to get her attention. "Don't worry. Men have been doing that since time began. Now, did any of the other ladies stop at the pile?" She turned her eyes to the mound of items.

Cora's gaze followed hers. "A couple glanced at it,

but I don't think any of them actually inspected what is there." Cora hurried to catch up with Sarah, who had started toward the pile of odds and ends.

The closer they got, the more Cora understood why the other ladies hadn't wanted to dig in the things. Water stood on every surface and mud filled every inch. She looked down at her shoes and sighed. "Um, Sarah, this might not be a good idea."

"Don't give up yet." Sarah directed her son, "Joe, get that board over there and lay it here." She pointed at an open space in front of her.

He obeyed, understanding that his mother was going to use the board as a form of bridge over the muck.

Cora looked about for a board of her own and found it in the form of a narrow door. Why anyone had brought a door this far was beyond her understanding. Now that she had it, Cora was thankful that it had gotten this far. Careful not to get a splinter, she followed Joe's lead and put it where she wanted to walk.

For the next ten or fifteen minutes, the two women surveyed the articles. They found all kinds of things, but none seemed useful for life on the trail. She'd about given up when she heard Sarah gasp.

Joe ran to his mother's side, probably fearing his mother was in some kind of danger. "Ma! You all right?"

"I'm fine, Joe." She smiled fondly at her caring son and then waved to Cora. In a loud whisper, she ordered, "Come see what I found."

Seeing his mother was fine, Joe started to turn away. He took two steps before Sarah hissed, "Joseph, stay here. We're going to need your help." She looked about as if to see if anyone else had noticed her excitement.

Cora came up behind the other woman and tiptoed to look over her shoulder. A large chest rested in front of Sarah, sitting atop another large chest. "What do you think is in it?"

Joe answered, "Probably junk."

Sarah shook her head. She pulled the chest open. "Look!" Excitement filled her voice.

Cora's heart jumped when she saw the bags of flour, sugar, salt and other foodstuffs.

Joe whistled low. "I'll go get Flynn to help me get it back to the wagon train."

Sarah whispered loudly, "Don't make a big deal out of this. Just tell Flynn that Cora needs him."

The boy nodded, then ran through the muddy water toward the fort and Flynn.

"That boy is going to ruin those boots." Sarah shook her head, but a proud smile graced her lips.

"What else do you think is in the box?" Cora asked, praying for dried fruit and honey. She wanted so badly to make a pie for Flynn and the baby. Her cooking skills were really good now and she'd love to test her campfire baking skills. She smiled at the thought. Sarah had been right weeks ago when she'd said they'd get used to the trail way of life.

Sarah turned around and sat on the trunk. "No idea, but I'm wondering what is in the chest below it, too."

Cora's gaze moved to the trunk in question. "More food?" she suggested.

"Maybe—or fabric, or books, or perhaps clothes. It must be something they didn't want to get wet or ruined." Sarah grinned. "Whatever it is, they thought it was valuable. They had that canvas over the top and then that was covered by those boards. I was looking for another board to lay down when I picked it up, and I saw the canvas and wondered what it was covering."

Cora felt her own excitement building, reminding her of being a kid at Christmas. She and Sarah tried to act normal as other people passed by going into the fort. Cora waved at Sarah's sister Abigail as she approached with her husband. She could tell that Abigail wanted to come over, but her husband said something to her, and instead of joining them, she waved as they passed by.

Flynn walked up holding Noah, with Joe grinning beside him. "I hear you ladies would like to move that old chest back to the wagons."

"You didn't tell him what's in the trunk?" Sarah asked her son.

Joe rocked on his heels, his eyes twinkling. "Nope. Thought it might be a nice surprise."

Sarah stood and motioned for Cora to join her husband. She followed, making sure to stay on the board. "Go see for yourself," Cora told him.

He handed the baby to Cora. "Looks like an old trunk to me," Flynn said as he made his way across the board.

Cora bounced Noah in her arms. The baby must have sensed her joy, because he squealed his own happiness.

Flynn still looked doubtful. Dark clouds covered the sun, threatening more rain. More than likely Flynn wanted to get back inside the fort before they all got wet.

He lifted the lid and his eyes grew round. A big smile spread across his face, revealing even white teeth. Flynn quickly dropped the lid back into place and said, "Come on, Joe. Let's get this old trunk back to the wagon."

"Yes, sir." Joe beamed like a possum eating his favorite fruit as he hurried to help Flynn.

They lifted the chest and proceeded back across the board. "Which wagon do you want us to take this to?" Flynn grunted.

Sarah answered, "Yours. We have plenty of that stuff in ours. Hurry back. We might need that other trunk carried, too."

Cora marveled at the way Sarah took charge. She'd seen schoolteachers boss their students around like that but never men, not even half-grown men. Cora realized Sarah was already heading back to see what was in chest number two. She hastened after her across the boards.

Her friend was bent over, holding the lid up with one hand and digging in the box with the other. When she heard Cora approach, she said, "This one has clothes, books and spices inside. Do you want any of this?"

"Of course. Do you think the clothes will fit me or the baby?"

Sarah smiled. "Only one way to find out. Let's take it to the wagon." She picked up one end of the box but then seemed to remember that Cora was holding Noah. "I guess we'd better wait for Flynn and Joe." Sarah turned around and sat on the trunk.

"Did you say there are books in there?" Cora asked as she rocked the baby, who was close to his usual nap time. "I've missed my books."

Sarah smiled. "Yes. I think Martha might be able to use a couple of them to teach the kids. I didn't get a good look at all of them, so there might even be some storybooks. I'm sure the men won't let us take them all." She added the last bit as if to warn Cora not to get her hopes up.

"Our wagon isn't that full. I might be able to talk Flynn into letting me keep them," Cora answered just as Flynn returned.

"What are you wanting to take?" He stood with one hand on his hip and the other on his gun holster.

Cora offered him what she hoped was a pleasing smile. "The chest Sarah is sitting on."

Cora walked down the board and smiled. "It has spices in it."

His eyes lit up.

So far, Cora had been using what little salt they had sparingly. She didn't want to run out and they had no other spices for her to season their meals with. Cora knew he wouldn't pass up something that might improve her cooking.

Joe groaned his frustration at the need to haul another trunk rather than going to explore the fort. He looked to the sky. "It looks like it might rain any moment."

Flynn slapped him on the back. "Then what are we waiting for? We need to hurry if we want to beat the rain."

Cora grinned. "Thank you." She patted Flynn on the arm before heading back to the wagon train.

A moment later, she almost laughed out loud when she heard Flynn call to Joe. "Come on, Joe. Put your back into it, and let's get this back to my wagon."

Sarah caught up to her and grinned. "You have that man right where you want him, don't you?"

It wasn't a question that needed an answer, so Cora

simply hugged Noah's sleeping body to her and smiled. "Well, it does have spices."

She heard Joe grunt and ask Flynn as they passed by, "How many spices are in this box?"

She and Sarah broke into giggles.

Flynn looked to Cora, and catching her eye, he winked as they passed. He enjoyed the rich color that entered her cheeks at his bold action. The sweet sound of her giggle warmed his heart.

Joe tugged forward on his end of the chest. "Flynn, this box weighs a ton. Do you think we could get it to the wagon today?"

He laughed. "Sorry, I got distracted." Flynn continued with Joe to the wagon. Cora was a pleasant distraction. Over the course of their travels, he'd grown fond of her. She was kind, generous and hardworking, and she never complained when he asked for her help, even when it meant getting her dress covered in mud as she helped push the wagon through the rain-drenched ruts of the other wagons. She was a wife any man would be proud of.

They placed the trunk beside the first one and opened the lid. Spice bottles nestled in an uncovered smaller box on top of books that took up half the space. On the other side of the chest were neatly folded clothes.

Joe sighed. "Books. I should've known Ma would find books in all that stuff."

The women arrived and Flynn stepped back. He really wanted to get back to the fort and the men he'd been chatting with earlier. They were talking about the trail ahead and what could be expected.

Not only had that been of interest to him, but his hope was to figure out who was the most informed on the comings and goings at the fort. That man might know if his killer had already passed through or not. Even though the sheriff had been sure he was on their wagon train, Flynn wasn't. The man could have departed from Independence before the train left. Flynn couldn't afford to ignore any possibility.

He glanced at Joe, who looked longingly at the fort. Flynn grinned as he said, "Ladies, if you are done with us, Joe and I would like to get back to the fort."

Sarah waved them away, and Flynn watched as Joe made a run for the fort. He assumed Joe had agreed to meet up with Ruby. That boy was smitten with the girl, and they'd been seen several times walking by the river in the evenings.

"Would you come get me in an hour?" Cora asked Flynn. "Noah will probably be awake by then and I'd like for us to get a few supplies." She slipped the sling over her head and cradled Noah close.

"I'll be happy to." He reached inside the wagon and quickly spread a quilt out for the baby. When he was satisfied Noah would be comfortable, Flynn moved to let her lay him down, but Cora handed Noah to Flynn instead.

"Thank you. It's easier for you to lay him down." She offered him a sweet smile and then hurried to see what Sarah was pulling from the last trunk they had carried over.

Flynn doubted Cora even noticed when he walked away and headed to the fort.

❧

Chapter Ten

Later that night, after taking Cora and the baby with all their new supplies back to the wagon, Flynn returned to the fort for the last time. He'd not learned much earlier and felt discouraged. He'd met lots of soldiers, Indians, travelers and trappers, but few matched the physical description of the man he was looking for, and none of them seemed like the killing type.

Dusk descended and he knew he'd have to retire to the wagon train soon. Flynn walked back to the trading post he'd visited earlier with Cora. She had liked a bracelet there but had said it was too expensive. Even so, he had watched her admire the bracelet again right before they'd left.

He walked up to the counter and looked through the glass top. The dark brown leather bracelet was still there. He saw that it had a brass heart insert with a vine etched in the brass metal.

"Can I show you something in there?" the owner asked, stepping up to the counter.

Flynn nodded toward the jewelry. "I'd like to get a closer look at that bracelet."

The man reached inside and pulled it out. "Your wife seemed to really like this piece." He handed it over.

"She did." Flynn ran his finger over the metal. He wanted to make sure there were no sharp spots in the brass.

"I can scratch her name or anything else you want in that, if you'd like."

Flynn looked at the man. He didn't look like a master engraver to him, and Flynn wasn't sure that whatever the shopkeeper wrote on the metal would be pretty. No, Flynn decided he would pass on that service. He looked at the price and frowned. Cora was right to say it was expensive.

Thankfully, he had quite a bit of money tucked away in the hidden compartment of his wagon. He had visited the bank right before leaving, making sure he would have plenty of money to get home with after reaching Oregon.

Half an hour later, Flynn walked out of the shop a little poorer but happy to know he would soon see a different kind of smile on Cora's face. Night had descended and Flynn waited just outside the door for his eyes to adjust to the darkness.

He leaned against the wall and watched as other men hurried about their evening chores. He knew he should get back to the wagon train. Cora would have the evening meal ready and waiting for him. Pushing away from the wall, Flynn started walking toward the main gates. He noticed a shadow move between two of the buildings. Careful not to be noticed, Flynn stepped onto the porch of the nearest building and melted into the shadows.

He watched as Doc finally emerged from the buildings. What had he been doing, skulking around in an alley? Flynn looked at the two buildings and then realized that Doc had come from between the blacksmith shop and the livery. But why? What could he need from either of those shops?

Flynn followed Doc out the huge gates of the fort, then caught up with him. "Good evening, Doc. How did you enjoy the fort?"

Doc almost dropped the cigar box from under his arm. He seemed to compose himself swiftly, though. "It was nice. I had my first good meal in weeks." He pulled a cigar from his coat pocket. "Care for one?"

"No, thanks." Flynn watched Doc's eyes as the flame from his match lit up his face.

The doctor puffed heavily on the cigar. "Aw, I know they are bad for my lungs, but I needed this one." He laughed. "I'm sure a nonsmoking man wouldn't understand."

Sweet smoke drifted down on them. Flynn had seen other men smoke cigars but had never been tempted to do so himself. They walked slowly to the wagons.

Doc glanced sideways at him. "You were at the fort kind of late."

Flynn nodded. "So were you."

The doctor stopped and studied the end of his cigar. "I was. I have spent the whole day debating if I should buy this box of smokes. I finally gave in. The blacksmith is privately selling them, so I had to go to the side entrance to avoid notice. He doesn't want anyone to know." He stopped and took another puff from the cigar. "You know, like the trading post owner."

That didn't make a lot of sense. Each establishment in the fort was allowed to buy and sell goods at their leisure. He frowned. "Why would the trading post owner care if the blacksmith is selling cigars?"

Doc shrugged. "I got the impression the two men aren't friends and the trader doesn't like competition, but who knows." He took one last puff of his cigar, then used his boot heel to rub the burning end off before tucking the remains in his front pocket.

"How's it going in the Clarkson wagon?" Flynn asked as they both turned to go back to the wagons.

"Good. Mrs. Clarkson isn't as all fired up as she was when we started out. I think she's lonely but hasn't shown how she feels to the other women. Harold is a worrier. I fear that man is going to have a heart attack before we get to Oregon, with the way he fusses about."

Harold hadn't struck Flynn as a worrier. He liked things done his way, but when shown a better option, Harold had always given in. Flynn didn't think worry was a character flaw of the older man, but then again, he didn't live in the same wagon camp with him, either. "I noticed Harold moved closer to the end of the train, even though it wasn't rotation time yet. Any idea why?" Flynn stopped again.

"Yep. The missus is always one of the last ladies to get her camp broke down and everything put away. Samuel came by and told us we would have to be at the tail of the wagon if we couldn't get started faster."

Later, as he made his way to his own wagon, Flynn thanked the Lord that Cora wasn't lazy. She got up early every morning and had breakfast going, sometimes before the rifles were shot off to wake camp. During the day, she searched for dry wood as they walked, so they were never without kindling to start their fires. Since she had learned how to cook over an open flame, Cora often made biscuits. Thanks to her hanging a bucket with the remaining morning milk on the side of the wagon, they always had a little butter in the evenings. He felt blessed to have her as a wife instead of the Clarkson woman.

Flynn smiled when he saw her beside their fire, baby Noah on her hip sucking his fingers. The thought that this was a temporary family saddened him a little. He'd grown fond of Cora and the baby. They still had several more months of traveling together. When it was over, would he be able to leave his new family? Maybe he shouldn't continue acting as if this was a real marriage and they were a real family. Something about that thought tore at his heart.

Over the next few days, Cora realized that something was bothering Flynn. He came back for supper later and later each day, and today he hadn't come back at all. Plus, he had quit taking the baby with him and said very little as he ate his meals. She sighed heavily.

Joe looked up from his seat across. "Something bothering you, Mrs. Adams?"

More often than not, Joe had begun to eat his meals with her, instead of her husband. The growing boy was always hungry. She offered him what she hoped was a pleasing smile. "Not really. I just wondered when Flynn would be coming back tonight."

"Oh, he must have forgotten to tell you that he's on guard duty again tonight." Joe scraped the rest of his food from his plate and into his mouth before handing the dirty dish to her. "Thanks for dinner. I'm going to go check on the oxen. I'll be back shortly."

"You're welcome." Cora watched the young man

head off toward the riverbank. She suspected he was
in a hurry to meet Ruby. Sarah had commented that if
she wanted to find her boy, all she had to do was head
toward Ruby's family's wagon.

Cora began gathering up the dirty dishes and putting them into the washtub. Noah was already sleeping. She planned on reading the book *The Woman in
White* by Wilkie Collins. She'd been pleased to see
that there were enough novels in the trunk they'd gotten at the fort to keep her reading all the way to Oregon. *The Woman in White* looked interesting, as if it
contained a mystery.

"Mrs. Adams."

Cora recognized the heavy Irish accent. Even
though she hadn't heard it in weeks, she knew Mrs.
Clarkson stood behind her. She turned slowly to look
at the other woman. Sad green eyes looked back at her.
"Hello, Mrs. Clarkson. Would you like a cup of coffee?" She motioned for the other woman to join her by
the cooking fire.

"That's very kind of you." She slumped down on
the wooden crate Joe had vacated earlier. "I know we
didn't get off to a good start, but please, call me Annie."

What had happened to the high-spirited woman
Cora had met in Independence? Annie looked much
like a racehorse that had been ridden hard and put away
wet. Her red hair looked dull and lifeless, hanging limp
and matted; her green eyes had lost all their sparkle.
Cora felt sorry for her. Life on the trail clearly hadn't
treated the Irish woman very well. "Then you must call
me Cora." She handed Annie a tin cup of warm coffee.

Annie took the cup. Her fingernails were broken,
and her hands looked dirty. The dress she wore hung

off one shoulder, indicating she had lost weight. "Thank you." She took a long sip and sighed.

"Is everything all right at your wagon?" Cora asked as she sat down, too.

The other woman shook her head. "No. Harold is furious with me, and with good cause, I suppose. So I had to go somewhere."

Shocked, Cora asked, "He kicked you out?"

"No, he's just angry and needed some time to cool down, so I came to see you. I don't know what else to do."

Cora sighed in relief, happy that Annie had not lost her home in the wagon, though still confused as to why the woman had come to her. She would have thought Annie would have gone to see her friend Mrs. Grossman. Obviously not. Cora poured herself a cup of the strong coffee, took a sip and asked, "What can I do to help?"

Annie set her cup on the ground by her feet and leaned forward with her head in her hands. Her shoulders shook as she silently wept.

Cora stood and walked around the campfire. She gave Annie a handkerchief, placed her arms around the woman's shoulders and simply hugged her until she quit crying.

What had her husband done to her? She hated to think Annie's husband was abusive like Grace's had been. Before she judged Harold, Cora decided to wait out Annie and see what the real problems were.

Once Annie's sobs seemed to have paused, Cora went back to her seat and asked, "What's happened to make Harold angry?"

Fresh tears began to slide down Annie's cheeks, but

she managed to answer, "Everything I do is wrong. When he married me, Harold said I'd never have to work another day of my life, and now he calls me lazy for not being the perfect wagon train wife, like you."

"I am far from perfect, Annie. If Sarah Philmore hadn't taken me under her wing, I'd still be burning our meals and not getting enough rest."

Cora had heard that the Clarksons were having problems. Both Sarah and Flynn had mentioned that they had been moved to the back of the wagon train. Sarah had accused Annie of being lazy, and later Flynn had mentioned Annie might could use a friend because the other ladies had rejected her, disgusted by the way Annie stayed in the wagon and slept most of the day away. Rumor had it that Harold and Doc took care of their campsite, fixed their meals and washed their own clothes.

It sounded like Harold had had enough and wanted his wife to take on her responsibilities. But Annie didn't act indignant about being asked to pull her weight. Instead, she seemed confused and sad. Cora continued to wait Annie out.

"Well, perfect or not, I want to be like you." Annie picked up her coffee cup and took another sip. "Harold says he should have kicked me out of the wagon and kept you." More tears made their way down Annie's face.

"Men say things sometimes that they shouldn't. I will be happy to help you, Annie. What did you fix for supper?" She watched the other woman wipe the tears from her face.

"Beans from a can and coffee."

Cora forced herself not to cringe. That wasn't a meal

for a man who had worked all day. Instead of showing her feelings, she asked, "What did you fix for lunch?"

"I gave Harold a bag of beef jerky." She sniffed as fresh tears threatened to spill over. "He grabbed the bag and said I hadn't put any effort into this trip. That's why I opened the beans and warmed them up for supper. And he still wasn't happy."

Cora couldn't stop the sigh that passed her lips. She understood Harold's frustrations, and she also understood Annie's. She couldn't fix Harold, but maybe she could help Annie. "Annie, when I first started trying to cook, Flynn wasn't very happy with the results, either."

Annie interrupted her. "But your man loves you. It didn't matter that you couldn't cook. He didn't get mad. Harold married me for a jewel to hang on his arm, but who can look like a million bucks in this dreary sandstorm we face every day?" She wrung her hands and moaned. "So much for thinking he'd fallen in love with who I am and not what I represent."

Cora's heart had stalled at Annie's first words. Flynn did not love her. But if she were really honest with herself, she had developed feelings for him. She was not sure they were love, because she hadn't let herself analyze them, but the feelings were of some foreign nature, for sure.

She chose her words carefully. "Annie, what concerns you most about what you're going through at the moment?"

Annie thought for a few minutes, then sighed heavily. "That I'm no better off now than I was at the saloon. I am still alone with no one to love me." She pleated the dress in her lap and sniffled. "I jumped out of the frying pan, into the fire."

Annie had been a saloon girl? A soiled dove? Cora's first reaction was surprise and a little discomfort, but she quickly shoved the thoughts down. So what if she had been a saloon girl? She'd left that life behind and chosen a new path, which was commendable. Realizing she'd been quiet for too long, Cora said, "Well, there's one thing you're wrong about. You are not alone. I am here for you and I feel sure Sarah will be, too, if you open yourself up to us."

Annie looked hopeful for a moment, and then her countenance fell. "It's not been my experience that other women want to be friends with women like me. Especially respectable women like you and Sarah." She focused on her clasped hands.

"Annie, look at me." Green eyes full of hope, pain and unquenchable sadness stared back at her. "Only you can change what people think about you, be it Harold or the other ladies."

"But how can I do that?" Annie spoke in a broken whisper.

"My grandmother told me one time to draw a circle and get inside it and say, 'This is the person I need to work on.' She said for me to try with every situation to do to others what I'd like them to do to me."

Confusion shone in Annie's eyes. "I don't understand."

"If you don't want to be viewed as a saloon girl, then don't act or dress like one. If you want Harold's love, then love him and do things that will please him. Those are the things you need to work on." Cora placed her hands over Annie's. "But, Annie, the most important person you need to please is God."

Her voice matter-of-fact and tired, Annie answered,

"God doesn't want anything to do with the likes of me. I have broken almost every one of His commandments. The only one I haven't broken is 'Thou Shalt Not Kill.' I'm sure He wants nothing to do with me."

"That's where you are wrong. The Lord loves you and gave His son for you. He wants to make your life complete and whole. He wants to love you and be with you."

"I don't know, Cora." She stood, raised her chin and stared at Cora. "But I'll study on what you've said. Thanks."

Before she left the camp, Annie turned back around. "Cora, Harold doesn't want anyone to know that I worked at the saloon."

"I won't tell anyone." She smiled at Annie. "Everyone deserves a second chance."

"Really?" Annie tilted her head sideways and studied Cora's face.

Cora answered, "Really. I won't tell, but I do have a question." At Annie's nod of agreement, she asked, "How long have you been married?"

Annie sighed. "Oh, we got married the night before the wagon train left Independence. We have been together for a while, but Harold decided to actually marry me the night before."

"Because you both wanted to start over." It was a statement that Cora instinctively knew to be true.

Annie nodded. "Yeah. I thought if I got married, I could leave my past behind."

Cora smiled. "You will. I'll help you as best as I can."

"How?"

"Well, first off, you have to change your sleep pattern. Sleep at night, stay awake all day." Cora grinned. "Maybe when you master that you can teach Noah how to do it."

Both women laughed. Cora prayed she could help Annie change her habits and teach her to cook, like Sarah had taught her.

Cora followed her away from their wagon. "Annie, if Harold is there when you arrive, tell him you are sorry and that tomorrow morning things will be different."

Annie nodded. "Are you going to help me?"

"I am. Get up when you hear the shots go off, fix your hair and fry up bacon for the men," Cora ordered. She looked Annie right in the eye and said, "Do not go back to sleep."

"I won't, but I don't know how to fry bacon." She wrung her hands in the folds of her dress.

Cora smiled. "I do, so come here as soon as you are dressed, and we'll fry up a skilletful that you can take back to Harold and Doc."

Annie hugged her. "Thank you."

"You're welcome." Cora hugged her back and then watched as the other woman headed back to her wagon. Annie had a happier bounce in her step as she left.

Cora continued to watch. She hugged herself, massaging her arms that were so full of love when they surrounded little Noah or when she handed Flynn his coffee each morning.

Suddenly, she felt blessed to have the people around her in her life. She would be thankful today. She would make an extra effort to be kind to Annie.

Chapter Eleven

After three days of Flynn avoiding her, Cora had had enough. She asked Martha to watch Noah and then sat down on the back of the wagon and waited for him to come in for supper. While she waited, her thoughts went to Annie and how much she had changed since the woman had reached out for help.

Annie now got up at the crack of dawn, put a hot breakfast before Harold and Doc, broke up camp and walked with Cora to learn more of what to do on the trail. Annie was lucky that she didn't have any children; Cora loved Noah with all her heart, but he added work that she knew Annie wasn't ready for yet.

Flynn walked into camp and looked about. "No supper tonight?" he asked after not seeing his usual plate.

Cora smiled pleasantly. "Have I let you go without supper yet?"

Wariness filled his voice as he seemed to sense a trap. "No, but there is always a first time for everything."

She shook her head. "Well, tonight isn't the night for no supper." Cora walked to the stewpot and dished him up his meal. She added a hot buttered biscuit to his plate and handed it to him. Then she did the same for herself.

Flynn sat down and poured coffee from the pot. He handed her a cup and then picked up his plate once more. Without saying another word, he proceeded to eat.

Cora set her cup on the ground and asked, "Are you going to tell me what I've done that has displeased you?"

He swallowed before answering, even managing to look surprised, if not a little guilty. "You haven't done anything."

"All right. Then why are you avoiding me? And ignoring Noah?" She waited, watching him struggle with what to say.

After several long minutes of silence, Flynn seemed to reach a decision. He sighed heavily. "Look, I don't want the boy to get too attached to me. It messes with children's minds when people they love and count on up and disappear. You and I agreed we'd go our separate ways after we reach Oregon. I just didn't realize how fond I would become of the little tyke and he of me. It tears me up inside just to think about it."

"You don't want to hurt Noah?" Torn by conflicting emotions, Cora wished she could hide the pain his words inflicted. On the one hand, she felt extreme joy that Flynn loved Noah. But on the other hand, her heart ached because her own feelings for him apparently were not reciprocated. She had thought she might mean more to him, but it appeared she had been wrong.

"No, I don't want to hurt Noah." He looked down at his plate. "Nor do I wish to hurt you."

Cora didn't know what to say, believe or feel. Had he heard the anguish in her voice? Seen it on her face? Was he now trying to make her feel better? She forced herself to settle down and hear him out.

When she didn't say anything, Flynn continued. "I worry that because we've become close friends it will grieve us both when we have to say goodbye and move on with our lives."

She took a deep breath. "Flynn, when we get to Oregon, Sarah, Abigail and Annie are going to each go their own ways. We all know this and yet we continue to build strong friendships on the trail. Getting to know people is a part of life and my ma used to say that sometimes people enter our lives for a season and then they move on. That's just life. And though we're sad to see them go, we can cherish the time we got to have together. I want us to cherish this time. We can't keep going like we've been the last few days. It's breaking my heart." Cora looked deeply into his eyes. "I can't continue this journey watching you shut us out of your life."

His eyes narrowed and he studied her face. "You want me in your life, Cora, knowing the pain it will cause when we separate?"

Cora decided honesty was the best medicine.

"If at the end of this journey, we still wish to annul our marriage, I will do so with a grateful heart that I had the privilege to know one of the greatest men I've ever met. And I will tell Noah until he is grown, of the man that loved him and protected him during part of his first year of life. But one thing I don't think I can face is spending what little time we have left not enjoying the very friendship that makes me feel glad to be alive."

A muscle flicked in Flynn's jaw and he set his plate on the tongue of the wagon. He seemed lost in thought for a moment. Then he drew his shoulders up and put both hands in his pockets. She couldn't tell if her speech made him happy or right the opposite.

He finally spoke, his voice husky and apologetic. "You're right. I have missed you both something fierce. I'm sorry, Cora. I just didn't want to hurt you or the boy."

Cora's smile was a little shaky. She wasn't well versed in how to understand men; she just knew honesty usually paid off. But she couldn't blurt out that her feelings for him had changed or that they continued to grow each day she was around him. She looked straight at him and hedged the best way she knew how. "That is sweet. You are so kind and tenderhearted, Flynn. Like I said, I will always think of you as a friend, even after we part. We will all be fine. You'll see." Even as she said the words, she knew she would not be fine. Her feelings for him were certainly becoming more than friendship. When their journey came to an end, would she truly be able to accept not ever seeing Flynn again?

Chapter Twelve

Flynn stood with his hands on his hips, watching each wagon as it lumbered across the river. By this point, his was the fifth wagon back. The first hundred or so had already made it across, but only by the grace of God. Wheels had broken midstream and had to be changed right there in the water. Items had been passed off to other wagons in order to lighten the load and tilt the wagon enough to slide the broken wheel off. One wagon had flipped on its side; another had lost a water barrel in the current. They were on the second day of crossing, and so far, there had been no fatal accidents. But he had witnessed the water change, the current swirl in a different direction, and he dreaded this crossing.

The last river they crossed, they had lost one of the wagons and one of the drivers in the fast-running waters. It had held the train up several days while they held a memorial service and arranged for another family to take in the widow. The water here was much deeper and the current a lot stronger.

"Heave ho!"

Flynn heard the shout as he watched the driver maneuver one of the longer wagons up the bank on the other side. He took a deep breath and tried to relax. He had watched carefully and he believed he knew the path to take. The wagons that stayed to the deeper water on the north side fared better than those that took the shorter route plagued with unseen rocks, which had caused many broken wheels.

Flynn watched Joe drive the wagon up to the bank and then traded places with the boy. "Joe, take my horse and ride on the south side of me," he instructed as he handed him Winston's reins. "I'm going to take the wagon through the deeper waters."

Joe nodded and kept the horse to the side as Flynn slowly urged the oxen into the water. He felt the blood drain from his face as Cora climbed onto the seat beside him. "What are you doing!" he yelled.

She lifted her chin and boldly met his gaze. "I'm riding beside you. I saw you pacing back and forth studying the river on both sides of each wagon, and I heard you say two people were needed on this seat so one could spot the dangers on each side."

Even as she spoke, he felt the tongue of the wagon begin to float. He prayed the wheels would stay on the riverbed. He tightened the reins, calling encouragement to the oxen. "Good girls. Come on, now. Just a little farther. Confound it, woman! My nerves were bad enough already."

"You talking to them or to me?" Cora asked, making light of the situation.

That sass. Normally, he loved it when they teased each other—but now was not the time.

"There's a boulder. Can you see it?" Cora pointed ahead. "Just there."

"I see it." Using the reins, he turned the oxen just slightly. In truth, if it hadn't been for Cora's sharp eyes, he would have hit the boulder.

As they passed by the rock, the wagon jolted and Cora made a small squeaking noise in her throat. He knew she had just suppressed a scream, betraying the fact that she was just as nervous as he was. Flynn's stomach churned in dread. "Do you see how dangerous it was for you to climb up here?" He waved one hand wildly. "Of all the harebrained notions..."

"There. It must be a hole." Cora's eyes darted to him, her voice intense. "See how the water swirls only in that place? Can you move around it?"

Flynn called to Joe. "Can we safely come your way a bit?"

Joe had already ridden the horse ahead and circled back to them. "If you dodge that little whirlpool, it's flat with no obstructions from there on."

Flynn tried to relax his jaw, which seemed to have locked. His throat felt raw with unuttered shouts. Suddenly, Cora's fingers dug into his arm as they reached the bank. The oxen, recognizing their escape from danger, needed no urging to pull the wagon out of the water. As soon as they cleared the bank, Cora bounced on the seat, clapping her hands. When Flynn brought the wagon to a stop, she threw her arms around his neck.

"You did it! Flynn, you did it!" Her sweet breath tickled his face.

Flynn hesitated a moment before enclosing her in a long hug. The relief he felt at the wagon's safe passage and her safety caused his senses to reel as if short-circuited. He jumped down from the wagon seat and held up his arms, inviting her to join him on the ground. She placed her hands on his shoulders, her eyes shining with happiness. He lifted her down and took her face between his hands. His lips brushed against hers, light and tender.

"Aw, cut it out, you two." Joe clicked his teeth together, and then he shouted, "No!"

Flynn broke the kiss and turned just in time to see the Philmore wagon do a slow flip before it floated downstream, parcels, bundles and other objects littering the river. Joe tore off down the river on Winston.

Cora moved closer to Flynn, her arms tightening around his waist. "Oh, Flynn. Those were their supplies to outfit the new store. They've lost it all."

"Maybe not. Look, Cora." He pointed to the river. "There are several horsemen retrieving the things in the river. Why, Joe handles that horse as well as I do."

Cora pulled away from him. "Thank the Lord I sent Noah over with the Philmore children on the ferry. I need to get Noah and Martha so that we can help Sarah repack their supply wagon."

Flynn realized he hadn't even thought of Noah. Thankfully, Cora had had the insight to send the baby across on the small ferry. The raft-like ferry was only capable of carrying small loads of women and children.

Once Cora had climbed on the wagon seat with him, his heart and mind had centered solely on her. A thought flashed briefly through his mind. Was she coming to mean more to him than he'd realized? He loved Noah, but everyone loved babies. What he felt for Cora was…something else entirely. And that kiss had rocked him down to his toes.

Cora walked barefoot downstream. She stayed close to the bank in case there was a hidden current but squished her toes in the sand, then allowed the water to wash it off. The shadow from the trees overhanging the creek kept the sun off her and cooled the stream. What was it about cool water washing over hot feet that caused a girl to feel soothed? She smiled at the thought and allowed the sounds and beauty to lure her into a state of pure relaxation.

How many times as children had she and Gracie sneaked off to the river and played in the water's edge? Or rather, *she* stayed close to the edge but her adventurous sister wound up in deeper water, falling about and getting soaked. That was how their mother always knew they'd been down to the river playing instead of doing their chores. She scolded them but they never minded because oftentimes their mother joined them, laughing and hiking up her dress to avoid wetting the hem.

The memory was sweet, and Cora vowed to keep it close to her heart. Someday she would tell Noah about his mother and how she'd loved swimming in the river. She sat down on a large rock that jutted out from the bank and allowed her feet to remain in the river's cool water. After several long moments of solitude, Cora pulled her knees up, laid her head on them and closed her eyes.

She decided to have a talk with her heart. What was it doing? Every time Flynn entered their camp, why did it do a little flip? Her pulse had a mind of its own, too, and raced with joy when he smiled at her. Her lips had tingled for hours after the kiss they had shared the day before. Cora didn't want to call her reactions love, but she feared that was exactly what it was. Why else did he occupy her thoughts every waking moment? And each time he took charge with quiet assurance, the respect she felt for him climbed several notches. He knew so much, and he helped anyone who needed it.

He walked confidently, tall and broad-shouldered. At the end of the day, the shadow of his beard gave him an even more manly aura. She often found she wanted to place a hand on his jaw.

Had his fiancée touched him like that? Did Flynn still love her? Could he have kissed Cora so soundly if he loved another? She struggled with her thoughts and decided to face facts.

And the number one reality was she was falling in love with her husband, whose only plan was to catch a killer and annul their marriage as soon as they got to Oregon. Cora tried to convince herself that the kiss had been a reaction to the stress of driving the wagon through the rugged waters. It had meant no more to him than if he'd hugged his sister after facing a great trial together.

But to her it had been earth-shattering.

A large splash caused Cora to jump.

She looked up to find a young girl with blue eyes, crooked teeth and wheat-colored hair staring across the water not far from where she sat. The girl smiled at her. "I'm sorry. Did I disturb you?"

"It's all right. I was lost in thought and didn't hear you arrive." Cora welcomed the intrusion. If she were honest with herself, she really didn't want to explore her emotions anymore.

The girl picked up another rock and tossed it into the water. She heaved a sigh, then said, "I'm Rebecca Williams."

"Is that the best you can do, Rebecca Williams?"

"What do you mean?"

Cora stood and picked up a smooth stone. She weighed it in her hand. "I mean, is that your best attempt at skipping a stone across the water?" Cora planted her feet securely, and with a sidearm toss and a flick of her wrist, she sent the rock skipping across the water.

Rebecca gasped. "That's wonderful."

"Haven't you ever skipped stones before?" Cora picked up another smooth rock. This was something she and Gracie had practiced every evening while getting water for their ma.

"No, I've never tried. I thought only boys could do that." She stared at Cora expectantly, one brow raised, her tongue tip protruding from the side of her mouth.

Cora couldn't help giggling at her awestruck face. Once she had stopped laughing, she asked, "Want me to teach you the trick of stone skipping?"

Joy replaced the question that had earlier contorted the girl's face. "Oh, yes, please." Rebecca scooped up more rocks and came to stand beside Cora.

Cora spent the next thirty minutes showing Rebecca how to stand, pull her arm back at a twenty-degree angle, flick her wrist and release the stone. At first Rebecca was awkward, but after a while she could skip stones almost as well as Cora.

"I wish I could get it to skip thirteen times." Rebecca threw the stone and counted the six skips it made before groaning her disappointment.

"Why thirteen? Is that your favorite number?"

"I don't really have a favorite number, but I'm thirteen years old, so it would be nice to make it skip that many times and add one to it after each of my future birthdays." She let another rock fly across the water.

Cora climbed out of the water, sat in the grass and put her socks back on. Oh, to be thirteen again, she thought. She'd had chores back then but nowhere near the responsibilities she had now. Plus, when she'd been thirteen, her ma, pa and sister had all still been alive, and the future had seemed bright with possibilities.

Sadness filled Rebecca's voice. "You are with the big wagon train, huh?" She watched Cora pull her shoes back on.

During her rock skipping tutorial, Rebecca had informed her that she was part of the smaller train that had stopped a little way behind theirs. Before that day, Cora hadn't realized that there was another group so close behind theirs, but it had made sense to learn that Rebecca wasn't part of their group. The wagon train Cora was on held so many families with children that there was no way she could know them all, but she was pretty sure she would have remembered Rebecca, had she ever met her. No other girl on their train had that color of hair.

Once her shoes were on again, Cora faced Rebecca, who stood on the bank, looking out over the water. "Yes, I am."

Another stone went skipping across the river. "I wish I could go with you on the bigger train."

Cora walked over to her and dropped an arm around

her shoulders. "I wish you could, too." She meant it. Rebecca had been fun to spend the afternoon with. But it was just a fanciful wish. Cora was sure that Rebecca's ma needed her. Whatever made the girl want to leave her family and join the other group would more than likely be forgotten tomorrow.

Sad blue eyes turned to face her. "Please, I won't take up much room and I don't eat much."

Cora drew back in surprise. She looked closely at Rebecca's face. "You would miss your family."

She shook her head. "Ma and Pa are in heaven. I said my goodbyes to them a month ago. They got really sick. Everyone on the train says they're surprised the whole train didn't die. They say it could have been a lot worse, but to me it seems like it was more than bad enough."

Cora looked around at the sunny field, at the overhanging trees. She heard the birds singing, but what she heard loud and clear was the desperation in the girl's voice. That and a heavy dose of despair. "Oh, I see."

Rebecca pulled away from her. "No, you don't. For the past month, I have been cast from family to family in our wagon train like a dirty rag that no one wants. My parents are dead and I'm all alone now." Rebecca swallowed a sob. "I don't know what's going to happen to me when we get to Sacramento Valley. I heard one of the men tell his wife they could easily marry me off to one of the gold diggers there. But his wife said I would end up a slave, cooking and washing until I'm old before my time. They actually argued about it and he walked off mad. The next day I was shifted to another family with six kids. I had to care for them and give them their baths."

Rebecca paused and Cora knew there was more she wasn't saying. "Are you still with that family?"

Rebecca bent and picked a flower from the tall grass as they walked back toward the trains. A flush not due to the heat of the day swept over her cheeks. "No, I was moved again yesterday."

"But why? It seems like that would have been a perfect situation for you, with a family that could use an extra set of hands. In exchange for your help with the kids, you have board and upkeep. Food. What happened?"

"The husband hugs too tight. It made me uncomfortable, so I told his wife I didn't like it. Next thing I knew, I was passed to another wagon." She rubbed her arms as if to remove the feel of those unwanted hugs.

"Oh, honey, I'm so sorry." Cora had held her own pity parties on this trip, but she suddenly realized that compared to Rebecca's situation, her own was actually good. Great, for that matter. "Where are you now?"

"I'm with an old granny and her husband. I help her with cleanup. She's a good cook. But I have to sleep under the wagon. She doesn't need me much—just at meals, and she said tomorrow would be washing day." Rebecca sighed, clasped her slender hands together and continued, her voice choking, "I'm all alone in the world."

At the beginning of this journey, Cora had felt the same way. Her twin was the last of her family, and with Gracie's death, she'd felt entirely alone. Cora touched Rebecca's arm. "You would be surprised how much I understand." They were almost back to the wagon train and she could see Flynn talking to Joe. He threw his head back, his laugh ringing out over the field. "I'm a twin. My sister died the day before we left on this trip."

"But what about your parents?"

"They died when Gracie and I were sixteen. After that, our grandmother cared for us for a few months until she passed away." She took Rebecca's hand, swinging it between them. "So I know where you're coming from. It's a lonesome place."

They had reached Flynn and Joe, and both men stood as they arrived. "Flynn, I'd like you to meet someone. This is Rebecca Williams." Flynn offered a handshake that Rebecca accepted. "Rebecca, this is my husband, Flynn Adams. And this is Joe Philmore."

"Howdy." No sign of the earlier anguish was in Rebecca's voice as she shook Joe's hand. A soft pink flush filled her cheeks as she ran her gaze over his young, handsome face.

"How do—" Joe seemed to have lost the ability to speak and he cleared his voice loudly.

"Mrs. Cora taught me how to skip rocks. I bet I can skip mor'n you." Rebecca challenged Joe, and to Cora's amazement, he accepted the contest.

"I highly doubt that a slip of a thing like you could beat me at skipping rocks." He puffed his chest out like a Domineck rooster.

Martha walked up with Noah and handed him to Cora. His little eyes were full of sleep, and she knew he would go down for his nap without a fuss. "So, what are you all doing?" She looked from Joe to Rebecca.

"I'm going to show this gal how a professional skips rock," Joe bragged.

"Oh, good. If you're going to the river, I'm going, too. It will be nice to cool off." The trio headed back the way Cora had just come from. Rebecca, Martha and Joe were chatting away a mile a minute. Cora's heart felt a bit lighter, but she knew Rebecca's problem was not solved. She had found new friends for now, but the situation wouldn't last. The wagon trains would part after they crossed the mountain, one going to Oregon and the other to Sacramento Valley in California. Then what would happen to the girl?

Chapter Thirteen

"Cora, I know you mean well, but we can't take the girl in." Flynn paced the campsite. Cora fumed at the tone of his voice, courteous and patronizing at the same time. "I know you have a big heart, but I really don't think you've thought this through."

With her hands planted firmly on her hips, Cora demanded, "I *have* thought it through, and I don't see the problem. Why could she not join us? Flynn, she doesn't have anyone that cares about her except for me."

He sighed. "I know you do, but what happens when we get to Oregon? Are you going to raise both kids alone? It's going to be hard enough on you to shelter and feed just one." He hated the idea of her trying to provide for two children. He would try to help her find a place to live, but an extra child meant an extra mouth to feed, another person to worry about, on whatever salary she was able to earn. Or had Cora forgotten their agreement? Was she expecting him to stay and help her care for both children, to provide for all of them as a family? Was she starting to see them as a married couple who would stay together forever?

She dropped her hands from her hips. Disappointment filled her face, and she turned her back on him.

He walked up behind her and put his hands on her shoulders. "Please don't cry. Think about it from my viewpoint for just a minute. I can't take her with me when we go our separate ways in Oregon. I'll hopefully be bringing a killer home with me to stand trial—how could I expose an innocent girl to that? And even afterward, there'd be no place for her in my life. My job isn't good for families." How many times had he told himself that his job was the reason he couldn't fall in love with Cora, even if kissing her had made him want to be a real husband?

Cora stepped away from him. "I'm going to bed. Noah's been teething and he'll be awake in a little bit." With that, she climbed into the back of the wagon and shut the flaps.

Flynn knew she was upset and possibly angry, but he could not help that. They were not the family who could take in a thirteen-year-old orphan. However, just maybe he knew a man and woman who could. He walked to the back of the wagon and softly called out, "Cora, I'll be back in a little while. I have to go check on something."

Her muffled voice answered. "All right."

Joe stepped out of the shadows. "Want me to stand watch?"

It was uncanny how he appeared and disappeared as if on cue. The boy never ceased to amaze him. He had watched Joe from day one, and the boy had never let him down. And the way he'd helped his father and brother the day they'd brought the wagon across the river still impressed Flynn. Joe had spent hours searching downstream for his family's possessions and had found more than anyone else. His mindset was that of a mature man, and it was hard for Flynn to see him as the young boy he was. "Thank you, Joe. I shouldn't be long."

Joe nodded. "Tell the Cartwrights I said hello." He winked and sat down on the crate at the back of the wagon.

Flynn stopped short and stared at Joe in astonishment. "How do you do that? Are you a mind reader?"

"Not at all. It's just everyone knows that Mr. and Mrs. Cartwright's daughter, Bonnie, died a few weeks back. Seems to me like they have a hole in their hearts and their lives that Rebecca can fill. Plus, you're a kind man. Smart, too. Why not kill two birds with one stone?"

It amazed Flynn that Joe's thoughts had traveled the same path as his own. Joe was shaping up to be a smart man, too. Then again, the way he'd acted around Rebecca might get him into hot water with Ruby, so maybe he still had a few things to learn. At that thought, Flynn walked away chuckling.

Luke Cartwright sat beside the fire, drinking coffee. Flynn didn't see Carolyn and surmised she'd retired early. They were a quiet couple, always minding their own business—but time and time again, they had shown themselves to be kind, decent people. They always followed the rules of the train and were the first ones to step up and help if there was a need.

"Mind if I join you a spell?" Flynn asked as he walked into their camp.

Luke poured another cup of coffee. "Not at all. What

brings you our way, Flynn? Trail Boss want me to take a watch?"

"No, nothing like that." Flynn took the offered cup. He looked around and lowered his voice before asking, "Where's the missus?"

Sadness entered the man's eyes. "She's turned in early tonight."

Flynn nodded. "My missus did, too—only mine did so because she's angry with me."

Luke sighed. "They spend half of our married life being angry with us. Hope it's nothing too serious for you." He took a sip from his mug.

Flynn knew he could continue to beat around the bush or just tell Luke why he had come to their camp. He chose to be straightforward. "Cora's angry because she wants us to take in a young'un."

Luke waited.

Flynn waited.

After about five minutes of waiting and silence, Luke finally spoke. "What's the story with the young'un?"

"She's a thirteen-year-old girl traveling with the California Train. Poor thing lost her parents a month or so back, and she's been bounced around since then, trying to find a place to land. My wife wants her to land with us, but Cora has her hands full with Noah and I'm worried the girl would be too much for her. You know how girls that age like to sass and test a person." He took a drink and stared into his cup. "Mind you, I feel for the child, her being an orphan and all, but I just don't think Cora has the experience to handle adopting a teenager."

"Hogwash." Carolyn stepped out of their wagon. "Cora Adams can handle any task she cares to take on, and everyone here knows she's got a gift for children. So, what's the real reason you don't want her to take the girl in?" Her brown gaze sized up Flynn, and if the look in those flashing eyes was anything to go by, he came up lacking.

He shook his head. "No reason beyond what I've said. Taking in a teenager is a big task, especially one who's grieving. She most likely has issues that will need full-time care and watching after."

"Cora is both stable and able to handle all of what you just mentioned. She'd love the child just like her own." Her voice broke on those last two words, and Carolyn came and put her hands on her husband's shoulders. He in turn reached up and covered her hands. The gesture touched a place in Flynn's heart, and he rubbed a hand across his chest.

Luke chuckled. "Enough, Flynn. You won't win with my Carolyn by making excuses. Just tell us what you want."

He shrugged. "All right. I want you to take Rebecca Williams."

Carolyn's voice came out a squeak. "Us?"

Flynn took his hat off and twisted the brim in his hands. "She needs parents and you need a daughter."

A tear trickled down Carolyn's face. "We had a daughter."

"And you could have another one." Flynn kept his voice soft and prayed it came out kind and caring. "She needs a ma, Carolyn. I know Rebecca could never replace Bonnie and you could never replace her ma. But I also know you both could be good for each other."

Luke stood and wrapped his arms around his wife. She turned her face into his shoulder. "Let us sleep on it, Flynn," he said, nodding at Flynn to indicate the discussion was over.

Flynn turned to walk away. Maybe this had been a bad idea. Had he hurt Carolyn? He hadn't meant to. He'd meant to help Rebecca and make peace with Cora.

"Flynn?"

He turned to face Carolyn. She wiped tears from her face. "We'll take her."

The words were such a shock that he almost thought he'd misheard them. "Are you sure?" If he lived to be a hundred, Flynn felt sure he'd never understand women.

Carolyn clung to her husband's waist. "I'm sure." She looked eagerly into her husband's eyes. "Are you fine with this, honey?"

Flynn took a couple of steps back to them. "Cora says the girl has been passed around the other train to the point where Rebecca feels like no one wants her. I don't want to see her hurt again. She needs a forever home."

Luke tightened his arms around his wife, drawing her closer. "She'll have one with us. We'll not be passing her on when the going gets tough. Our Bonnie taught us that children like order, responsibilities and love. Rebecca will have all three."

Flynn smiled. "I believe she will. Now, would you mind coming back with me and explaining it to Cora?"

Luke actually laughed out loud. "I think you can handle it, Flynn. That was some mighty fine persuasion you just handed us, so you'll do just fine with your missus."

Carolyn smiled. "Thank you for thinking of us, Flynn. I'll come over in the morning and Cora and I will find the girl and bring her home with us. It will be all right. You'll see."

"Thanks to the both of you. You're good people. I'm glad we met up." Flynn walked back to his wagon, the tension gone from his shoulders and the tight knot in his stomach soothed.

Flynn lay on his belly looking down at the village below. He could see ten tepees beside a stream of water that connected to the one the wagon train was camped beside. Women milled about doing chores, and older men sat in front of their tepees smoking and talking. Young and old women alike worked over cooking pits and the children played nearby. He looked to Levi and whispered, "Tell me again why we're here."

"We're scouting."

He shook his head. "You mean spying."

Levi motioned for him to stop talking and crawl back the way they'd come. As soon as they were far enough away not to be noticed by the villagers, they stood. Levi led the way back to their horses.

Once they had put some distance between themselves and the village, Levi asked, "Did you notice anything odd about the village?"

Flynn thought back. It had seemed peaceful. The women were going about their normal chores, and children had been playing with a stick and some sort of ball while the old men smoked and talked. His eyes narrowed as the penny dropped. "There were no young men in camp."

"Exactly. I'm curious if they are out hunting—or if they are surrounding our wagon train, waiting for nightfall so they can attack." Levi sighed. "I prefer to think they are hunting."

"Any ideas on how we can find out?" Flynn's mind was already working on what he could do to protect his own. He didn't like the idea of Cora and the baby being at the camp without him, and the possibility of an Indian raid happening while he was gone scared him.

Levi grinned. "We scout until we find them." He turned his horse and headed back toward the wagon train. "When we get about a mile away from our wagon train, we'll both spread out and see what we find."

Flynn nodded. "If you don't mind my asking, why did you ask me to scout with you today? Don't you normally do this alone?" Aware that they had just left the Indians, Flynn waited for an answer even as he kept his head tilted just so that he could hear anyone approaching them from behind.

"You are the most alert man on this train, with the exception of myself and Samuel." He pushed his hat back and looked over at Flynn. "Even now, you are making sure we aren't being followed."

So his behavior was transparent. That was a dangerous thought, especially if it meant that others had picked up on it, too. Catching a killer would depend on his target not realizing he was being hunted. Flynn would have to do better, if he planned on catching a killer and keeping Cora and the baby safe.

"Don't look so concerned. My job is to observe and learn everyone's mannerisms, attitudes and strengths on this train. You, sir, were a hard one to figure out." Levi grinned. "For a while there, I wasn't sure if you were a good guy or a bad one. Men like us are either one or the other."

They rode along in silence. Flynn had also been observing Levi. He'd found him to be silent, reserved and tough as nails. When the wagons had passed through the worst of the rivers, Levi had been in the center of the rushing currents, making sure each family made it safely to the other side. He had nearly killed himself trying to rescue the man who'd gotten caught in the rapids and drowned. While Levi hadn't been able to save the man, he had managed to bring his body to shore to allow his widow to give him a proper burial.

When they were about a mile from camp, Levi instructed, "You go right and I'll go left. If they are surrounding the camp, they may have scouts out, so watch yourself." Levi pulled his horse to the left and waved as they parted ways.

Flynn moved with caution as he made a wide circle around camp. He heard shouts on the wind and followed the sounds. His horse snorted and pulled on the reins. "Hold on, ole boy." Flynn pressed the horse to continue moving forward.

Within a few moments, he could see what the commotion was about. In a valley between two hills, the young men of the village were in pursuit of a small buffalo herd. From where he sat on the hill, he watched as they cut one of the mighty beasts from the rest of the herd. With the arrows they shot and the lances they threw, the buffalo soon collapsed onto the earth. Flynn was amazed at how quickly they were able to bring the big beast down. He grinned as they celebrated their kill.

His lips soon stiffened as he saw a bull come back. He snorted and charged toward the closest young man. Flynn urged Winston down the hill. He prayed he would reach the man before the buffalo. The Indian saw the animal bearing down on him and let out a shout. The other men turned just as Flynn rushed in between the man and the magnificent beast.

He prayed herding buffalo worked the same as herding cattle. As Flynn reached down, the man instantly understood his intention and grasped his forearm. With all his might, Flynn hauled the man up onto the horse. The young Indian swung up behind him and held on tight.

The massive buffalo snorted. He stopped, pawed at the ground and then turned right before reaching them. As if he knew he was defeated, the buffalo returned to his fleeing herd.

Flynn smiled as the warriors around him cheered and shouted. He didn't understand their words but knew they were happy and grateful by the smiles on their faces. The young brave slid off the back of his horse. Once he was on his feet, he motioned for Flynn to join them on the ground.

Flynn climbed off his horse and turned toward them. They slapped him on the back and some of them even shook his hand. Flynn wasn't sure what to make of the situation.

"Looks like you've made a few friends," Levi announced. He had walked his horse down to where they were without Flynn even realizing he was there.

Flynn grinned. "Just doing what comes naturally. I don't know what all the fuss is about."

Levi leaned on his saddle horn. "You saved the boy's life, and they are grateful."

"You saw?"

The scout nodded. "Yep." He pointed to a cluster of

trees. "There for a second I thought that bull was going to continue with his charge."

"So did I."

The braves began butchering the meat, so Flynn climbed back on his horse. He and Levi waved good-bye, then headed back to the wagon train.

"I'm glad that went well," Levi said as they rode.

"I'm glad you were in the tree line watching, just in case it hadn't," Flynn answered as he patted his horse on the neck. "You get an extra helping of oats," he told the horse.

Levi chuckled low. "What do you do for a living?"

Flynn sighed. "I'm a lawman, but I'd like to keep that information between us, if you don't mind."

"Is your reason for joining this wagon train anything myself or the wagon master should know about?" Levi pulled his horse to a stop.

"I'm on the hunt for a killer. He has killed multiple women between here and Texas. Rumor says he joined our train. I'll let you know when I find him." Flynn sighed. "*If* I find him. I don't have a lot to go on."

Levi clicked his tongue and the horse began to move again. "What about your new wife? Does she know you're a lawman?"

"Cora knows."

"And she doesn't mind? I mean, after you get to Oregon, will you be going back to Texas or staying?"

"I'm not sure yet." A big part of Flynn wanted to stay with Cora and the baby, but his life was in Texas, not Oregon.

Levi sighed. "My wife hates me going back and forth. I'm thinking this might be my last trip." He looked off into the distance.

Flynn knew Levi hadn't realized the turmoil his questions roused in him. He was falling for Cora and already loved the baby. If he told her how he felt, would she be willing to move back to Texas? That would mean traveling along a dusty trail again. And what about the dangers his job put him in? Would she hate not knowing where he was when he was out chasing bad guys? Would she feel safe on her own? Would she actually *be* safe? He hadn't been able to protect Miriam—would he let down Cora, too?

Chapter Fourteen

Cora gingerly placed her armload of plants in the back
tailgate of the wagon. She couldn't believe her luck in
finding rosemary, sage and lavender along the banks of
the river. Though she hadn't studied herbs, her mother
and grandmother always had them in their gardens and
used them as seasoning and sometimes even as medicine. Now she just needed cans to plant them in and to
carefully transport them the rest of the way to Oregon,
and she'd have the start of a fine herb garden.

She'd dug them up, careful to get enough of the root,
and for some reason, it made her extremely happy to
think of having them with her, tending to them. Maybe
that was why her mother and grandmother always had
a garden. Maybe she herself would enjoy gardening
someday.

Annie walked up beside her, seemingly in good
spirits. "What are you going to do with those weeds,
Cora?"

"They aren't weeds. They are herbs that I found
growing down by the river. I hope to plant them when
we get to Oregon." She moved so Annie could see them

lying on the tailgate. "But right now I need to find pots to plant them in. Otherwise they will die."

Annie wrinkled her nose. "What do you need them for? They're not that pretty."

Cora smiled at her friend's expression. "They're not to look at. They're used for healing and cooking purposes." She brushed dirt off one of the leaves, then continued, "You can use them to season meat. My grandmother even put them in desserts. I wish I had some of her recipes."

"You're smart, Cora. Wish I was smart like you." Annie picked up the lavender and smelled it. "This one smells like a flower."

Annie had done so much better these last few weeks, but some days she lacked confidence and needed a helping hand. "You're smart, too, Annie. Just in a different way. I admire how you talked Mrs. Smith into trading you dried peaches for coffee beans. You knew how much she wanted the coffee and what a fair trade with her would be. We all have different talents and strengths. What you are holding is lavender. It is used to help people relax, and it's also taken to help with pain."

"How do you use it for pain?" Annie asked, setting the plant back down.

Cora smiled. "You mix the dried lavender leaves with tea leaves and then boil them in water and drink it."

She saw the light click on in Annie's eyes. It had been so easy to teach her how to be a good wife. Annie was a fast learner. Once she realized that she could learn new ways of doing things, Annie had become a pleasant person to be around.

Just last evening, they had worked together and made two blackberry pies. This morning, Annie confessed that Harold had been doubly pleased at her efforts. It was as if something had finally clicked in Annie's brain and taught her to enjoy pleasing her new husband in little things that other ladies did as a matter of course. Such as taking him water to drink during the heat of the day or pulling his shoes off for him when he was too tired to do it himself. And to his credit, Harold had responded positively, and it was wonderful to see the personal growth in them both.

Cora smiled. "Now, as I said, all I have to do is find containers to plant these in."

Sarah walked up and smiled. "Will this work, Cora? I saw you bringing those back and figured you'd need things to plant them in." She held out a large coffee can, but Cora paused before accepting the gift.

"Isn't this what you use to put your loose tea leaves in?" Anything that had a lid was valuable. The lids kept bugs, dust and even children out of whatever the container held.

The older woman shrugged. "It was, but my tea got wet during the last river crossing and had to be thrown out. The can has just been sitting there empty, so you might as well use it."

"I have tea I'll share with you, Sarah." Annie took off in a run toward her wagon.

Sarah chuckled. "That girl has turned into the sweetest li'l thing." She stared after Annie, then turned back to Cora. "Here. Take this. It's large enough that you can plant all three herbs in it." When Cora started to protest, she raised her hand to halt her. "It doesn't matter if Annie shares her tea with me. Whatever amount she returns with won't be large and will probably only fill the bottom of this big can. I can find somewhere else to store the leaves." She pushed the container into Cora's hands.

Cora knew the sacrifice Sarah was making and appreciated her all the more. "Thank you. It's perfect." She turned back to the tailgate and added the can. Now all she needed was dirt to plant the herbs in.

Annie came running back with a small can. Sarah took the tin can and smiled her thanks. "You shouldn't give me this much, Annie."

The young woman smiled. "It's the least I can do. You and Cora have taught me so much. You're the best friends I've ever had. Besides, I'm more of a coffee drinker. Tea is something that I never really acquired a taste for."

Sarah laughed. "Well, thank you anyway. Why don't y'all come with me and we'll have us a small cup of tea before we have to start getting ready for bed. I'm sure I have coffee left that I can serve you, Annie. How 'bout it? Join me?" Sarah raised an eyebrow in question even as she reached an arm around Annie for a quick side hug.

The women chatted and laughed as they walked past the three wagons that separated Sarah and James's wagon from Flynn and Cora's. Though she'd be a happy lady to get off this train, Cora would miss the friends she'd made along the journey.

They walked up as Martha waved goodbye to a young man from a few wagons ahead. Her younger sisters sat in the dirt, each one with a tablet on their laps. Cora loved that she had a small part in teaching these kids, even if it was through Martha. She looked around for Noah. Not seeing him, she thought he and Daniel must be in the tent taking a nap.

She sat on the tongue of the wagon as Sarah put on hot water for the tea. Martha dipped into the tent, assumedly to check on the little boys. She returned quickly. Panic twisted her face as she said, "Noah's not in the tent!"

Cora felt her heart slip into her throat. "What do you mean? Where is he?"

"He was sleeping in the tent with Daniel and now he's not." She ran to the other side of the wagon, calling Noah's name.

"Get up, children. Find Noah." Sarah's command sank into Cora's fuzzy mind.

She ran to the next wagon and asked the two ladies there, "Have you seen Noah?"

Shock filled their features as they shook their heads no. "We'll help you look for him."

"Thank you." Cora ran back to Sarah, hoping she'd had better results, but no one had found him.

"Go, go." Sarah pushed her away. "We'll shoot into the air if we find him. Martha is headed to the river. The kids are searching behind us. Go frontward and ask if others have seen him."

Cora's heart beat frantically as she ran from wagon to wagon, asking if anyone had seen her baby. Smothering a sob when one after another they shook their heads no, she began to shake as fearful images built in her mind.

She saw Flynn and ran straight into his arms. "He's gone, he's gone," she wailed. Cora buried her face against the corded muscles of his chest. His arms encircled her, drawing her closer. Flynn would find him, she told herself even as she tried to control her weeping.

"Who's gone, Cora? What's wrong?" His voice was calm as he slid his hands along her arms and pushed her gently so he could see her face.

"Noah is missing. I can't find him." The terror of losing him swept through her, and it seemed as if darkness closed in around her. Cora felt herself slide down Flynn's body. She told herself that she couldn't faint now, not when Noah needed her—but the darkness took her anyway.

"Cora?" Flynn's breath caught in his throat as he carried her limp body back to their wagon. "Sweetheart, wake up."

She opened her eyes, confusion racing across her features for a moment. Then she seemed to remember Noah and began to struggle. "Set me down, Flynn. I'm all right." Her dark eyes showed the tortured dullness of disbelief. "We have to find him, Flynn. I can't lose him, too."

"We'll find him. He can't have gotten far." He spoke with quiet but desperate firmness while his mind played over all the things that could happen to a little fellow unchaperoned. Especially one who had been crawling everywhere lately.

"I have to get back to Sarah's wagon. Maybe they've found him."

Flynn knew she didn't believe that, but he hurried along beside her back to the Philmores' camp. His mind raced with all the horrible things that could have already happened to the baby. His heart wrenched at the thoughts. The oxen could have trampled him. He could get bitten by a snake. If he made it to the river, he might have fallen in.

When they got back to Sarah and James's wagon, Flynn forced his lips to relax. He hoped that if he looked calm it would comfort Cora. "Stay here with Sarah and I'll round up some men. We'll spread out a few feet apart and cover every inch to the right and left of us." He pulled her close and kissed her on the forehead. "Don't worry. We'll find him." He prayed fervently that he was right.

He looked to Sarah, who nodded her understanding that Flynn wanted her to watch over Cora. There was no telling what the young mother would do if the search for Noah ended in tragedy. He gave them both a quick nod and then went in search of the wagon master, gathering men as he went.

As they continued to look late into the evening, icy fear twisted around his heart. He had come to love that little boy as if he were his own. He took a swift, sharp breath. Noah *was* his. He couldn't lose him.

A shotgun blast split the sounds of the evening. Flynn's mind was a mixture of crazy hope and fear. His legs shook as he took off in a run back to the wagon. He ran to the place he'd left Cora, and there she sat, Noah clasped in her arms, a trembling smile on her face. His gaze traveled over her and Noah, and then searched her eyes. She held out a hand to him and it was all the invitation Flynn needed. He went onto one knee, his arms of their own will encircling Cora and Noah, thankfulness flowing from his lips. "Thank You, Lord. Oh, how we thank You."

Cora kept nodding and repeating his words. "Yes, Lord, we so humbly thank You."

"Where did you find him?" he blurted in excitement.

"Right over there." Cora nodded with her head. By then, a crowd had gathered round them and Flynn noticed Martha hanging back with tears of joy and relief streaming down her young face. It seemed everyone loved little Noah.

"He'd crawled up under that bush. Who knows what he was following, but thankfully, he was too tired to press on and went to sleep. The Millers' dog found him and started whining to get our attention. When I went to investigate, I found Noah curled into a ball, sound asleep."

They spent the next twenty minutes or so thanking the others, assuring Martha she was not to blame and passing Noah back and forth between the two of them. Flynn realized he didn't want to let Noah out of his sight and apparently Cora felt the same, because Flynn was the only person she allowed to take Noah from her.

They walked to their wagon, Flynn's arm around Cora's shoulders. She didn't pull away. A near tragedy had etched gratitude into their relationship. Flynn wondered briefly if this was the change he'd longed for the last few months. Satisfaction pursed his mouth and he felt his smile broaden in approval.

Chapter Fifteen

A soft noise on the side of the wagon pulled Cora from a deep, restful sleep. She fought against the need to wake up, since it was not a cry from Noah. She burrowed deeper under the blanket, refusing to look up to see what sound she had heard. But to no avail. She lay quietly for a moment listening to the sounds around her. It was probably just a limb from the tree they'd camped under rubbing against the canvas.

Cora could tell it was earlier than she usually woke, but thoughts rushed in of all she needed to do today. Besides fixing breakfast, getting the baby fed and clearing up their camp space before they hit the trail, she needed to trade or barter for heavier clothes for herself and Noah. The nights were getting chillier as they drew closer to Oregon.

On that happy thought, Cora decided it was time to rise. Careful not to wake the baby, she climbed out of the wagon and stretched the stiffness from her muscles. How she wished they had a mattress like other people on the train—but she knew they were better off traveling as lightly as possible.

Every wagon had started with at least two oxen, but some of the beasts had simply worn out from the burdens they were pulling or gotten into poisonous weeds and died. Thankfully, their oxen were still healthy. Flynn had said it was because their wagon was light, and he and Joe were careful to check the grasses where they grazed along the trail.

Not fully awake yet, she yawned widely. The full moon almost touched the horizon and gave her plenty of light as her gaze moved about the camp. It wouldn't be long till dawn chased the beautiful orb from the sky. One thing was for certain: on this trip, she had seen more beautiful country, experienced more fresh air and lived off the land more than she'd ever had in her life. It had been an unforgettable experience.

She walked around the side of the wagon to the water bucket. Her mouth felt as if it were stuffed with the dirt and grime she'd breathed in during their long journey. Cora lifted the dipper and took a long drink. Would she ever not feel as if she needed to wash the dust out of her mouth, nose and ears? She rubbed her eyes; even her eyelashes felt gritty.

Cora looked into the sky and found the Big Dipper. She thought of the Indian encounter that Flynn had shared with her and Joe last evening. He and the wagon train scout had gone ahead to inspect the trail and to learn what dangers lay ahead for them. The excitement in Flynn's voice and the movements of his body and hands as he told of the buffalo hunt and the large bull buffalo showed how much he'd enjoyed his day of scouting.

Cora had heard tales from the other ladies about the different tribes along the Oregon Trail that they could encounter. She'd convinced herself that they wouldn't run into them. She had been wrong. Flynn had met them and even saved one of the young braves. Pride grew in her heart as she thought about how heroic Flynn had been, putting his horse between man and beast.

She was grateful that the Lord had watched over Flynn and Levi and kept them both safe. Things could have gone badly, according to Flynn, if the buffalo bull had decided to continue charging toward him.

Another yawn reminded her it was too early to stay up. Just as she put her foot up to climb into the wagon, Cora noticed what looked like a pile of furs beside the right front wheel of the wagon. Chills covered her arms as she realized she was not alone. Cora raised her gaze from the furs and spotted an Indian woman who stood within a foot of her beside the wagon. The woman placed her finger over her lips and motioned toward the furs.

Cora looked about to see if anyone else were awake. Seeing no one, she walked toward the furs, all the while keeping her gaze on the Indian woman. Was Joe still under the wagon? Or had he left sometime during the night?

Moonlight illuminated the woman, who looked to be in her late twenties. Her black hair was pulled into a thick braid that trailed down her back like a rope. She wore a beautiful beaded dress that came about midcalf and then met a pair of leather boots. The woman indicated that Cora should lift the top fur.

Cora did as she asked and was surprised to see that the top fur was actually a cover flap for a bag made of furs. She looked to the woman once more.

She indicated that Cora should dig in the bag, and Cora obeyed. Inside was another bag made from a smoother animal skin that held fresh meat, and below that bag were what looked like more packs of dried meat. She looked to the woman and asked quietly, "For us?" When the woman didn't respond, Cora pointed to herself and then the meat and repeated her question.

The Indian woman nodded and smiled. Pretty white teeth flashed against her caramel-colored skin.

Cora's gaze caught a slight movement to her left. An Indian man stepped out of the shadows. He stood straight and tall under the nearest tree, with his arms crossed over his chest. His hard gaze seemed to look right through her. Had he been there before?

Cora quickly glanced around again. She wanted to call out to Flynn, but he was away on guard duty. She considered and then discarded the idea of calling to Joe, not wanting to risk the boy getting hurt. Joe would be no match for the warrior, in strength or experience. The warrior took a step back as if he could read her mind. It seemed he wanted to reassure her he was no threat.

The woman moved silently forward and touched her arm. Cora's gaze jerked to her face. She smiled as if trying to reassure Cora and extended a pair of shoes, small enough for a baby. Cora took them and realized they were moccasins. She examined the fine crafts-manship of the leather. How did the woman know that Noah was in need of shoes? Cora raised her head with a smile of thanks, but both the Indian woman and man had slipped away into the darkness.

"Are you all right, Cora?" Joe dropped his hand on her shoulder.

She jumped at both his touch and the sound of his

whispering voice so close to her ear. How long had he been standing behind her? Was he the reason the Indian man had revealed himself? Cora took a deep breath and let it out slowly as she scolded herself for not looking around more carefully. She made a mental note to be more aware of what was behind her. "I'm fine, Joe."

He placed his hand under her elbow and moved Cora back inside the circle of wagons. "Why don't you go back in the wagon and try to get some sleep?" Joe suggested.

Cora saw he held his rifle at the ready. She smiled at him. "Are you kidding? I couldn't sleep another wink. How about I make a fire and start the morning coffee?" Afraid he might go after their visitors, she asked, "Would you sit with me until Flynn returns?"

Joe nodded but kept his gaze focused on where the Indian man had stood. "I'll get the bundle they left for you."

"Thank you." Cora began making the fire. She still had warm coals from the night before, so the process was much easier than if she had had to start out with a cold firepit.

Joe brought the fur bag and set it down. It was much bigger than she'd first realized. "What do you think that was about?" he asked, looking over his shoulder as if expecting more Indians to come into their camp.

"It probably had to do with Flynn and Levi helping them yesterday. I think this is their way of saying thank you." She put the coffeepot on the grate to heat up and sat down on one of the three crates. Cora looked at him. "How long were you standing behind me?"

He grinned. "I was at the front of the wagon when you came out. I had heard something and was investigating when you saw the Indian woman. Her friend and I spotted each other right away, but with both you ladies between us, I didn't dare fire the rifle. I hope you weren't feeling too afraid." He sat down, facing the woods that surrounded the wagons.

Cora didn't tell him she'd thought he was asleep under the wagon; that would have hurt his pride. "I knew you were close by. I just didn't know where. I'm glad you were behind me and I'm glad you didn't shoot him. Thank you for watching out for us."

Joe shook his head. "I wouldn't have shot him, unless he did something to threaten you or Noah. Pa says all human life is important and we need to respect it." He paused. "Honestly, I hope I never have to use this gun on anyone. I'm not sure I could live with myself if I killed a man."

She understood how Joe felt. Her thoughts went to the killer in their midst. Thankfully, he hadn't attacked any of the women on the train. While she hoped he would do something that would allow Flynn to identify and capture him, Cora prayed he wouldn't reveal his true colors by harming any of the women on the wagon train. She almost smiled at her line of thoughts. Reading mystery novels caused one to suspect everyone. There was no proof that Flynn's killer was even on the wagon train.

An hour later, the rifles went off, alerting the wagon train it was time to rise and get ready for another day of traveling. Cora knew Flynn would be back and in need of coffee and hot food to get him going. She didn't know how the men could stay up half the night and go again the next day.

Joe excused himself. He took the water bucket down

from the side of the wagon. "I'll fetch the water this morning, Cora."

She could tell he thought the Indians might still be lurking about. She decided not to argue. "Thank you, Joe."

As soon as he stepped over the tongue of the wagon and headed across the meadow, she pulled a packet of the fresh meat from the furs. The meat was steak-cut and Cora knew just how she would prepare it. She crept into the wagon so as not to wake Noah and took the spices from the crate. There was garlic and black pepper and even onion powder. She all but rubbed her hands together.

Most every morning, they could smell the savory meats from around the camp from other families' hunting successes, but all she and Flynn ever had was leftovers from the night before, usually corn or tater cakes. Flynn seemed so intent on spending as much time as possible with the other men on the wagon train, fixing wagons, doing guard duty and scouting with the scoutmaster, that he hadn't done any hunting. She'd almost asked him to do so a time or two but then realized it was more important for him to search among the camp for a killer than to hunt. After all, they weren't starving. But this morning, there would be steaks to go along with their tater cakes. She prepared the meat with seasoning and placed them in the pan over the grate. She added a cup of water since the meat was dried, then put the lid on top and added a bit more kindling to get the fire hotter.

After a few minutes, Joe returned with the water. "Are those buffalo steaks I smell?" He licked his lips in anticipation while placing the water on the side-board of the wagon.

Cora grinned. "I believe so. I'm sure Flynn will know for sure." She wrapped the remaining steaks up and handed them to Joe. "Would you take these to your ma?"

Disappointment showed on his face as he took the uncooked steaks. "Yes, ma'am."

He started to walk away.

Cora didn't even try to hide her grin when she called after him. "Oh, and, Joe, hurry back or your steak will get cold."

He beamed happily and took off at a run to his mother's wagon.

"Where is Joe headed off to so fast?" Flynn asked.

He came from the opposite direction than Cora had been expecting him. She jumped and turned to face him. "Why do you always do that?" So much for being aware of her surroundings.

Startled by her tone, Flynn looked about and then asked, "Do what?"

"Sneak up behind me like that." She smiled to take the sting out of her words, then answered his earlier question. "He's taking buffalo steaks to his parents' wagon."

"Buffalo steaks? Where did you get them?"

Cora pointed to the buffalo robe sack. "We had visitors this morning."

Flynn walked to the robes and opened the top. He whistled low. "Levi will be glad to have some of this. I hope you saved him a steak."

She smiled. "Do you know if he's in camp?"

"He is. Would you mind throwing a steak on the

fire for him?" He walked up and placed an arm around her shoulders.

Cora couldn't resist leaning into him. "I already did."

"You're a good woman." He kissed her temple and then released her, as if embarrassed by his actions. "I'll go invite him to breakfast."

Before Cora could comment, Flynn had fled their campsite. She touched her temple where his lips had pressed moments earlier. Cora smiled. Maybe he was starting to feel for her what she felt for him. Maybe losing Noah, even for a few hours, had made them both realize just how much they needed to remain a family.

Flynn couldn't believe that he'd just kissed Cora for the second time. What was wrong with him? He had promised the marriage would be one of convenience only, and here he was, acting like a schoolboy with his sweetheart, stealing kisses whenever he could.

Levi rode his horse at the front of the wagon train. Flynn waved to him and the other man galloped to him at a fast pace. "Everything all right at your camp?" Levi asked, coming to a halt beside him.

"Sure is. Seems the missus had a visitor early this morning who dropped off fresh buffalo steaks. Feel like having breakfast with the Adamses this morning?"

Levi's gaze searched the area. "Did your wife say how many visitors we had?"

The concern in his voice had Flynn on immediate alert. "No, but truth be told, I didn't ask for details, either."

Levi's eyebrows pinched together. "That's not like you." When Flynn didn't respond, he continued, "I'll report our visitors to the wagon master." Levi turned his horse to leave but then turned him back around. "Weren't you on guard duty last night?"

"Yep."

"And you don't know how many got past us?"

Flynn shook his head, feeling lower than a snake. "I'll get more details."

"If that invitation to breakfast still stands, I'd like to come. I'd like to hear what your wife has to say about the Indians. How many she saw and such."

Why hadn't he thought to ask her those questions? Flynn nodded. "We'll be glad to have you."

The scout spun his horse and trotted off, leaving Flynn feeling incompetent. Why hadn't he or one of the other men spotted the Indians in their camp? How many were there? Had Cora been in any danger? And why had he assumed it was a friendly visit? Just because they came bearing gifts didn't mean they weren't scouting out the camp as the preamble to some attack.

Flynn walked back to the wagon where Joe and Cora waited. He stopped at a distance and watched his camp. Noah had woken up while Flynn was gone and now sat on his mama's lap eating cornmeal mush and smacking his lips. Flynn noticed Joe still had his rifle lying across his lap, and even though he smiled and laughed with Cora and the baby, his eyes continued to search the woods behind her. Joe, a teenage boy, had more sense than Flynn did.

Shaking his head, Flynn walked the remainder of the way into camp. "Levi says he'll be happy to eat with us. He's got some questions about our visitors."

Joe's eyes were serious as he nodded. "I'll tell him everything I know."

Cora nodded, as well, her eyes holding a touch of fear and caution. "Do you want to hear it from us first? Or do you want us to wait for him?" she asked, searching his eyes.

Flynn swallowed. "He'll be here any moment. No need for you to have to rehash it twice."

She nodded and gave the baby another spoonful of mush. "I don't believe they were here to cause any trouble."

Levi entered the camp in time to catch that and replied, "Maybe not, but we still need to know how many you saw and what they said."

Flynn looked to Joe. "Joe, please tell me everything that happened."

Cora handed the baby to Flynn. He watched as she flipped the steaks in the frying pan. Was she angry that he'd asked Joe before asking her?

Joe stood and gave the scout his seat. "I heard a noise and rolled out from under the wagon. I circled around to the front, thinking whoever I heard would expect me to come around the end of the wagon. Then Cora came out the back end. She got a drink. I watched as an Indian man placed the bag beside the wagon. He motioned for a woman to come out of the shadows. Then he just melted back into them. It was like one minute I saw him and the next he was gone."

Levi nodded. "They can do that. Go on."

"Cora saw the woman and the bag. While they were talking, I walked up behind Cora. The man stepped out of the shadows, I guess just so that I would know he was still around. Anyway, after she talked to Cora, they both left. I've been keeping a watch out just in case they come back."

Still ignoring Cora, Levi asked Joe, "It was just the two—a man and a woman? You didn't see anyone else?"

Joe shook his head. "No, and they weren't anything but friendly." He took the plate that Cora handed him and smiled his thanks.

Levi turned his attention to Cora. "Do you have anything to add to Joe's story?"

Cora dished up potato cakes and a steak on two other plates. She handed a plate to Levi and set Flynn's on the crate she'd abandoned. "Joe summed it all up nicely." She took Noah from Flynn. "If you gentlemen will excuse me, I'm going to go get fresh water from the river." Cora shot Joe a look before she took the water bucket from the side of the wagon and joined her friends as they passed by.

Levi turned to Flynn. "Did I offend her?"

Flynn shook his head. "Cora's always busy in the mornings. I'm sure she just wants to get her chores done before we have to leave." His gaze met Joe's. The young man raised an eyebrow but kept his thoughts to himself.

Levi ate his breakfast in silence. Flynn noted that both Levi and Joe continued to watch the outside ring of the wagons. Flynn knew he'd messed up. He should have asked Cora for more details about the Indians who had visited before being prompted by Levi. His gaze moved to where she'd left with her friends.

Levi finally spoke. "We're not going far today. I talked to the rancher who owns this land, Mr. Browning, about camping on his property for a few days. The animals need rest and the ladies are getting tired. Some of them have asked for time to wash clothes and relax with their children." He scooped up the last of his potatoes and chewed thoughtfully. His gaze met Flynn's. "That might give you time to sweeten up your new bride." Levi laughed at his own observation. He placed his plate by the firepit and smiled. "Please thank your wife for the fine meal, Flynn—it was a real treat." He started to walk away and then stopped. "I've decided you aren't to have guard duty for a couple of turns. It's obvious you need to rest."

Flynn nodded. He didn't mind being off guard duty one little bit. He was never one to sleep during the daylight hours, and the eight-hour night shifts turned into sixteen hours nonstop without rest. It took him several days to get over that lack of sleep. Besides, if truth be told, he liked being close to Cora and Noah at night. He loved that responsibility. But he still felt guilt over failing to protect them when the Indians had come. Even though there didn't seem to have been any danger, he still felt as if he'd let Cora down…just as he'd let Miriam down.

Chapter Sixteen

Cora stared across the river at the ranch house. Nestled against the side of the mountain, the long house looked welcoming. Cattle grazed in the pasture while a garden rested on the east side of the building. She sighed. What would it be like to live in such a place?

She shook her head at the thought. Cora had been thinking on what she'd do once they reached Oregon. She couldn't apply to be a schoolteacher because most school boards didn't allow married women or widows with children to be teachers. So she'd been wondering if she could become a live-in nanny or maybe take in mending to support herself and Noah.

Cora sighed. She was tired of trying to find something she was good at besides teaching, so, at the moment, she would simply focus on the present and be thankful that the wagon master had decided to stop for a few days. There was plenty of work for her to do, but since they had a couple of days, Cora decided to take the afternoon and simply rest by the cool water.

Thankfully, Martha had agreed to take care of Noah. Cora smiled at the memory of the young girl promising she wouldn't let the baby out of her sight. Martha said it now every time she took the baby. Losing Noah once was enough to keep the girl fully alert whenever she babysat. This journey was leaving a deep impression on them all, in different ways.

Cora slowly walked to the river's edge. Fall was underway in full force; the leaves had lost their green colors and had turned bright shades of yellows, reds, oranges and browns. The scent of cool air filled her nostrils.

Fall was her favorite time of the year. Seemed like the wind of time changed, the air was clearer, and the leaves falling reminded her of the Scripture about putting off the old and putting on the new.

When the wagon train began to have serious problems, like sick children, dead livestock, death by drowning and fatal snakebites, Sarah had decided it was time for the ladies to form a Bible study and prayer group. She explained that it was up to the women to raise prayers of protection over their wagon train and that Bible learning was good for all of them.

They had studied that verse about old and new one morning this week and Sarah had done a great job explaining. It had created an eagerness in Cora to learn more about the Word. Sarah had mentioned the seasons and what each one brought with the change. And with that thought in mind, Cora prayed that they would make it to Willamette Valley before the first snow.

"Care if I join you?" Flynn pushed away from a nearby tree. His handsome face offered a smile, but uncertainty shone in his beautiful eyes. He came close, looking down at her intently.

Cora hadn't seen Flynn since breakfast, when he and

Levi had come into camp demanding answers about the Indians who had given them gifts. They had asked Joe, a boy, for answers instead of her. It hurt that Flynn thought more of what Joe had to say over her own words. She moved away, her jaw tightening with each step as she continued toward the water.

He hurried and kept up with her. "You're angry."

Should she deny it? Let him think all was well? Or tell him the truth? Cora stopped and inhaled a deep breath. She knew it would sound childish to explain she was offended and angry because he had not asked her first about what had happened this morning. Her reaction reeked of immaturity, since she had evidence in the past of several times when he *had* considered her advice or feelings. She knew he wasn't dismissive of her—he'd proved it time and time again. So why did this one occasion hurt down deep within her heart?

"I thought so." Flynn walked beside her. "Look, I know I should have asked you what happened instead of Joe, but that's not the way men think—not when it comes to questions of safety. And Joe, well, Joe is proving that he's growing into a fine man, and Levi and I both wanted to show him our respect for him by treating him as such. He protected you and Noah this morning."

Cora held her tongue. She wanted to say Joe was still a boy, but truth be told, she hadn't thought about how Joe would have felt if they had asked her first instead of him. Would he have felt they thought of him as a kid, even though he'd proved he was a man today?

It still bugged her, even as understanding came. She just felt she was the adult and she had protected Noah. Not Joe. But since neither of them had needed protecting, her or the baby, neither she nor Joe had truly protected anyone. So her feelings of hurt were ridiculous, weren't they? Her emotions were a jumble, and even though they made perfect sense to her, she knew Flynn would never understand. "I see" was all that she could force from her lips.

Flynn knelt and picked up a handful of pebbles. He walked a little away from her and began skipping the stones across the water. His gaze moved to her several times and then he'd look quickly away.

Cora realized he could be doing anything right now but instead he was at the river with his surly wife. Why? Did he really care this much about her feelings that he'd stay with her, even though he thought she was angry? She was a novice at this thing called love. She'd never even had a boyfriend, having allowed her studies and then her teaching career dictate that fact, but now she had a husband and had no idea what to do with him.

She sat down at the water's edge and watched two wild ducks fly down and land in the center of the river. The squawking shattered the quiet, but their beauty was well worth it.

"Have I ever told you my pa has a ranch like this one?" Flynn sat down on the bank beside her.

"No. I don't know much about your family," she admitted. The male duck followed the female around the water. They quacked as if talking to one another.

"Pa owns one of the biggest ranches in Texas. He always planned that I'd inherit and work it for him when he got too old to do it himself." His gaze moved to the cattle in the field closer to the ranch house.

"You had other plans?"

"I only ever wanted to be a lawman. When I was eighteen, our town sheriff made me a deputy. Chasing bad guys, making sure shops were closed for the night and generally helping others made me happy. Chasing my father's cattle all over the ranch did not." He sighed as if remembering the hard work he'd had to do on the ranch.

"What did your pa say when you told him you wanted to be a sheriff?" Cora picked at the rocks around her. She chose a white one and a red and a black one while she waited for his answer. She wondered if she could make a necklace out of the stones as a memento of the trip.

Flynn sighed. "He wasn't pleased. But he knew I'd never be happy working his ranch, so he told me to go get it out of my system, hoping that maybe someday I'd come back." Flynn chuckled.

Cora grinned. "So you're kind of like the prodigal son." She wondered if Flynn would ever give up being a lawman. The set of his jaw led her to believe he probably wouldn't.

Flynn turned his head sideways and looked at her. "Something like that, only I've gone back to the farm—just never gone back to ranching."

She rotated the rocks in her hand. "What was it that you didn't like about ranching?"

He shrugged. "I think my main objection was that I didn't want to work my pa's ranch. I wanted to do something that wasn't handed to me."

Cora took her shoes off. If she was going to sit by the water, she was going to get her toes wet. She dropped the stones in her shoe.

"What about you?" he asked. "Did your parents have different plans for your life than you did?"

She sank her feet into the sandy edge of the water. Cold moisture squished between her toes. Soon it would be too cold to enjoy the fresh mountain waters. "My parents owned a small store in town. Gracie loved working there, but I hated it. The only times I was happy was when I got to work on the ledger or when Ma ordered new books. Pa didn't care for the job of bookkeeping and Ma preferred ordering. Gracie liked waiting on the customers, so Pa had me do the books." She smiled at the memory.

"Do your parents still own that store?"

Cora's smile slipped from her face. "No. They both died from a fever when my sister and I were sixteen. After their funerals, we lived with our grandmother for a few months, until she died also. I asked our teacher if she would train me to be a schoolteacher. She agreed, and she and I lived together in the house the school provided while Gracie went to live with our uncle and aunt in Independence." She leaned forward and let one hand trail in the water. "We lost touch with each other for almost three years. Then one day I received a letter from Gracie saying she was getting married and she asked me to come live in Independence."

"That's how you ended up there?" Flynn pulled his knees up and rested his forearms on them.

"More or less. I didn't go until a teaching position opened up." Cora wiggled her toes in the cold water.

They sat quietly listening to the water gurgle over the rocks. Cora thought about telling Flynn what had happened next. How Gracie had married Hank and then found out he was a mean drunk. What would he think if she told him that Noah wasn't the first baby that Gracie carried but he was the only one she hadn't lost before birth?

Gracie had claimed that accidental falls had caused the first two miscarriages, and Cora had believed her until she'd moved to Independence. Once there, Gracie had confided in Cora that Hank hit her when he was drunk. How she managed to carry Noah and deliver him without Hank killing the baby was a mystery to Cora. Maybe Noah was the gift from God meant to finally convince Gracie she needed to get away from her husband. But sadly, she had waited one day too late and it had cost Gracie her life.

Flynn placed his arm around her shoulders. "I have a present for you."

She looked over at him. "You do?"

He nodded. "I've been hanging on to it, waiting for the right moment to give it to you." His grin was infectious, and Cora found her mouth curling into a smile.

"Is that moment now?" she asked, leaning into his warm side. Cora pulled her feet from the water.

He stood, then tugged her to her feet. "Close your eyes and hold out your hands."

"Flynn Adams, you better not put anything gross in my hands." Cora laughed and then did as he asked. She waited, holding her breath. What could he possibly give her?

"I am sorry for this morning, Cora." He slipped something over her wrist.

Cora wanted to peek so badly but she'd agreed to keep her eyes closed. "Can I open them now?"

He turned her hand over. "Not yet." His strong fingers fiddled with whatever it was he'd placed on her wrist.

It felt like he had fastened something leather on there. Had he made her a bracelet?

"All right. You can look now." Flynn still held her hand in his.

Cora recognized the beautiful bracelet from the fort. "Oh, Flynn, you shouldn't have. This is too expensive."

He smiled broadly. "Not if you like it. If you do, it's worth every penny."

She threw her arms around his neck and hugged him tight. "I love it. Thank you." Cora decided at that moment that she wanted to tell Flynn that Noah was her sister Gracie's baby, and that Hank might be following them to Oregon to take the baby back. Then she wanted to tell him how much she had grown to love him. It was his sweet spirit and kind ways that had proved to her that Flynn was a wonderful husband. He was nothing like her brother-in-law. She took a deep breath, ready to confess everything, but just before she could get the words out, Doc called to Flynn.

"Flynn, Harold needs your help repairing a wheel."

Not wanting the doctor to see her bare feet, Cora quickly released Flynn and grabbed her socks. She quickly pulled the stones out and then put both shoes on her feet.

Flynn knelt down beside her and kissed her on the cheek. "Stay here if you want and relax." His voice was low, intended for her ears only. His gentle smile softened his features and she gloried in the shared moment. He then turned back to the wagon train.

Cora watched him go. She'd missed her opportunity

to tell him about Noah and her fears of Hank catching up with her. Not to mention that she loved him.

Doc laughed. "No need to look so sad. He'll be back in a little while and you can have your romantic time with him."

Frustration at Doc welled up in Cora and she had a hard time not letting it show. She wished he would follow Flynn and leave her alone. Why wasn't he helping Mr. Clarkson fix the wheel, instead of enlisting Flynn's help? Doc had helped a lot of people on the train with sickness, sunburns and scrapes, but Cora realized that not once that she knew of did he help the men with manual labor. When labor-intensive work came up, Doc managed to find somewhere else to be.

She stood as the ducks flew away. Doc watched them fly. "Ducks are interesting birds."

Cora nodded. "I think they are pretty."

"Oh, they are." Doc looked at her. "How are you feeling?"

Surprised by his question, Cora answered, "I feel all right."

"Good. Did you know that your friend Annie Clarkson is with child?" He picked up a stick and waved it about, reminding Cora of someone practicing with a sword.

"Are you sure?" Cora knew Annie had been feeling peaky in the mornings but hadn't thought that she might be pregnant. Showed how much she knew about these things.

He laughed again. "I am a doctor, Mrs. Adams." He played with the stick for a few moments more, then tossed it away. "Of course I'm sure."

Cora was happy for her friend. Annie would make

a good mother. In a way, Cora envied her. She would love to carry a baby in her body. Noah was a year old now. She hadn't made a big deal of his birthday; not because it wasn't important, but because she'd woken up sad the morning of his birthday that Gracie was missing her son's first birthday. She feared she would cry if someone mentioned it, so she hadn't told anyone about the significance of the day. Just the thought of how her sister would have loved celebrating every milestone in Noah's life broke Cora's heart.

"Well, I best be getting back to camp." Cora jumped. Lost in her thoughts, she'd almost forgotten Doc was there. "I promised the Welsh woman I'd come by and check on her little girl. She was coughing yesterday, but I'm hoping the hot water and honey I recommended have soothed her throat." He ran his gaze up and down Cora's body. "You sure you're feeling all right?"

Cora nodded. The way he was looking at her sent a chill down her spine.

He shook his head. "Let me know if you start feeling like Mrs. Clarkson. I would think you'd be with child by now, too." Doc chuckled at the expression of shock on her face. He walked back to camp, leaving Cora outraged at his boldness.

"Hi, Cora."

Cora turned to find Rebecca carrying a basket of clothes to the river with a small washboard sticking out the top.

Had she heard Doc's parting words? "Well, hello there, young lady. I see you're getting a jump start on chores. If I'd known you would be here, I'd have brought Noah's things to wash."

"Ma says we will finish quicker if I wash mine

here and she does hers and Pa's at the wagon. When the washing's put back up, we're going to play back-gammon and eat popcorn. It's our treat for the day's work." Rebecca's features became animated as she shared her excitement with Cora, and it wasn't lost on Cora how easily the girl called Mrs. Cartwright "Ma." It appeared Flynn had chosen wisely with that situation. The Cartwrights had voiced their intentions of adopting Rebecca legally when they arrived in Oregon.

"So you love being with the Cartwrights?"

Rebecca straightened herself with dignity. "They reward me when I do good, or when I work hard, help-ing them with what they're doing or with chores, and when I mess up, they don't get upset. Instead, they en-courage me to try again. Just like my real ma and pa." She pulled her shoes and socks off and stepped into the river. "Jumpin' Jehoshaphat!" she squealed. "This water's cold as ice."

Cora laughed as the girl hopped about, her dress tied in a knot at her knees to keep it from getting wet. "You might want to hurry and get out of there before you catch your death of cold." The water hadn't seemed that cold to her, but Rebecca was making such a fuss that Cora couldn't help laughing.

A question she had wanted to ask nagged at her, but for the life of her she couldn't remember what it was. She turned to leave and then it hit her. She whipped back around with hands on her hips. For a moment, she savored the feel of the leather bracelet on her wrist. "Where did you get popcorn?" Oh, how she loved pop-corn! But not once had she smelled the delightful food in camp.

Rebecca clamped a hand over her mouth, her eyes

wide. She shook her head. She dropped her hand, shoulders sagging. "I wasn't supposed to tell anyone. Tonight, while everyone is at the get-together, Ma, Pa and I planned to come back to our wagon and have popcorn and play games. We only have three ears of the stuff and that's not enough to share with everyone."

"Don't worry. I won't tell, nor will I ask you to share. Did the Cartwrights bring it from Independence?"

"No," Rebecca said. "Ma traded two buckets of apples to the rancher's wife for the popcorn and some lard and sugar. Ma's going to teach me how to make apple dumplin's." She grinned proudly. She'd changed so much during her stay with the Cartwrights.

"That's wonderful, Rebecca. I'm sure you'll be cooking as well as your ma in no time."

Cora watched the girl start her laundry. Rebecca didn't look up from the task, so Cora walked back to her wagon. With luck, Flynn would be finished with Mr. Clarkson and Martha would return Noah. She suddenly had a longing to spend quality time with her own little family. The chat with Rebecca had inspired her. And if she could, she'd get some of that popcorn from the rancher's wife.

Chapter Seventeen

"Annie, would you like to close us in prayer?"

Cora carefully watched Annie's reaction to Sarah's question. If she acted the least bit nervous, Cora would step in and pray herself, even though she still felt uncomfortable praying in front of others. But ever since Annie had joined their prayer group, Annie had eagerly soaked up every bit of information she could on the Bible and the Christian way of life. To Cora's surprise, she readily agreed to pray.

Haltingly at first, she came up with a simple prayer asking God to forgive her and then went on to seek His blessings. It was short, but Cora observed a few covertly wiped tears from several of the ladies and had to clear her own throat of the lump suddenly lodged there.

Annie's fresh outlook on God's forgiveness of her sins reminded the ladies of their own gift of grace. They left the meeting each morning with a sense of encouragement, and the burdens of each day of traveling seemed lightened somehow.

Cora left the meeting and rushed to her wagon. The train wasn't traveling today, due to heavy rains all night. Trying to drive through the muddy roads would only damage the wagons, and they would get nowhere. If she worked fast, she could catch up on washing clothes and cleaning the wagon. Dust was an inch thick on the floor and even in her bedclothes. But it looked like the sun would shine bright today, and if she hurried, her wash would be dry before nightfall. Martha and Sarah had given her several outfits for Noah but not enough to last an entire week. So Cora washed them out in the evenings when they stopped for the night. She'd been hampered by last night's weather, and if she didn't get some baby outfits washed, Noah would have nothing to wear.

She pulled down the tin bucket that hung on the side of the wagon and filled it halfway with water from the water barrel. She'd left water simmering over the grate while she went to the prayer meeting and she carefully added the hot water to the bucket, along with a few pieces of lye soap that she mixed in with her wooden paddle until she had suds.

"You do that as if you've done it all your life." Annie stepped up beside her and watched as Cora added Noah's outfits to the water. Cora left them to soak and added more water to heat for the second washing.

"Well, I have done it a few times before this trip, but never for this many people." She hoped Annie didn't want to chat and that she'd leave Cora alone to get her work done. "While Martha has Noah, I like to get the work that uses hot water out of the way. He toddles around way too much for my peace of mind."

"I'm still not good at the clothes washing. I don't wring them out well enough and it takes forever to dry, but Harold helps me if he's able to."

Cora took her paddle and swished the clothes around. And then one by one she wrung them out tight and dropped them into the bucket of rinse water. So absorbed was she in her task that it took her several seconds to realize Annie had walked off. Had she offended her friend by ignoring her? Oh, well, she would make it up to her later. When she had the last little romper in the rinse water, she added diapers to the wash to soak. She strung her line from the back of the wagon to the edge of Annie's wagon. Should Annie decide to do her own wash, she would attach her line from her wagon to Cora's. As she hung Noah's rompers on the line, she wondered how much longer he would fit into them. He grew like a weed.

When the diapers were done, she fetched a fresh bucket and washed Flynn's two shirts and a pair of his pants. She had never questioned him, but it seemed odd that he had wound up on this wagon train with only the clothes on his back. She knew he had bought the two extra shirts and a pair of pants at the first fort.

Even as she thought of the fort—and the crates she and Sarah had discovered there—she glanced around furtively. Could she possibly make cinnamon apple dumplings for just Flynn, Noah and herself? There had been spices of every kind in one of the crates he had toted back to their wagon. And apple trees were all around them. If Cora had her druthers, she'd stay right here in this area. Along with apple trees, there were hickory nut trees, and if she wasn't mistaken, she'd spotted a few persimmon trees, as well. The rolling hills and green grass went on as far as the eye could see and Levi had found fresh spring water before breakfast this morning. She knew several of the ladies were apple picking, and she would, too, later if there were any left, though laundry had to come first. This opportunity to get even her bedcovers washed was too good to pass up.

She had a husband and a child to care for and she loved it. She'd never have thought how satisfying it was to cook meals for them to enjoy as a family, to see Flynn in clean clothes she'd washed herself and to dress Noah and know that he was well cared for. And though their wagon wasn't that big, she had organized it to meet their basic needs.

She went to Annie's wagon and called out, "Annie, are you not washing clothes today? If not, can I stretch your line?" There was no answer, so Cora pulled the line hung on the sideboard of the Clarksons' wagon and attached it to the back of hers. She hung up the freshly washed blanket she and Noah slept on and Flynn's blanket, along with their two towels and a few washcloths. She straightened and rubbed her back. Cora was no stranger to hard work, but this was a dilly.

"Annie?" she called again. Maybe she could talk Annie into apple picking with her by promising to share the apple dumplings with her. Her husband would probably appreciate the treat. Annie was learning to cook just as Cora had done, and oftentimes it ended in disaster. "Annie, where are you?" Maybe her friend had gone with one of the other ladies.

Cora grabbed her bucket and took off toward the apple tree closest to their wagon. She knew there were bigger and better apples nearer the creek, but for her, these would do fine. A briar scratched her leg and Cora sucked in a deep breath. "Ouch." She reached to push the briar away, and to her surprise, it held blackberries.

She walked a bit farther and there was a small patch of briars loaded with blackberries, her favorite berry. "Oh, merciful goodness. How absolutely wonderful! I can make a blackberry cobbler this evening and still have some left over to make blackberry syrup." Instead of apples, Cora picked berries till her bucket was almost full. She would make two cobblers and share one with Annie.

Cora decided that she'd tell Sarah about the patch when she went to pick up Noah. With the kids' help, Sarah would be able to make cobblers and syrup, too.

Feeling accomplished and quite proud of herself, she hurried back to the wagon to get started. Flynn would eat well today and that thought brought a feeling of happiness to her heart.

Harold Clarkson walked up to where Flynn busily guided his oxen to a greener spot of grass, before taking them back to the wagon for the night. Doc had arrived a few moments before Harold but as of yet had offered no help. "Howdy, Harold. Did you need Doc to help you with something?"

If Doc would go on about his business, Flynn could get a lot more done without stopping to answer Doc's constant barrage of questions. And lately there had been some bizarre ones that made little sense.

"Have either of you seen Annie?" Harold's voice held worry as well as frustration.

Flynn shook his head. "No, can't say that I have—not today."

Doc shook his, as well, muttering under his breath that some women should never become wives. Harold ignored him but Flynn's indignation was stirred that

Doc would openly criticize another man's wife. Where was his common courtesy to a man who was taking him to Oregon without getting anything in return? Doc was supposed to be Harold's relief driver, but so far, Flynn hadn't seen Doc work with the oxen at all.

"Last time I saw her, she said she was going to the river for water, but when I got back from the afternoon watch, she'd not returned. The water bucket is gone, too, so I can only assume she hasn't come back. I thought maybe she stopped by to visit with Cora, but she's not at your wagon, either." Harold looked expectantly at Flynn, as if Flynn might have answers to share.

"Well, Cora is at the Philmores'. Maybe Annie's with her."

"I'll go check." Harold walked off in the direction of the Philmores' wagon.

Flynn started back to work and noticed that Doc still watched Harold.

"Something on your mind, Doc? Everything working out with you traveling with the Clarksons?"

"Did you know Annie is a soiled dove?" Doc's scowl increased as he said the words.

"That so?" He hadn't known, but he couldn't say that he much cared. Over the last couple of months, Annie and Cora had become friends. Flynn had seen Annie go from lazy and helpless on the trail to a woman who worked hard and made a traveling home for her husband. Her past mattered a lot less to him than the fact that she was trying hard to build a good future.

Doc stood. "Well, I think I'll head to bed. I'm sure Harold will find her soon."

Flynn frowned. Doc had changed since he'd known

him in Texas. Gone was the man who cared for his patients. He now seemed to not care about anything—including his looks, his behavior or how others might see him. Plus, he seemed unusually interested in the women on the train and judgmental about their pasts to the point of downright rudeness. The old Doc he remembered would have been concerned for Annie and would have offered to help find her.

"Good night, Doc." Flynn waited for a moment, carefully analyzing that gut feeling he got at times when he was around Doc—the feeling that there was something…off. Something wrong. He didn't want to feel that way. Doc was his friend. Maybe he needed encouragement.

Flynn's conscience pricking him, he tied up the oxen and followed Doc to camp, pondering ways to soothe the older man's feelings so he wouldn't be so grumpy. Maybe he could invite Doc back to their camp and Cora could offer him some of the blackberry cobbler she'd had left over from supper.

It had been the best thing he'd eaten in a long time. He happened to glance up and saw Doc heading away from the wagon train. Doc skulked about as if on a secret mission. Flynn's instincts told him something wasn't right.

He followed at a distance and stayed within the shadows of the wagons.

Come to think of it, Doc had acted strange all day. He seemed to be edgy and even more quick-tempered than usual. The doctor stopped and looked back over his shoulder. Flynn pressed his body into the shadows.

His thoughts went to all the conversations he and the doctor had shared while on the trail. Doc had actually mentioned his own visits to the towns where two of the women had been killed. The coincidence hadn't struck Flynn before, but it was hitting him hard right now. He felt a suddenly sinking certainty that Doc was the murderer he'd been trailing for over two years. This doctor who had befriended him was the same man who had killed his fiancée. What he didn't know was why. And why kill the other ladies, too? Had he just enjoyed the act of killing so much that he'd continued to do so?

Leaving the safety of the wagons, Doc ventured off toward the woods. Flynn melted into the darkness as he continued to follow the doctor. The moon lit their paths as they wove through the trees, moving farther from the wagon train.

Flynn watched Doc closely but suddenly he seemed to disappear. Using caution, Flynn continued forward, looking for the older man. Then he saw it, a small cave in the side of the hill.

Darkness enveloped him as he quietly entered the small opening. He detected a light ahead of him and moved toward it.

Doc must have left a torch at the opening of the cave to use later. Flynn's heart sank as he realized Doc had been here earlier and had explored the cavern, prepared it. But for what? What was he hiding in the cave?

He stopped when he heard Doc talking to someone. "I'm back. Harold has finally decided to start looking for you."

Flynn slipped deeper into the shadows and inched toward the light and Doc's voice. A woman's whimper reached his ears and Flynn's pulse kicked up. The sound of ripping reached his ears.

"Doc, why are you doing this to me?"

"Because you are no better than her."

Flynn moved forward until he could see Doc and Annie on the cave floor. Tape and a rag lay beside her. He could only guess that Doc had gagged her and used a bandanna to hold the rag over her mouth. Thankfully, Doc had his back to Flynn.

Annie cried, "No better than who? I don't know who you are talking about." She sat on the ground with her feet and hands tied. Her hair had fallen down about her shoulders in red, curly waves.

"You know who." Doc walked around her like a buzzard circling a dead animal. "You are all just alike."

Her head swiveled about as she tried to follow his every move. Her voice pleaded with him, "Doc, I don't know who you think I am like. I don't even know how we are alike."

"Yes, you do! You sell your bodies and don't care who you hurt in the process." Doc stopped in front of her and pulled a knife from his boot.

Annie pushed backward on her bottom. She shook her head. "I don't do that anymore."

"You will. When the going gets tough, you'll go right back to the nearest saloon. You all do. It's in your blood." He stared off into the distance, as if seeing something in his past.

She shook her head. "No. I love Harold and he loves me. I'll never go back."

Doc forced a harsh laugh. "Yes, you will. God only knows why, but you will."

Her voice took on a more confident sound. "I gave my life to Jesus. Cora says I'm a new person. I left that old life behind and I'm saved from it."

Flynn inched closer to them. He prayed she could

stall long enough for him to be able to jump Doc and keep him from killing her like he'd killed Miriam.

"Do you really believe that?" Doc squatted in front of her.

She nodded. "I do."

He stood. "Then you are a fool. If you're saved, why hasn't Jesus rescued you from this?" Doc indicated the cave and himself. "You know, I planned to take my time with you, but soon Harold will have the whole wagon train out looking for you, like they did Cora's brat. And they'll find you. I can't have that. I have to keep you from hurting others."

"What others? I'm not going to hurt anyone." Tears filled her voice. "Please, Doctor. You know Harold and I are going to have a baby."

His voice went still. "Of course I know. I'm the one who told you. He and I have talked about the baby. The poor man thinks motherhood will settle you, but I know that's not true."

Flynn had been wondering how Doc had known about Annie's past. Now he knew that Harold had confided in the man whom he considered to be the family physician, never realizing that in doing so, he'd put his wife and unborn child in danger.

He was close enough now he could run at Doc and knock him to the ground. He braced himself but stopped short when Annie asked Doc in a soft voice, "Who hurt you, Doc?"

Doc's wild eyes searched her face. "You really want to know?"

She nodded.

He laughed and shrugged his shoulders. "I guess it won't hurt to tell you. After all, you aren't going to tell anyone." Doc frowned. "My ma. She promised Pa she'd never leave us and go back there, but she did."

Annie tugged at the ropes on her hands. "I'm not your ma."

It was as if Doc hadn't heard her as he continued, "Do you know what that does to a man? Not only was he heartbroken and shamed, but he became bitter. He went from a loving father to a man who beat the devil out of his only son. Pa said I'd never be good enough as long as I loved her. I'd be sinful just like her."

"Doc. Your pa was wrong. Her going back had nothing to do with you and didn't make you evil." Annie scooted farther from him. She was obviously searching for a way to get past him and out of the cave.

Doc walked away from her. His back was to Flynn and Annie now. His voice sounded far away as he muttered, "No, Pa was the wisest man I knew. He told me to become a doctor and clean the world of the evil women in it."

Flynn frowned, trying to understand what this all meant. Miriam wasn't a "soiled dove," so why had Doc killed her?

Doc toyed with the knife but seemed to be lost in his past. Flynn waited to see if Doc would confess to killing the other women. If he did, Flynn would be able to arrest him for murder and see that Miriam's killer would never hurt anyone again.

Annie continued to push herself farther away from her captor.

While Doc was distracted, Flynn stepped from the shadows, revealing himself to Annie. He held his finger over his lips and cut the ropes from her feet and hands. Then he motioned for her to leave the cave.

Annie sank into the darkness of the tunnel and disappeared.

Flynn stepped out of the shadows and blocked the exit.

Doc turned slowly. "How long have you been here, Flynn?"

"Long enough to send Annie back to the wagon train."

The doctor sighed. "You shouldn't have done that." He flipped the knife so that the blade was facing down.

Flynn placed his hand on his gun. "Tell me, Doc, why did you kill Miriam?"

Doc looked down and shook his head. "She was a lady of the night, Flynn."

"No, she wasn't." Miriam was a sweet girl. The moment she entered his town, Flynn had been smitten. She'd opened her small dress shop, and everyone had loved her. Miriam attended church every Sunday and never even entered the red-light district. How could the doctor think ill of her?

"Oh, but she was. I had a patient in Grapevine, and I saw her enter the town. She went to the saloon and worked all night. It was then that I saw her true colors." He shook his head. "The night she died, I told her I'd seen her." Doc laughed harshly. "Can you believe she told me she was a new woman?"

Flynn didn't believe him, didn't want to believe him.

Still, Doc pressed on. "They all say that, you know?"

"How many women have you killed, Doc?" Flynn pulled his gun from his holster.

Doc shrugged. "I've lost count." His gray eyes searched Flynn's. "They all needed to die. I killed Miriam for you, Flynn. She would have hurt you and any children you might have had with her. So I did you a favor."

Flynn shook his head. "No, Doc. You killed her and the other women for yourself. Your mother hurt you and your father hurt you. You wanted to hurt others to stop your own hurting."

Doc laughed bitterly. "Did you know that the first one I killed was my mother? She tried to tell me that it was Pa's fault that she had to go back to that life. I couldn't let her go around telling such lies."

Flynn didn't know what to say. He'd always thought that when he found Miriam's killer, he'd feel better, but all he felt was sadness for this twisted, broken man. "You know I have to take you in, Doc."

Doc turned sad eyes on Flynn. "I won't hang for murder, Flynn."

"That's not up to me to decide, Doc. A judge will determine your fate." Flynn motioned at the knife in Doc's hand. "Drop the knife, Doc, and let's get out of here."

Doc sighed. He bent over at the waist.

Flynn assumed he was going to lay the knife on the ground. Shock shook him when Doc thrust it into his own chest. He fell backward with a grunt.

Flynn hurried to his side and helped him lie flat. "Doc, you didn't have to do this."

Doc's voice quivered. "I'm old, Flynn. I'd never make it in prison, and this is much better than the hangman's noose."

"Doc, please—ask the Lord to forgive you before you die." Flynn couldn't believe he was reminding the man who had killed so many that God would forgive

him for his sins. But it felt like the right thing to do.
Like what Miriam would want.

The older man gasped. "He won't forgive me. I've
done too much."

Flynn shook his head. "Doc, one sin is no greater
than any other. He will forgive you. Ask before it's too
late." He felt frantic. Flynn didn't want Doc to die in
sin. He wouldn't wish hell on any man.

Doc closed his eyes. His lips moved but no words
came out. He took his last breath. His hand fell to his
side.

Flynn sat back on his heels. Had Doc been asking
God to forgive him? Flynn prayed he had. He picked
up the torch and started out of the cave. His two-year
hunt was now over, and it left him feeling more hol-
low than he'd expected. But still, there was some clo-
sure in getting answers at last. He decided not to let
Doc's reveal of Miriam's past distort his memories of
the sweet woman that she had been to him. Instead,
now that he'd found her killer, he felt ready to finally
say goodbye.

Chapter Eighteen

Cora loaded the last of the items into the wagon. The wagon train had not been allowed in the rancher's pastures, nor near the house, but the road to pass through had several surprises along the way. For one, there was a shed filled with items former wagon trains had left behind. She was able to salvage a few chairs, some blankets, dishes, and boots for herself and Noah. A few utensils and a cast-iron frying pan.

Within an hour after leaving the ranch, they began to climb the mountain, and the air became chilly. Cora walked a few miles beside Flynn as Joe drove, then rode beside him as Joe walked. Even though she loved watching the scenery, it wasn't long before she knew she'd have to get in the wagon and close the flaps. If she kept Noah out in the cold air, he would get sick for sure.

The higher they went, the rougher the road became, and Cora had to lay the chairs on their sides and wrap the dishes and other breakable things in the furs the Indian couple had left.

When they pulled over for lunch, Flynn stuck his head through the flap. "Got room back here for one more?" At Cora's nod, he joined them, to Noah's delight.

The baby immediately crawled on Flynn's lap, demanding, "Up."

Flynn picked him up and twirled him around within the tight circle a few times, filling the air with Noah's giggles and Flynn's deep laughter. Finally satisfied, Noah commanded, "Down," and crawled a few feet away to play.

"It's getting colder the higher up we climb." He rubbed his hands together rapidly. "I hope it doesn't get any worse." His expression changed and became almost somber. "Will you and Noah be all right? About the only thing you can do till we get across is huddle under blankets."

Cora nodded as she made them a cold lunch in the wagon. She pulled out the leftover biscuits from breakfast and stuffed them with leftover ham. "How long will it take us to get across?"

Flynn took the offered biscuit sandwich. "The wagon master said barring no accidents or delays, it'll be around five days. That is if the weather holds up." Flynn pulled one of the furs over his lap. "Lord willing, this is the last leg of the journey."

She watched him take a big bite from the biscuit. "Then Noah and I will be just fine. But with this chill in the air, I'll keep him inside. I'd rather not have a sick baby when we arrive."

"I think that's wise." Flynn finished off the sandwich and then reached for her hand, then chuckled. "I figured I'd warm your hands between mine, but yours are warm and toasty." He went to pull away. Cora held on to him. She placed her other hand on top of his.

"Then I'll warm yours." The movement caused her to bump shoulders with him and he leaned in and kissed the tip of her nose.

"You're sweet." A smile ruffled the corners of his mouth, but his eyes clung to hers, analyzing her reaction. Shyness swept over her, and instead of answering, she laid her head against his shoulder. They sat like that, together, sharing each other's warmth until the signal was given to travel once more.

Flynn jumped out of the wagon and returned a few minutes later with a dipper full of water. "I thought you might like a drink before we head out."

Cora found one of her glass jars, took a sip from the dipper and then poured the remainder of the water inside. "Thank you. That will hold us until we stop again."

He nodded and reclosed the flap.

Once they started going again, Noah climbed into her lap. He yawned and curled against her body, much like he had when she'd first started using the sling.

Cora picked up her novel and leaned against the wagon wall to read but found that she couldn't focus on the words. Her mind wouldn't shut down and concentrate long enough. After putting the book aside, she spent the next hour dreaming of her new life in Oregon.

Sometime later, Flynn called to her to come open the flap and look out.

She unzipped the flap enough that she could look through. They both laughed as a little body wriggled around in front of Cora and pulled the flap open even more. Flynn sat on the bench and pointed forward. Cora gasped at what she saw. Across the gorge was a huge waterfall that cascaded as far as the eye could see. It was absolutely breathtaking. Noah's excited "Ohhhhhh. Wa…wa" had Cora reaching to pick him up, wanting to share this new sight with him.

In a voice filled with awe, Flynn said, "Look, Noah, at what God made." He pointed just as Noah pointed.

Cora's smile broadened in approval and a sweeping pull at her heart made her almost dizzy. She reached out to touch Flynn's arm and kissed the side of Noah's face. "Isn't it beautiful, Noah?"

"Boo'ful." The boy clapped his hands together in delight.

The closer they came to it, the louder the sound of water crashing down became, echoing in their ears. "Have you ever seen a waterfall before, Flynn?" Cora asked wonderingly.

"Not one on this level. We used to dam up water in the creek just to watch it flow over, but I've never seen anything like this." There was wonder in his voice that reflected in his expression. He spread his hand to take in the entire scene. The last of the yellow and gold leaves on the tall trees fell, giving notice that winter was just around the corner. A squirrel stared at them from one of the higher limbs and then swiftly disappeared behind the tree.

Having always lived in the flatlands, Cora hadn't seen such wild, untamed beauty. There was little sky to be seen, as the trees blocked it out. She felt closed in, a bit claustrophobic, but entranced by such a breathtaking creation. How could anyone not believe in a supreme God when they beheld such beauty?

Noah puckered his little mouth as the waterfall disappeared from sight, but before he could pout or cry, he was distracted by Martha and her younger siblings running beside the wagon.

"Mrs. Cora, Mrs. Cora, look!" They each held something in their hand.

Flynn slowed their wagon to almost a complete stop. He pulled Noah through the flap and then allowed Cora to climb from the back of the wagon. She turned to see what they had. Their hands were full of little pink things that looked like thumb-sized vases.

"What are those?" She took one from Martha and felt it. It was smooth.

"Ma says these flowers are called piggies." Martha held one up to Cora's nose and Cora drew back. Martha laughed infectiously. "They smell good. You put them in a jar without the lid and they make your whole house smell good."

Cora sniffed at the one she had in her hand, and sure enough, it had a light tulip smell.

"Here, you can have these, and we will gather more for Ma." Martha and the rest of the kids dumped them into her hands before Cora could protest.

Cora climbed back in the wagon. Already her hands and face felt frozen. The wagon had been reasonably warm but now held a very cold chill. She put the flowers in an empty tea tin and put the lid on it. She wasn't sure if they were poisonous and didn't want to take the chance with Noah. The baby now put everything he could get his hands on into his little mouth.

She then laced the flap back up and went to retrieve Noah. Before she could say anything, Flynn said, "Here, you best take Noah. It's too cold for him outside."

"My thoughts exactly. Thank you for letting me collect the flowers from the girls." He seemed so pleased with himself, especially after Cora's praise. The closeness they'd experienced lately filled a spot in Cora's heart that had felt empty since her parents passed away. And the way he showed her attention in front of others caused her to think her feelings were returned.

Flynn had grown more important than anyone else in her life other than Noah. She wanted to please him, be around him, share her thoughts and dreams with him. When he was out of sight, she knew the moment he returned even before she actually saw him. The awareness was so strong, it made her heart sing with delight. The little touches of his hand on her arm, the kisses to the top of her head as he looked down on her, all these things were new and exciting, and she thought on them and kept them close in her heart. She loved him, and that knowledge gave her relentless enjoyment.

Flynn drove until they stopped for the evening. Dusk had settled as they unhooked the oxen and led them to water. Even though he was bone tired, his steps were light as he headed back to camp. His thoughts had bounced along with the ruts the wagon hit: happy thoughts and plans and questions. He loved the response from Cora when he showed her attention and he knew he'd never felt this way toward any other woman.

Because of the narrowness of the trail, they couldn't park the wagons in a circle and instead left them in a straight line. Some were perched on the side of the mountain coming up one side and going down the other. Flynn had stopped almost in the flat section. His eyes widened when he made it to camp.

"Is that sourdough bread I smell?" He leaned around

Cora to look in the pan. "And cooked apples?" He rubbed his belly. "Ohhhh, we're eating good tonight. To what do we owe this pleasure?"

"Since it's too cold to walk, I worked in the wagon and used my starter to let the bread swell. I also peeled the apples earlier and they've been marinating in sugar and cinnamon. We only have a little meat left and I'm trying to make it last, so I added water to the pot and threw in a few potatoes and a carrot. We're running out of most all food supplies." She sucked in her bottom lip, capturing it between her teeth.

"We're now only four days away. We'll have enough."

"You think our wagon will hold up?"

"You saw me checking the wheels, didn't you?" At her nod, he rushed to assure her, "I did that because we were starting over the mountain. Had there been a safety issue or a need for new spokes, I'd have taken care of it then, but the spokes only needed oiling. We're in good shape."

Flynn took the plate she dished up and they ate in silence. He sopped the last of the stew gravy with his bread and sat back full, his hunger satisfied. "That was one fine meal. I'm thankful that you learned to cook outside over a grate."

"Thank you. But give me a little credit—I learned fast. You didn't have to eat too many burned meals."

He chuckled. "That's true. Thanks to Sarah."

He watched her out of the corner of his eye and drew his legs up, laughing when her mouth fell open and she threw the dishcloth at him. Flynn loved how playful Cora had become. She no longer looked over her shoulder, and the fear and panic had vacated her beautiful eyes. He knew she cared about him. What was she going to say when he confessed he cared for her, too, and wanted to remain her husband for the rest of his life?

Much as she loved the beautiful mountains, she'd never been so happy to hear they were nearing the bottom and entering the Willamette Valley. The call came back through the wagons and activity increased. People began to walk beside their wagons, a few even running ahead.

When Flynn helped her from the wagon and set Noah on his shoulders, she couldn't stop the tears from flowing. Finally, they had arrived. But Cora wasn't quite prepared for what she saw.

Flynn had long since set Noah on the seat beside Joe and he, and Cora continued walking. Suddenly, they weren't tired, and their walk seemed jubilant. They traveled six or more miles till the wagons began splitting off and going different routes. In those six miles, they passed seven or eight farms. The land was still green and lush, and the houses they passed now were made of planks instead of logs. Most were two stories. There were glass windows and wraparound porches. They crossed a river about two miles in and it had a wooden bridge. A farm near there had a huge gristmill built in the river.

Flynn raised his eyebrows at her with a huge grin across his face. One farmer's field lay full of pumpkins and gourds. The air had warmed up considerably once they were off the mountain. Flynn removed his coat, then took her hand. Ahead of them, the Clarksons' wagon pulled to the side and stopped. Joe followed behind with their wagon. When Cora realized what was happening, a lump lodged in her throat and she bit her lip to keep from crying.

"Well, my dear friend, this is where we part ways." Sarah's voice was suspiciously thick, and she wrapped Cora in a tight hug. "You take good care of yourself and baby Noah, and take good care of your man, you hear?"

Martha had pulled Noah off the seat and swung him round and round before squeezing him tight and planting kisses all over his face. Then Annie and Harold Clarkson joined the fray, hugging, crying and kissing everyone. Cora couldn't hold back the tears anymore and cried openly. Noah, seeing her distress, screamed and could not be consoled till everyone started laughing. When her two best friends went in separate directions, reality set in and Cora climbed onto the seat beside Flynn, with a huge weight on her shoulders.

This was where their arrangement was supposed to end. If he decided to annul the marriage, how would she and Noah make it? And what would she do with this heart full of love for Flynn? She had exactly eleven dollars to her name and didn't know a soul where they were headed. Flynn had to check in with a sheriff and file a report about Doc, and other than that, he knew no one or nothing about the place, either.

As they came into the town, Cora felt a bit of hope blossom. There were streets with clean sidewalks and buildings. The main street was redbrick and the general store large, with signs advertising items of all kinds. There was a barbershop, round red-and-white columns announcing it as such. The town looked bustling and prosperous. Maybe there was a chance she could find some life for herself here. She looked down at Noah and his eyes were bright as his little hand waved at each building they passed.

Flynn pulled the wagon in front of a boardinghouse. While he went in to secure them a room, Cora prayed like she'd never prayed before. "Lord, please let Flynn love me as I love him. Help us make a home here. Father, I will do my best to honor You with our lives and will raise our children to love and obey You."

The smile on Flynn's face as he came out to them and his words, "I have us a room," filled her with powerful relief. He wasn't leaving them, or at least not yet. "Thank You, Jesus," she whispered under her breath.

Chapter Nineteen

Cora laid Noah down on the bed. A real bed. Not a pile of quilts but a bed with a mattress. She made sure he slept soundly and then walked to the window and looked with delight down below at the busy street. She and Noah had bathed in a tub and he had been gleeful, splashing and jabbering. Once they were clean, she had sat beside the fireplace until her hair had dried. To say she felt like a new woman would be putting it lightly. But it had been almost two hours now since Flynn left them, stating he would give them time to clean up and rest a bit. Where had he gone? What was he doing that would take so long?

He'd made sure she and the baby had everything they needed to be comfortable; he'd even checked the room for cleanliness and for any sign of insects that might have come in seeking warmth. Then he'd said he would be back shortly. She assumed he'd gone to take care of the oxen and the wagon. But that didn't take two hours.

Already she missed Sarah, Annie, Rebecca and all the other friends she'd made on the Oregon Trail. Especially Martha. She would have kept Martha if she could have. But they'd all parted ways with hugs and tears. Rebecca had clung to her long and hard, thanking her and Flynn for finding folks who cared about her again.

Cora had no idea what the future held for her and baby Noah. Hank hadn't caught up with them, so she assumed they were free of Noah's father. She wished with all her heart that she could tell Flynn that she loved him and that she didn't want to end their marriage of convenience, but he'd not expressed those kinds of feelings toward her or given any indication that her feelings would be welcomed. Flynn Adams was married to his job. Now that they were in Willamette, they would part ways soon. Tears filled her eyes and she turned from the window.

She moved to the bed and lay down by Noah. The softness of the mattress soothed her tired body, but she found herself unable to nod off. Cora had too many decisions to make to fall asleep. She found herself regretting that she'd not told anyone that her marriage to Flynn wasn't real, even after Doc died and the secretive reason for Flynn's presence on the wagon train was revealed.

If she had told her friend the truth, would Sarah have offered to take her with them? Probably. But going with Sarah and her family wasn't what Cora wanted to do. She wanted to stay with Flynn. She loved him, and if he would agree, she'd stay married to him until the day she died.

Right then, Cora made the decision to tell him everything: that she wasn't Noah's mother and that Hank had murdered her sister. She'd wanted to tell him so many times on the trail but never seemed to find the right time. Now was the time.

Someone pounded on the door. Cora looked to see if the noise had woken Noah. He continued to sleep soundly. She pushed herself off the bed and straightened her dress before pulling the door open.

Cora gasped. A bitter, cold despair stirred in her soul. Standing in the doorway was none other than Hank, and with him he had the sheriff. It was as if her thoughts had conjured him up. She looked at the sheriff's badge to make sure he was a real sheriff. Then her gaze moved to Hank, who grinned behind the lawman's back. He seemed to enjoy her struggle to capture her composure.

"Miss Cora Edwards?" The sheriff nodded at her. He held his hat in his hands and his eyes showed signs of weariness.

Cora stood to her full height. "I'm Mrs. Flynn Adams."

"It's her all right, Sheriff." Hank stepped around the sheriff, moving closer to her, and Cora took two steps back.

Hank pointed at the bed. "And that's my son. She killed my wife so she could have our son."

"What? No!" Cora's hand covered her mouth. She blocked Hank from advancing farther into the room and toward Noah. She lowered her hand. "Sheriff, I didn't kill her. Hank beat her until he passed out from drinking. Then she came to me and told me about her plan to leave on the wagon train. She'd already made the arrangements. Gracie asked me to raise Noah right before she died. He's trying to get away with murder. I would have told the sheriff in Independence, but I was afraid, and Gracie begged me to leave with Noah so he

couldn't hurt her little boy. Grace told me she didn't report Hank beating her because the sheriff there always
sided with the husbands." Cora knew she was rambling
but couldn't stop herself. She had to save Noah from
his father and herself from the hangman's noose.

Hank shook his head. "That's not true. You killed
her and took our son. You were always jealous of your
sister." He stepped sideways to go around her, but Cora
blocked him once more.

"Please, Sheriff. This man is a liar, a drunk and a
murderer."

The lawman looked from one of them to the other.
"Is there anyone that can vouch for you, Mrs. Adams?"

"Are you asking if anyone else saw Gracie die or
heard her ask me to take Noah as far away from Hank
as I could go?" She heard her voice quiver. Felt the tears
burn the backs of her eyes and knew she was doomed
if the sheriff believed Hank's lies.

Before the sheriff could answer, Flynn walked into
the room. "What's going on here?"

He walked over to Cora and stood beside her.

Cora felt the anger radiating from Flynn. His eyes
blazed, and his nostrils flared with each breath he took.
But who was the focus of his anger? She couldn't tell.
Was he angry with her, for lying to him? Did he know
what had happened, or was he about to find out now?

She wished with all her heart that she had told him
about Hank and explained that Noah wasn't really her
son but her sister's. She looked to her husband for understanding, but he stared at Hank as if daring him to
take another step toward his family.

Hank heeded the unspoken threat and stepped back.

He puffed his chest out but stood beside the sheriff as if looking for protection.

The lawman sighed. "Are you Mr. Adams?"

Flynn answered, "Yes, and I'd like to know why you and this man are here scaring my wife and son."

"It seems your wife and Mr. Marshall are telling two different stories of how Mrs. Marshall died." He removed his hat, wiped the sweat off his brow and replaced the hat.

"That boy is mine, not yours," Hank bellowed from behind the sheriff.

Flynn turned to Cora questioningly. "What is he talking about?"

He spoke with staid calmness, but Cora could tell it was a deceptive calm. Would he believe her, once he knew the truth? Would he forgive her? Cora whispered, "This is Hank, Noah's father. He killed my sister and now wants Noah."

Flynn stared deeply into her eyes. She noted his set face, his clamped mouth and steady expression. What was he going to do? Could he fix this? She wanted so badly to lean on him, but he stepped away. Her throat seemed to close up. A heaviness centered in her chest. She dropped her lashes quickly to hide the hurt.

When she glanced up again, Cora saw a smirk twitch across Hank's face as he said, "Your wife is a murderer and a liar, Mr. Adams." He turned to the sheriff and in a loud, demanding voice said, "I want her to hang for killing my sweet Grace. And in the meantime, I deserve my son. That woman has stolen him and caused me to lose months of his life."

Noah chose that moment to wake from his nap. He sat up and looked wide-eyed at the adults who filled the small room. His face scrunched up and his lower lip quivered.

Did he recognize his father? Or remember the loud voice filled with anger? Cora didn't know, but she hurried to the bed and scooped him up. She would fight for him with all that was within her; she'd do her best to protect him from Hank and harm. In a calm voice that she didn't feel capable of, Cora tried to soothe the child. "Shhhh, it's all right, baby." She rocked her body back and forth, feeling trapped.

Noah stuck two fingers in his mouth and buried his face in her shoulder.

"Mrs. Adams, you've admitted that this man is the boy's father. I need you to come to the office with me."

Cora wanted to scream. She knew that to a sheriff, "office" meant "jailhouse." If he locked her up, what would happen to Noah? Cora nodded. "I'll go with you, but Flynn is more of a father to Noah than Hank ever was." She held her head high as she scooped up Noah's bag and walked out the door, leaving the men to hurry after her.

Flynn entered the jail cell with Cora, who clung to Noah. She'd refused to give the boy to the sheriff or to Hank Marshall. The baby had screamed and clutched her for dear life every time one of them had tried to take him. Flynn finally told the sheriff to let her keep the boy for the time being. Thankfully, the lawman had agreed.

It tore his heart to see her so distraught. Love, fear and anger battled for his attention. Fear that Hank might get her hanged for murder and anger that she'd not been honest with him about Noah's true mother and what had brought her to the wagon train. They had been together for months. How could she have kept something this important from him? Especially knowing he was a lawman. Why hadn't she trusted him?

He sat down on the bench beside her, aware that Hank stood beside the sheriff's desk. Fortunately, the man was too far away to overhear their conversation, if they kept their voices low. "Start at the beginning and tell me the whole story. I need to know everything."

Cora's voice sounded lost as she said, "Gracie was my twin sister. When she married Hank, everything was perfect at first, or at least that's what she led everyone to believe. When I moved to Independence, I saw the truth and I begged her to leave him. Then she had Noah. She came to me many times after he was born, hurt and scared. Hank made sure never to hit her in the face. He didn't want people to know he beat her. He broke her wrist once and always left bruises on other parts of her body. Hank likes to drink and he's a mean drunk." She paused; her gaze searched his.

Flynn concealed his true emotions from her. He didn't want her to see the anger he felt toward Hank. In a soft voice, he said, "Go on." A lone tear made its way down Cora's cheek. It took all he had not to wipe away her tears, pull her into his arms and tell her he'd do all he could to protect her and the baby.

"The day I met you, Gracie had come to my house in the wee hours of the morning. She was hurt—fatally hurt, with only minutes left to live. Gracie told me Hank had threatened to kill Noah and she had fought him off. This beating was the worst I'd ever seen." She shivered but then pressed on. "I put her on my bed. Her breathing was labored, and she'd been beaten so severely that we both knew she wasn't going to recover. I wanted to go to the doctor, but she wanted to tell me the plans that she had made to escape with Noah. Gracie had already made the deal with the Clarksons to come here with them. She asked me to keep Noah safe and to take him. Before she could tell me more, she died. I couldn't let Hank have the baby. I had to keep my promise to Gracie and keep him safe. I had to leave Gracie there without a proper burial. All I can do is hope that Hank took care of that." She paused, took a deep breath and then pressed on again. "I didn't know she'd used my name as a cover until Mrs. Clarkson called to me. She'd told them that she was a widow and wanted a fresh start."

Noah squirmed against her. The little boy reached for Flynn, demanding, "Hold you."

Flynn took the boy in his arms. He understood her need to protect the boy. "Why didn't you tell me?"

Her voice cracked. "I was afraid."

Those three words tore a hole in his heart. He nodded and hugged Noah, then pulled the boy back to look in his little face. "You be a good boy. Stay with Ma."

Noah threw his little arms around Flynn's neck. "Pa."

Flynn felt a knot develop in his throat. For the first time, Noah had called him Pa. He patted the baby's back. "That's right! Pa."

The baby gave him a wide smile and then reached for Cora again.

Flynn gave her the baby and then turned to leave. Making his voice hard and cold, he announced, "Sheriff, I'm done in here."

The sheriff opened the cell door. It was all Flynn

could do not to look back at his small family. He knew he broke Cora's heart by not showing her any warmth, but he had to make Hank believe he didn't love or trust his wife anymore. This would take some hard dealing and wisdom.

"Well, what's going to happen to her, Sheriff?" Flynn sat down in the chair beside the bigger man's desk.

"That depends on a few things. I'll need to find out which of them is telling the truth." His gaze moved to Hank, who looked as smug as a cat with a canary in its mouth.

"I'm not one to tell a man how to do his job, Sheriff, but I am curious why Mr. Marshall isn't in jail also. After all, she claims he's the one who killed her sister. If accusation is enough to land someone in jail, then he should be there, too." Flynn had the satisfaction of watching the grin slide right off Hank's face.

"Now, hang on just a minute. I've been waiting here three days for my son to arrive. If I had killed my wife, I could have stolen my son while you were on the trail. I had plenty of opportunities. But I did things right—I went to the law, which is something *she* never did." He crossed his arms over his chest and stared back at Flynn.

Flynn shrugged. Now he understood why he'd had that feeling of being watched at various moments throughout the journey. How long had Hank traveled alongside the wagon train? And how was it that none of the guards had seen him? Either Hank was exceptionally good at hiding or he was lying.

"I'll send a telegraph to the sheriff in Independence and see if we can get some answers. Until then, the little lady stays here." The officer looked at Hank. "Don't leave town. If you so much as sneeze wrong, you'll be in that other cell."

"I'm not going anywhere. I want to see her hang. What about my son?" Hank walked to the bars of the cell.

It took everything in Flynn not to get up and drag the man away. He didn't believe for a moment that Cora was capable of killing her twin sister. He also didn't doubt that Hank would harm the boy, if he got him.

Flynn laughed. "You want the sheriff to give you the boy so you can hightail it out of here? How stupid do you think he is?"

Flynn looked at the sheriff, who raised a bushy eyebrow at him. Clearly the man was wise to his tactics, but he didn't respond. That was to Flynn's favor.

Hank pointed his finger at Cora. "So you are just going to let her keep him?"

The sheriff pushed his chair back and stood up. He walked across the room to the potbellied stove and picked up the coffeepot. "Why not? Both are safe in there, and she's clearly the one that baby trusts." He walked back to the desk and poured himself a cup of the thick brew.

Flynn stood also. He walked to the door and opened it. "Well, I need a shave, haircut and a bath." He left before anyone could respond. Taking long steps, Flynn walked to the side of the building and waited until Hank left. He watched as the man swaggered his way to the saloon. He could tell Hank believed he'd won.

Once he was inside the saloon, Flynn reentered the jailhouse. Cora sat in the corner of her cell while Noah crawled on the floor to the bars. His heart ached seeing her in there, looking sad and rejected.

The sheriff didn't even look up from his paperwork. "Figured you'd be back as soon as he left." He looked up. "I'd like to see your badge before we continue."

Had Cora told the sheriff that he was a lawman, too? His gaze met hers and she shook her head no.

"No, she didn't tell me. Either you're a greenhorn or you know we can spot each other a mile off." He took a drink of his coffee and frowned.

Flynn chuckled. "Well, I'm not a greenhorn, but I have been on a dusty trail for months, so I might be a little rusty." He sat down in front of the desk. "You don't believe Hank Marshall's story any more than I do."

"You've got that right. I didn't like the man when he walked through that door three days ago and I like him even less now." He turned to Cora. "Are you sure there isn't anyone who knows that Grace Marshall came to you that night?"

She stood and picked Noah up off the dirt floor. "No one else saw her. Gracie didn't want anyone to know that Hank beat her or that she was leaving him. She told the Clarksons she was a widow and wanted a fresh start."

"Then it's going to be hard to prove that he's the guilty party rather than you." The officer sighed heavily. His glance raked over Flynn. "Do you have any thoughts?"

Flynn turned to face Cora. "I'm sorry I wasn't very kind earlier. I wanted Hank to think I'm angry with you and that I don't believe you." He watched her try to smile and fail miserably.

"It's all right. I don't blame you for being angry with me. I should have told you everything long ago."

The sheriff cleared his throat.

Flynn turned his attention back to him. "Cora says Hank is a drunk who likes to hit women."

The sheriff nodded. "Yep, that I believe. He goes in the saloon every night and half the time sleeps there at a table, stone drunk."

Flynn was glad that the sheriff had proof that at least one part of Cora's story was true. "I just saw him go into the saloon. If we wait a little while, he'll be on his way to drunk soon. We don't want to wait too long or he'll claim he didn't know what he was saying." Flynn knew he was rambling, but an idea was forming. "I've got it, Sheriff." The thought had just come to him and he knew exactly how he could get Hank to confess to killing his wife.

The sheriff chuckled. "You have a plan?"

"Yeah. Let's head over to the saloon. I'll explain on the way." Flynn turned his attention back to Cora. "If this works, you'll be out of the cell before tomorrow morning and Hank will be in it."

"I pray you are right," Cora answered, sitting back down on the hard bench.

Flynn wanted to tell her it would all be all right. That he loved her and had spent his time away from her this afternoon trying to figure out how to tell her and ask her to remain his wife. Now he wasn't sure what their future held, but he did still love her, and if it was possible, he'd keep his promise and have her out by morning.

"I'll send Mrs. Amor to come sit with you. She's nice and always brings food with her when she comes."

The sheriff pulled his hat from the hat rack beside the door and put it on his head.

Flynn followed him out the door. When they got outside, he asked, "At the saloon, what is your drink of choice?"

The sheriff slapped him on the back. "Tell Sam you want Sheriff Amor's special drink. He'll fix you right up. I'm going next door and telling the wife to make a visit to the jail. Don't do anything at the saloon until I get there. I'll stay in the background so that if you need me, I'll be there."

A few minutes later, Flynn walked into the saloon. He didn't normally go into taverns if he didn't have to. He never drank and dreaded doing so now to trick Hank, but the man would get suspicious if Flynn refused to have a drink. The bar covered most of the back wall, where brown bottles covered the shelves. Tables were scattered about the floor and a flight of stairs was off to the right. Flynn moseyed up to the bar.

"What can I get you, stranger?" Sam wiped the spot in front of Flynn.

Flynn spoke in a very low voice. "I'll have Sheriff Amor's specialty."

The bartender nodded. He turned his back on Flynn, pulled a bottle and glass from under the shelf. He turned back around and poured the brown liquid into the glass.

Flynn took the glass and sipped. He was ready to flinch at the bitter taste of what looked like whiskey but was happily surprised when his tongue encountered sweet tea. "Thank you." He downed the glass. "I think I'll have another."

"You might want to pace yourself. This stuff goes

right to the brain." Sam kept an admirably straight face as he poured him another glass.

Hank sat in the corner nursing his drink and looking anxious.

Flynn had to wonder if Hank was worried that Flynn might confront him or if he'd had enough drink to be bothered that his story might not be as believable as he'd thought. Either way, as far as Flynn was concerned, Hank should be afraid.

Flynn lowered his voice and asked, "What's that fella over there having?" He tilted his head sideways to indicate he was talking about Hank.

The bartender leaned forward and wiped at the stains on the bar. "Strongest whiskey I carry." He shook his head. "He's on his third glass and I believe he's run out of money." Sam winked at him and then pulled another bottle from under the counter. "Maybe you should share this bottle with him." He topped Flynn's glass off with the sweet tea and grinned. Then he shook the sheriff's special brew. "You best go slow on this stuff, though."

Flynn took the whiskey bottle and bellowed, "I might just do that." He took another drink from his glass. He lowered his voice so that only the bartender could hear him and said, "As soon as my friend arrives, which should be any moment."

Sam nodded his understanding. He left the whiskey bottle on the table and looked around. "Stranger, business is slow right now."

Flynn looked about also. He looked up the stairs and saw a pretty blonde looking down at him, and beside her, a not-so-pretty redhead. "Well, it's still early in the day. I'm sure it will pick up."

The sheriff walked through the door.

"See what I mean? There's my friend. Care to top me off one more time?" He dropped several coins on the counter and waited for Sam to pour from the iced tea bottle, then scooped up the whiskey and headed to Hank's table. Out of the corner of his eye, he saw the sheriff walk to the counter and sit on the bar stool at the end, closest to Hank's table.

Flynn reached Hank's table, his steps a little wobbly. "Care to share a drink?" he asked, waving the bottle in front of himself as if he were already half-drunk.

Hank eyed him wearily. "Why would you want to drink with me?" he demanded with a slight slur.

Before answering, Flynn thumped the bottle down on the table in front of Hank.

Flynn pulled out a chair, spun it around so that the back faced the table and then straddled the seat. He refilled Hank's glass with whiskey and said, "I want to thank you for revealing to me that my wife's a murderer." Flynn pretended to shudder. "Imagine what she's capable of if she killed her own sister. She might have killed me in my sleep." He allowed his words to slur slightly, too.

Cora's brother-in-law drank all the liquor from his glass and held it out, grinning, for Flynn to refill. "Naw, Cora's the mild one. Her sister, Grace—now, she's a fighter."

"Isn't Gracie the sister that Cora killed?"

Hank seemed to get his focus back. "Isn't that what I said?"

"Earlier, yes. And I want to thank you. I was getting tired of her and the boy, so you helped me get rid of her and you get your boy back. We both are winners." He took a drink from his glass, making sure not to gulp the contents. He needed to make Hank think he was drinking heavily also, if his plan was going to work.

Chapter Twenty

Cora watched as a woman she'd never seen before entered the jail. She was a little taller than Cora, with blond hair and blue eyes. Cora was thankful that her visitor wasn't Hank or another man. She couldn't get out of the cell, but that didn't mean someone else couldn't get in.

The woman smiled at her through the bars. "Come on. I'm busting you out." The twinkle in her eye said she was teasing…but then she pulled a key from her apron pocket and inserted it into the lock.

"I don't think that's a good idea." Cora picked up Noah and stepped farther away from the door.

The woman's smile grew even bigger. "It's all right. I'm Mrs. Amor, the sheriff's wife. He asked me to move you to our house. According to him, if your husband's plan works, the men don't want you anywhere near this jail when the real killer is brought in."

Cora felt herself relax. She smiled at the woman. "Where are we going?" She picked up the baby's bag and walked through the jail cell door.

Mrs. Amor made a funny face at Noah. He laid his

head on Cora's shoulder and grinned. "He is such a sweet boy."

"Thank you." Cora hugged Noah close.

"Let's get out of here. I am always telling Stephen he should clean this place up, but do you think he does? No, of course not. Once a week I come over, but this last week I've been busy, so the place is a wreck." She led the way out of the jail. "Be sure to close the door," Mrs. Amor said over her shoulder.

Cora closed the door and hurried to keep up with her. She was surprised when they went to the house next door. "You live next door to the jail?"

Mrs. Amor opened the door and held it for her to pass. "We do." She closed the door and led the way through the living area and into the kitchen. "Are you hungry?"

Her stomach chose that moment to growl.

Mrs. Amor laughed. "I'll take that as a yes. Have a seat and I'll fix us dinner."

Cora sank into the nearest chair. Noah began to push against her. Her gaze moved across the spotless floor. "Down," he demanded.

Not seeing anything that could harm the baby, Cora asked, "Do you mind if I let Noah crawl on the kitchen floor?"

"Of course I don't mind." Mrs. Amor placed a jar of pickles on the table.

Cora stood and stretched. "Can I help you?"

"No need. I'm serving cold brisket, potato salad and a few veggies—it'll be ready in a flash. Just relax. The men will be back soon." She paused and smiled. "I hope."

What could Flynn be doing that would make Hank

confess to murdering Gracie? Cora's mind had been occupied with the trip from the jail to the house, so she'd not thought too hard about what Flynn was up to. But now she couldn't ignore her fears. Hank was capable of murder, that much she knew, so was Flynn safe? She felt the dull ache of foreboding. She loved Flynn, had for a while, but when this was all over, would he forgive her for not telling him about Gracie, Hank and Noah? Would he still want to end their marriage? Did he care about her the way she did him?

"Why don't we eat now?" Mrs. Amor suggested. "You are going to wear a hole in my floor." She smiled, taking the sting out of her words.

Cora hadn't even realized she'd been pacing. "I'm sorry." She scooped Noah off the floor and sat down. "What do you think they are doing?"

Mrs. Amor filled a dessert plate with a spoonful of potato salad. "I can't say."

Noah reached his hand forward to grab the salad.

"Wait, Noah. We need to pray first." Cora took his small hand in hers. She looked to her hostess, who bowed her head.

Cora had to admit that Mrs. Amor knew how to pray. She prayed over their meal, asked for the men's safety and the success of the ladies' bake sale before saying amen. Cora helped the baby eat and nibbled on her own meal. Her eyes kept going to the door. "Are they coming here when they finish whatever they're doing?"

Mrs. Amor stacked dishes in the sink and began to wash them. She handed Cora a tea towel to dry the dishes and answered, "Yes. It may take a while. You know how it is to be married to a lawman."

"No, I don't. Flynn and I married right before we left Independence. I learned he was a lawman a few hours before the wedding." Cora dried the dish and sighed. "Honestly, I didn't know or understand what that meant, until now."

"Oh, honey, you still don't know." She handed Cora a plate.

Cora looked down at Noah. He played with the spoons Mrs. Amor had given him. Noah banged the floor and the cabinet, then looked up at her with a big grin. He was her whole reason for everything she'd done over the last several months: taking the Oregon Trail, marrying Flynn and going to jail. As she looked down at his sweet face, Cora knew she'd do it all again and more.

"Elsie! We're back."

Both Cora and Mrs. Amor turned to look into the living room.

"We're in here!" Mrs. Amor called back.

A few moments later, both Sheriff Amor and Flynn walked through the kitchen door. Noah saw Flynn and toddled across the floor as fast as his chubby little legs could go. He grabbed Flynn's pant leg and leaned into him.

Mrs. Amor smiled at her husband. "Are you two hungry? I put two plates on the back of the stove."

"As a bear," her husband answered.

Flynn scooped up Noah. His gaze caught and locked with Cora's.

"Come sit, Flynn," the sheriff ordered, pulling out a chair at the table.

She felt as if Flynn was the only one in the room. He nodded and then carried the baby to the table to join the sheriff and Elsie. Cora wished he would say something to her, anything.

Flynn gave Noah a quick hug and then set him back down on the floor. He took the offered chair and smiled when Mrs. Amor placed a plate of food in front of him. "Thank you."

Mr. Amor said a quick blessing and then the men dug into their food. Flynn could feel both women watching them, waiting for the details of the evening. The sheriff had told him not to volunteer any information; he enjoyed the game of his wife waiting and then demanding to know what had happened. The lawman said it was something they had done since they'd gotten married fifteen years earlier. Flynn didn't really understand but played along.

Cora picked up the baby and excused herself to go change his diaper.

Flynn felt bad for not telling her what had happened. That Hank was in jail and that she was off the hook for murder. Her anxious face pulled at his heart. "Excuse me." He pushed away from the table and followed Cora into the living area.

He stood in the doorway and watched her finish dressing Noah. The little boy squirmed and wiggled as she kissed his little face and head. He squealed as he rolled over and tried to crawl away. Flynn hated that if Hank had had his way, he would have lost them both.

Cora looked up and saw him standing there. The smile on her face faded. She let Flynn scoop the wiggly baby from the couch and place him on the floor. Noah took two steps before falling back on his diaper.

Flynn sat down beside her on the couch. "Hank confessed to killing your sister."

"He did?"

Flynn looked into her tear-filled eyes. "Yes. He claims it was an accident and that until he found her at your house, he didn't know he'd killed her."

"That's probably true. Hank would get drunk, hit Gracie, and then the next day, once he was sober, he'd be full of apologies and would assure her that it would never happen again. But it always did." Sadness filled her voice.

He scooted over and put his arm around her shoulders. "He'll never hurt another woman again." Flynn planned on making sure that the judge heard every word that Hank had confessed to him. Thankfully, the sheriff had heard his confession also. There was no way the judge would let Hank go free after Hank had admitted to killing a woman, by accident or not—and Sheriff Amor would be an excellent impartial witness.

Cora laid her head on his shoulder. "Will he be hanged?"

"That depends on the judge. He could be sentenced to a lifetime in prison."

Noah crawled back to Cora and pulled on her dress until he was standing. He stuck two fingers in his little mouth. She reached down and picked up the child. She cuddled him close. He was getting so big. He yawned and snuggled into her.

Flynn wanted to protect them both forever, but they had agreed to go their separate ways once they got to Oregon. "Cora, I'm sorry you didn't feel like you could trust me enough with your secrets."

Cora turned to look at him. "Oh, Flynn. It wasn't

that I felt I couldn't trust you. There's no one else I trust
more. But, at first, I was mourning my sister. Then I
was afraid if you found out I wasn't Noah's real ma,
you wouldn't want to bring me here, and I couldn't go
back to Independence. And I for sure couldn't let you
take Noah from me. I lived in a constant state of fear
that Hank would find us. I was afraid of everything
and everyone."

He didn't know what to say or how to respond. She'd
been afraid to tell him the truth. Every day they were
together on the trail, while he had been falling in love
with her, she had been afraid he would abandon her.
How did they get past this?

Flynn gently set her away from him. "Well, we are
here now. You are safe from Hank. I found Miriam's
killer, so I suppose our arrangement is complete." He
looked at her intently and then strode to the door.

She followed him. "Our arrangement is completed,
yes—but that means that now we can start fresh."

He frowned down at her in confusion. "How do you
plan on us starting fresh?"

Cora laid her hand on his chest. "You have proved
you can be more than trusted. That whatever you go
for, you get. And I have learned that you are a man
of your word. You don't abandon the people you care
about. So I would like to start our marriage again.
And I will work hard at proving to you that I, too, can
be trusted. I can be determined—and, Flynn, I don't
abandon the people I love, either."

Flynn looked deeply into her face. Gone was the
frightened, unsure woman he'd met in Independence.
In front of him stood the woman he'd grown to love.
She was strong and loyal, and even though she'd been

too scared to share her past with him, he knew she'd been as honest as she thought she could be. "You love me?" Lightly he fingered a loose tendril of hair on her cheek.

Cora smiled. "I knew I loved you that time we lost Noah. You were the person I ran to, you were the one I trusted to find him, and you were strong for me even though you were just as scared."

It took all his control not to grab her up and hold her tight. Cora Adams, his wife, had just said she loved him. If she were being honest, they could spend the rest of their lives truly falling in love or deeper in love if her emotions were as real as his.

Flynn turned and took one step toward the kitchen, his movements hurried and purposeful. Then he stopped as he realized that standing in the doorway, looking sheepish, were the Amors, who had listened to the whole thing. At the moment, Flynn didn't care. He wanted to shout from the rooftops that Cora loved him. No matter what uncertainties waited for them ahead, he knew love would conquer all of it. He'd seen it happen too many times between his parents. And it was what the sheriff had insinuated earlier in the day.

"Sir, and Mrs. Amor, would you mind if we leave now? The meal was lovely, and I thank you, but…" Flynn didn't get to finish his sentence.

"Go on. Get out of here." Both the sheriff and his wife shooed them out the door.

Chapter Twenty-One

Moments later, as dusk covered the valley, they were back in the room Flynn had rented. Cora wiped the milk from Noah's face and laid him in the center of the bed. She pulled the covers over him and then sat on the edge of the bed. Flynn added wood to the fireplace, then pulled the only chair in the room, a small rocking chair that Noah had instantly loved, and placed it in front of the hearth. He wedged himself into the seat with a chuckle. "This is a mama-baby chair for sure."

Cora laughed. Flynn held out his hands, and as soon as her reaching fingers touched his, she felt safe. The warmth of personal contact after all the uncertainties of the day comforted her.

"Cora, we need to get some things straight between us." One look at her expression and he hurriedly explained, "No, no, don't fret. I just need clarity on a few details. Cora, make no mistake. I love you. Nothing will change that till death. So, anytime we have discussions, it will never be to end things between us or to go our separate ways. If you will have me, I'm yours for life, but so often I've seen relationships fail for lack of communication and I don't want that to happen between us. Do you understand what I'm saying?" At her nod, he continued.

"So I'd like to ask if you're certain you are committed to me. And are you still afraid to tell me things? Will you keep secrets from me?" He hesitated as if torn by conflicting emotions.

Cora's heart filled with all the passion she felt for this man. In his moment of uncertainty, her feelings intensified. Wanting to put all his worries to rest, she leaned forward and took his face in her hands. She kissed his lips gently. Cora had never been so forward in her life and she felt the flush start in her neck and move up into her cheeks. So far, this was the most important thing between them, and she intended to make him feel completely secure in her feelings for him. She put all the love she felt for Flynn into her kiss. All the while praying he'd understand what her forwardness meant.

When she pulled away, Cora rested her forehead on his and said, "I know my past actions have caused you to doubt me and for that I'm so sorry. But know this, Flynn Adams—I will spend the rest of my life earning your trust."

He pushed out of the tight chair and hugged her close. "Cora, I have some news to discuss with you." He kissed the top of her head and then turned her so that he could sit her down in the rocking chair before moving a few feet away.

Cora gently set the rocker in motion. Her heart pounded in her chest. What more could he tell her? "I'm listening."

"Sheriff Amor told me today that the next town over,

Cascade Falls, is in need of a sheriff. The town's not as large as Willamette, but it is an established town. He says it is beautiful there and they have several waterfalls that cascade down the mountains. There are plenty of grazing sites for cattle and the place is green and lush. There's a house a couple of blocks out of the main section of town that goes with the job. Sheriff Amor has been covering that area himself, but with the way this town and Cascade Falls have grown, he thinks it's time for another sheriff to take the reins. He's offered the job to me." He paused, as if he'd forgotten to breathe.

Since he hadn't asked any questions, Cora waited for him to continue. She prayed that he was trying to lead up to the fact that he wanted to take the job and provide a home for her and Noah.

"What do you think? Do you want to stay here in Oregon? With me?"

Cora's heart sang. "I do want to stay here with you. But what about you? You don't want to go back to Texas?"

"I will have to return to Texas sometime in the future—but not to stay. When we arrived earlier, the sheriff gave me a telegraph that was waiting for me from the town I used to serve. It stated my job had been given to a more stable lawman. Still, I have to go back and see my parents and sister." Excitement filled his eyes and Cora was sure it wasn't there because he'd be returning to Texas to see his parents and sister.

Cora smiled. "How soon could we see the place?"

"Sheriff Amor said he would take us there tomorrow if we were interested."

She sat up and reached over to smooth Noah's hair.

It curled at his nape. He would soon need his first haircut. Her baby had begun walking, and much like Flynn had said early on, Noah ran everywhere. Cora had teased Joe, telling him he had taught the baby the bad habit of running when he should be walking. A smile touched her lips. Noah would have stability, go to school and maybe be joined by a brother or sister. She looked at Flynn, her courage and determination like a rock inside her. "This has an indefinable feeling of rightness about it, doesn't it? Do you feel it, too?"

He answered in an odd, gentle tone. "Yes, I feel it, too."

The next day, Cora could barely contain her excitement. The house was small but had a white picket fence and green shutters. It had a cookstove with an oven in the kitchen. She could bake Flynn blackberry cobblers every night with such a fine stove. In the living room, there were shiny hardwood floors, a rock fireplace and glass windows that looked out onto the street. And wonder of wonders, it sat on two acres. She could have a milk cow, chickens and a garden; Noah could have a dog, even a cat if he wanted.

There were some repairs needed and certainly a whitewash job, but with a little cleaning, they could move in now.

"Sweetheart, Stephen and I are riding over to the sheriff's office. Do you want to go?"

Cora turned to Sheriff Amor. "Is there a general store in town?" She wanted to see the whole town, but the main reason for asking was that she needed cleaning supplies.

He rocked on his boots. "Sure is. Two doors down from the office."

She caught Noah as he tried to run past her. The baby still wobbled when he ran or walked. "Then I'd like to go buy some Murphy soap, a pail, a broom and a mop."

Sheriff Amor threw back his head and laughed loudly. He slapped Flynn on the back. "Looks to me like the decision's been made. Might as well just swear you in, give you a badge and the keys to the jail."

And that was just what happened. By nightfall, Cora had the house clean and warm and smelling of cinnamon apples and beef stew. And she almost cheered when Flynn arrived in a wagon filled with odds and ends of furniture, donated by the townspeople eager to welcome law and order to their town.

Cora's heart sang with delight. Joy bubbled in her laugh and shone in her eyes and was reflected in the ones staring down at her. She laid her head against Flynn's chest and listened to his heartbeat. She was home.

Epilogue

One year later

Cora took a deep breath and then released it. Her baby was on his way and she was feeling the birthing pains. She resisted the urge to push because the midwife said it was too soon. Another pain shot through her tired body and she groaned.

"You are doing great, Cora." Annie stood at her head, holding her hand and cheering her on.

Cora tried to smile through the pain. She puffed out the words, "That's easy for you to say. You aren't having this baby."

Annie laughed. "No, I already had mine."

"How is Flynn doing?" Cora decided to focus on her sweet man instead of the pain of giving birth to his child.

"Oh, you know. He's pacing the floor and telling Noah his ma is going to be fine." Annie winced, reminding Cora not to squeeze her friend's hand too hard.

Cora looked to her midwife. "Can I stand up?"

The older woman returned her look. "It's better for

the baby if you don't, but if you want to stand, I won't stop you."

Annie grinned. "Then stand she shall." She helped Cora move her legs off the bed and rise to her feet.

Even though the midwife didn't think standing would help, Cora felt better. The pressure in her lower belly eased. "This helps." Cora smiled at Annie. She'd been pleased to learn that Annie and Harold had settled in her small town.

"I'm glad, dear. While you're up, I'll change out these wet sheets." The midwife began stripping the sheets off the bed.

Cora sighed. She'd sweated so much in the last three hours she doubted there was any more moisture left in her. A pain hit her hard. Cora bent over and groaned. She felt the baby's head between her legs and gasped. "Help. He's coming out."

The midwife dropped the sheets and hurried to help her. "Push slightly," she ordered.

It took all Cora's willpower not to push fast and hard. She didn't want to harm her baby, but her body was doing its own thing. Cora groaned as the infant slid into the midwife's waiting hands.

Helpless, and shaking like a leaf, Cora let the midwife work as she stood beside the bed with Annie holding her up. "Is it a boy?" She sighed.

"No, she's a girl." The midwife slapped the baby's behind. "Give me just a moment and I'll get her cleaned up for you," she said over the baby's cry.

Cora nodded. She had been so sure the baby would be a boy. Flynn would be impossible to live with. He'd known all along that it would be a girl.

"Do you have a name yet for her?" Annie asked.

"Flynn suggested that if he was right and the baby was a girl, we should name her Gracie, after my sister." Cora bit her lip as another wave of pain shot through her body.

"That's a lovely name." Annie frowned. "Are you all right?"

The midwife wrapped the baby in a blanket and carried her over to Cora. "Here, hold your daughter, and I'll finish making the bed."

Cora nodded. "Should I still be having labor pains?"

The midwife tucked the last corner of the sheet under the mattress. "That's probably the afterbirth." She put another sheet on the bed. "It should be coming out any moment."

"I don't know. This feels…" Cora groaned as her knees began to buckle.

The midwife grabbed the baby and laid her on the bed. "Hold her up, Annie." She began feeling about on Cora's stomach. A grin split her face. "Looks like we have another baby waiting to join us."

Cora gasped. "Another baby?" No one had said there were two babies in there. She couldn't be having twins. Could she?

"Don't fight the contractions, Cora. Relax like you did before."

She wouldn't call the way Gracie had been born "relaxing," but Cora tried to do as she was told. A pain tore through her already sore body. She gasped for air and pushed. The midwife was ready.

A second baby entered the world. There was no

need to slap her bottom because she entered the world screaming her unhappiness at being last.

"It's another girl," the midwife announced. She held the wiggling baby close. "Annie, help Cora into bed and let her hold the first baby while I get this one cleaned up."

Cora allowed Annie to help her into bed. She smiled as her friend handed her baby Gracie. Her new daughter was beautiful. She had dark hair, like her father. While Cora counted the baby's fingers and toes, Annie cleaned the floor beside the bed and straightened up the room.

"Can Flynn come in now?" Cora felt tired and wanted to show him his daughters before she fell asleep.

The midwife brought the second baby to her. "Yes. I'll go get him."

Cora smiled, a baby in each arm. "Thank you so much for helping me."

She was rewarded with a pat on the shoulder. "It was my pleasure, but you did most of the work. All I had to do was catch and clean them up."

Within moments of the midwife leaving, Flynn arrived. He held Noah in his arms and wore a look of shock on his face. "Twins?"

Cora nodded. "Didn't the midwife tell you?"

He shook his head. "No. I guess she wanted them to be a surprise."

Noah squirmed in his arms. "Down."

"No, son. Look at your sisters." Flynn tried to get the boy to look at the babies, but Noah was more interested in getting out of his father's arms.

"Would you like for me to take this young man to the kitchen for a cookie?" Annie asked.

Flynn smiled his thanks as Noah wiggled from his arms into Annie's.

The midwife stood in the doorway. "I could use a cookie, too."

Annie laughed. "Then let's all go to the kitchen for a cookie party."

When the door closed behind them, Cora said, "I hope you don't mind having three children, instead of two."

He kissed her forehead. "I am thrilled we have twin girls and a sweet, active, into-everything little boy."

Cora laughed. "He was a handful, I take it."

Flynn grinned and touched the top fingers of the baby closest to him. "Have you thought about what we should name them?"

"Well, Gracie, after my sister—and for the other one, how about Hope?" She kissed the tops of both their heads.

Flynn nodded. "Why Hope?"

"Hope was my mother's name. Unless you want to name her after your mother." Cora yawned.

Flynn smiled. "We can use hers as a middle name. How does Gracie Christina Adams sound to you?"

"Beautiful."

He smoothed the hair off Cora's forehead. "Thank you for giving me Gracie and Hope. I love you very much." Flynn kissed the top of her head.

Cora smiled. "I love you, too." She was tired but didn't want Flynn to leave. Another yawn escaped her.

She didn't protest when Flynn took Hope from her

arms and laid her in the small crib beside the bed. Then he did the same with Gracie. The two babies snuggled close in the small space. She knew they'd need a bigger crib in the near future, but for now, the girls were content to remain close. Cora loved her small family. In the last year and a half, she had gone from being a single schoolteacher to a mother, a wife and a mother again. And Flynn had made it all possible.

"Before you go to sleep, I wanted to tell you that you don't have to worry about me being a sheriff anymore."

Cora forced her tired eyes open. "I don't?"

"No. A couple of days ago, I bought Kingfisher's farm, and while you were in labor, I quit my job. Well, sort of. I told the new town council to start looking for my replacement. Together, I believe we can make the Kingfisher farm into a fine horse ranch." Flynn sat down on the side of the bed.

"But you love being a lawman," she protested, even though her heart was singing with happiness.

Flynn took her face in both of his hands and leaned his forehead against hers. "Yes, but I love you and our family more. I want to spend every day with you and the kids. Being a sheriff is exciting at times, but not being around my growing family isn't what I want. I have a better understanding now of why my pa ranched after he and Ma married." He paused and searched Cora's tired features. "What are you thinking?" Concern filled his husky voice.

Cora smiled. "I was just thinking how blessed I am to have you. I love you so much."

"I love you, too. The Oregon Trail was the best thing to happen to me. Thanks to it, I have a beautiful wife and three wonderful children. What more could a man ask for?" Flynn watched her eyelashes slowly rest on her cheeks.

A soft smile covered her mouth and she whispered, "More children?"

* * * * *

LOVE INSPIRED

Stories to uplift and inspire

Fall in love with Love Inspired—
inspirational and uplifting stories of faith
and hope. Find strength and comfort in
the bonds of friendship and community.
Revel in the warmth of possibility and the
promise of new beginnings.

Sign up for the Love Inspired newsletter
at **LoveInspired.com** to be the first
to find out about upcoming titles,
special promotions and exclusive content.

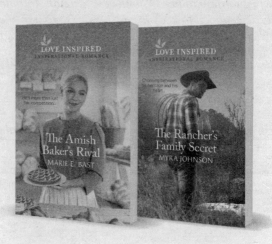

*Newly guardian to her twin nieces, Hannah Antonicelli
is determined to keep her last promise to her late
sister—that she'll never reveal the identity of their
father. But when Luke Hutchenson is hired as a
handyman at her work and begins to bond with the little
girls, hiding that he's their uncle isn't easy...*

Read on for a sneak peek at
Finding a Christmas Home *by Lee Tobin McClain!*

On Wednesday after work, Hannah drove toward home, the
twins in the back seat, and tried not to be nervous that Luke
was in the front seat beside her.

"I really appreciate this," he said. His car hadn't started this
morning, and he'd walked the three miles to Rescue Haven.

Of course, Hannah had insisted on driving him home. What
else could she do? It was cold outside, spitting snow, and he
was her next-door neighbor.

"I hate to ask another favor," he said, "but could you stop by
Pasquale's Pizza on the way?"

"No problem." She took a left and drove the two blocks to
the only nonchain pizza place in Bethlehem Springs.

He jumped out, and she turned back to check on the twins,
trying not to watch Luke as he headed into the shop. He was
good-looking, of course. Kind, appreciative and strong. And he
had the slightest swagger in his walk that was masculine and
appealing.

But he was also about to go visit his brother, Bobby, if he kept his promise to his ailing father. And when she'd heard about that visit, it had been a wake-up call: she shouldn't get too close with him. The fewer chances she had to spill the beans about Bobby being the twins' father, the better.

He came out of the pizza shop quickly—he must have called ahead—carrying a big flat box and a white bag. What would it be like if this was a family scenario, if they were Mom and Dad and kids, stopping for takeout on the way home from work?

She couldn't help it. Her chest filled with longing.

He climbed into her small car, juggling the large flat box to make it fit without encroaching on the gearshift.

She had to laugh at the size of his meal. "Hungry?"

"Are you?" He opened the box a little, and the rich, garlicky fragrance of Pasquale's special sauce filled the car.

Her stomach growled, loudly.

"Pee-zah!" Addie shouted from the back seat.

"Peez!" Emmy added, almost as loud.

"That's just cruel," she said as she pulled the car back onto the road and steered toward Luke's place. "You're tempting us. I may have to order some when I get these girls home."

"No, you won't," he said. "This is for all of us. The least I can do is feed you, after you drove me around."

Her stomach gave a little leap, and not just about the prospect of pizza. Why was he inviting her to have dinner with him? Was there an ulterior motive? And if there was, would she mind?

Don't miss
Finding a Christmas Home *by Lee Tobin McClain,*
available October 2021 wherever
Love Inspired books and ebooks are sold.

LoveInspired.com

For readers of *Lilac Girls* and *The Lost Girls of Paris*

Don't miss this captivating novel of resilience following three generations of women as they battle to save their family's vineyard during WWII

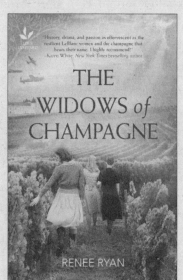

"With complex characters and a stunning setting, *The Widows of Champagne* will sweep you into a wartime story of love, greed, and how one should never underestimate the strength of the women left behind. I couldn't put it down."
—Donna Alward, *New York Times* bestselling author

Coming soon from Love Inspired!

LOVE INSPIRED
LoveInspired.com

LI42707BPA